GAUNTLET

By Ellery Prime
Illustrations by T2A

Chromatic Press Inc.
Toronto, Canada

Gauntlet
Written by Ellery Prime
Illustrations by T2A

Originally serialized in Issues #001 (July 2013) - #011 (June 2014)
of *Sparkler Monthly* Magazine

Editor - Lianne Sentar
Copyeditor - Ashley Hisson
Logo Design and Cover Layout - Lissa Pattillo
Book Design - Lillian Diaz-Przybyl

ISBN: 978-0-9938611-2-3

Chromatic Press Inc.
Toronto, ON
Canada

E-mail: editorial@chromaticpress.com

Visit us online at www.chromaticpress.com
and www.sparklermonthly.com

♦ ♣ ♠ ♥

Table of Contents

♦ ♣ ♠ ♥

Chapter 1 7
Chapter 2 39
Chapter 3 69
Chapter 4 101
Chapter 5 133
Chapter 6 155
Chapter 7 175
Chapter 8 193
Chapter 9 215
Chapter 10 237

Square One : A *Gauntlet* Bonus Story 275

Bonus Comics 286

♦ ♣ ♠ ♥

Chapter 1

♦ ♣ ♠ ♥

"Taxi!"

A well-dressed woman in high-heeled sandals cut in front of Clio, throwing a harassed, almost suspicious look over her shoulder. Clio watched, her hand slowly falling, as the woman waved down the cab that pulled up.

Clio raised her eyebrows in amusement. The woman's abrupt maneuver didn't bother her.

"Excuse me," Clio said, taking a step back from the woman teetering on the curb. The woman at least had the grace to look a little embarrassed at the show of politeness.

"Sorry. Were you waiting for...?" Even as she threw out the half-hearted apology, the woman was reaching for the cab's door, her manicured nails aggressively signaling her true intent.

Clio shook her head and smiled. "No, no. It's all yours."

The woman's face relaxed into softer lines, and she smiled back. "Isn't the heat terrible?" she commented. "If you're going east, we could share."

For a moment, Clio was tempted. Her sandals were comfortable, but she'd done a lot of walking that day already, and she *was* prickly with heat. She could be home, showered, with her feet up, and a book in her lap in fifteen minutes.

A part of her admired the woman's boldness--her selfishness, even--that had mellowed into this offer. Her rudeness seemed a part of her air of busy importance, from the expensive briefcase she carried to her perfect makeup and hair.

"Thank you." Clio laughed, rejecting the thought only a little ruefully. "But I'm a glutton for punishment. I like to walk."

They exchanged awkward nods, and the woman disappeared into the back of the taxi. Clio watched as the woman immediately lit a cigarette pulled from an expensive silver case, her thin, elegant fingers flashing that perfect manicure again. Clio could imagine the woman was rushing to an important meeting around a huge table in front of floor-to-ceiling windows. Someday, it could be Clio who rushed through the city with an air of distracted importance.

The taxi expertly merged into the speeding traffic. Hot, still air steamed from the sidewalks. Clio turned her face, trying to a find a breeze, as she continued on her way home.

Pink twilight washed the tall buildings scattered along the jagged sprawl of the skyscrapers. Clio enjoyed the muted feel of the sun on her back through the thin fabric of her white summer dress. Her exposed shoulders bore their own flushed color because she'd forgotten to bring sunscreen again. Spaghetti straps rubbed with slight discomfort against the tender skin, but it was satisfying, in a way--like the waterlogged fatigue after a day of playing in the water during childhood summers.

She laughed to herself about viewing the world through rose-colored glasses. She strode down the street, her backpack swinging from her hand with a confidence borne from three months in the city. She could provide for herself despite the fact that she had no ties here beyond her love for the city itself. She felt special here--grown-up. Her fresh, sleek haircut, blunt along the edges, swung with brisk jauntiness against her bare shoulder blades.

In moments like this, when she felt almost fearless, all of her insecurities briefly faded. She felt like she could hold her own against anyone.

Like that woman in the cab.

One day she would be just as polished, just as confident.

She wondered for a moment what it would be like to have that extra edge of knowing that others truly saw her as an adult, that they would take her seriously--that they would see *her.*

If she had to be honest, she sometimes felt like she was playing at being an adult rather than actually being one.

I came here. I'm doing this, all on my own.

Instead of comforting her, a shade of unease prickled her at the thought. A brief, vague recall of past awkwardness and inexperienced fumbles caused her stomach to twist in remembered embarrassment. Her determined bravado wavered.

Clio brushed the half-formed memories aside with an unconscious shake of her head, as if to clear out the unpleasant drift of her thoughts.

Right now was enough. The shine of just being where she was hadn't worn off. Even a simple action such as crossing the street seemed new and interesting, and produced a secret thrill inside her.

The city never failed to tease her with its impressive skyline and twisting corners, urging her to know it better. It was everything she had ever expected and so much more. The shops and smells and people enticed her while her sandals tapped against the pavement, taking her toward the comfort of her little apartment. She remained in her pleasant reverie until a catcall from a passing car startled her.

Her ankle wobbled on an uneven piece of sidewalk. Clio gasped, her hand flying up and waving for balance before she steadied. Blood rushed to her cheeks.

"Are you all right?"

Clio smiled at the friendly face of the white-haired man who stood in an open doorway. A strong, savory aroma rolled out from the restaurant behind him, punctuated when a small wave of laughing customers exited by his side. Her empty stomach made an almost soundless rumble.

"Yes, thank you," she replied. "I'm fine. Just clumsy."

Her smile remained a while longer as she passed by. The frank appreciation in the man's eyes as they traveled over her face and body was something that she only acknowledged on the most abstract level. Converting stares, even comments, into a message of general goodwill was an exercise in mental gymnastics. She knew that, but it was better than allowing herself to be weighed down by the cumulative weight of the male gaze that seemed ever-present.

With the ease of practice, she shrugged off those thoughts. More tantalizing smells brought her hunger to life. She was tempted to claim a seat in one of the small eateries that lined the gently curving avenue, but a quick glance at the sky made her hesitate. The buildings weren't so rosy now. A deeper, bruised purple had darkened their shapes and the globe of the sun was hidden behind the tall back of a pointed skyscraper.

She continued on, walking a little faster, until the delicious scent of baking bread drew her into a small bakery. Inside, she breathed deeply and smiled at the woman at the counter. A baking sheet holding fresh, steaming rolls enticed her to buy three, and the woman added a savory, curry meat pastry to her bag. Clio thanked her profusely and tucked the warm treats into her backpack.

Her brisk steps took her along a cobblestoned alley, past a neat, protected square lined with eclectic shops and waddling pigeons. The opposite alleyway spilled into the bustling pedestrian traffic of a street packed with restaurants, bank kiosks, and small clothing boutiques. Traffic roared past, filling the air with the smell of exhaust. Her nose wrinkled.

She still marveled at the intimate juxtaposition the city offered. Manicured perfection erupted into dirty gravel and upturned asphalt as giant machines drilled into the city's core. The elite transformed into the rough and tumble so unexpectedly, often within the space of a block or two. It made Clio glow with pride to know she was learning to navigate here, developing that sixth sense that allowed city dwellers to make their way through the confusing jumble of streets and avenues. It made her one of them. She belonged.

It was that internal compass that made her neck prickle with just the faintest touch of unease when she came to an obstruction. She stopped in front of looming concrete cylinders, rubble, and raw earth. Orange-vested men called out to each other and matching cones barred the way. Clio frowned, not seeing a way through the construction.

The pedestrians around her seemed unfazed. Some crossed at the green light, turning right, as the honking cars piled up next to her. The rest smoothly veered to the left, down the bisecting avenue. Indecision stalled her. Just as she decided to dash across the road with the last of the stragglers, the traffic signal flashed its warning. She cursed under her breath.

The respectable number of people who took the left-hand path reassured her. She turned to follow them down the block, picking up speed as she diligently planned the changes to her trip home.

The early summer evening still promised a decent amount of time before the sun's light faded into dusk. She *had* taken this walk before--once or twice--though only in the bright bustle of midday. Even so, her chin came up and she walked with a stubborn determination. It was silly to be concerned at all, despite the offhand rumors about the area's somewhat unsavory reputation.

She had never been warned of this neighborhood *precisely*. It was cheek by jowl with an established thoroughfare, after all, and stretched but a few blocks to the south of that major artery. The buildings were squatter here, more mysterious with their unadorned gray facades and narrow windows. Their function was less clear than the taller, more striking buildings that lined busier streets, but their grouping seemed to indicate they belonged to each other. Exterior walls formed narrow walkways between the flat-roofed structures. Were they apartments, or perhaps an institution of some sort?

All she needed to do was turn and cross the unremarkable huddle of buildings. She knew the sidewalk would funnel her through their midst and deposit her back on track, almost at the doorstep of a major subway station. She could be home within ten minutes.

"Ice cream? The heat is still so bad at this hour."

Startled, Clio looked at the man standing behind a street food stall. She'd unknowingly come to a halt in front of his kiosk.

"Oh." His friendly face steadied her, and Clio smiled back. "No, thank you. But I will take a water, please."

He pulled out a bottle from his cooler, exchanging it for a couple of limp bills. Her fingers wrapped around the narrow shape, dislodging the clumps of wet ice that clung to its surface. "Thank you."

"Do you live near here?" he asked.

The inquiry didn't feel intrusive because the man's eyes--which seemed warm and kind--watched her with a mix of curiosity and concern.

"Not very, no. I'm just passing through." Clio shifted her weight nervously as a line appeared between his brows. "I went to the gardens today, and I'm heading home now. It was so nice out that I thought I'd walk. I had to take a little detour, though."

She suddenly felt a bit foolish--offering unnecessary information--but somehow the earlier comfort she'd taken in their simple exchange had disappeared.

Her awkward feelings deepened when the man's smile faded entirely. He nodded toward the path she was set on.

"It can be confusing around here if you're not familiar with the twists and turns," he said. "I'd recommend you go back that way and cross over two blocks. The bus there runs straight east, if that's where you're heading."

Pride made her quickly defend herself. "Oh, but I have been through here before, and the station is just on the other side. Thank you, though." She smiled to soften her rejection of his advice.

"It's different in the evening. You might lose your way."

His voice seemed to grow sterner, and she gave a short laugh. She took a half-step back as unease bloomed in her stomach. "Well..."

She glanced over her shoulder. There were fewer people on the sidewalk now. She could still see the busy intersection where the traffic stalled and turned due to the construction; the workers swarmed over the site with reassuring activity. But between her and the way back stood a group of lounging young men. She had passed them before, but, surrounded by the other pedestrians, she had barely taken note of them.

If she *did* want to retrace her steps, she would have to walk past them without the comforting camouflage of other walkers. The young men loitered against the wall of a building about halfway down the block, laughing and roughhousing with each other. Clio hesitated, not quite willing to admit to any feelings of intimidation.

It was ridiculous. She had to go one way or another, and she was letting someone else's worries affect her. She turned her head in the opposite direction, back at the shadow-blanketed neighborhood she'd been wary of in the first place. The clustered, unmarked buildings suddenly seemed too close together. They appeared to crouch in a secretive huddle, excluding anything that didn't belong.

"Well..." Her gaze dragged back to the construction. "I think--"

Before she could complete her thought, one of the young men turned his head and met Clio's gaze. An unpleasant thrill shot down her spine. One by one, each of the men turned to see what had captured their friend's attention. Clio jerked her head around abruptly and met the kiosk man's now neutral expression. Light laughter burst out behind her.

"Thank you for the water." Clio forced a smile and made her body turn as naturally as possible. "Have a good evening."

She felt the weight of his stare on her as she moved to the narrow walkway between the mass of buildings. Out of the corner of her eye, she saw the loitering boys go back to their conversation and pay her no mind. She breathed a sigh of relief and gave herself a mental shake for getting worked up about something so small.

She realized she'd been clutching the water bottle hard enough to dent it. She loosened her grip and the abused plastic crunched back into place. She tucked it into a pocket of her backpack and resituated the bag on her shoulders, deliberately distracting herself from the vague unease as she walked between two of the squatting buildings.

She emerged into a smallish square. Her heart lightened when she saw an older woman carrying groceries. Clio smiled at her.

The woman merely stared at Clio and passed in silence.

Two small boys played in a corner, bouncing a ball off one of the walls. A distant female voice called out and echoed through the square. The boys grabbed their ball and ran off, cutting across Clio's path and disappearing down a side alley. A drifting cloud chose that moment to dampen the fading sunlight, and a humorless laugh escaped Clio. She stubbornly kept walking toward the narrow alley in front of her.

She *wasn't* scared. The place was just a little creepy.

The cloud slipped away, allowing the low-hanging sun to cast long shadows over the square. Clio watched her own shadow march up to the alleyway and disappear into its dark mouth.

Only a few more minutes, she told herself. Then she would be on the train and whizzing toward home.

Clio thought up a game to guess how many steps it was to the end of the passage. She counted them out steadily while her sandals kept time on the cement. She remembered that she needed to turn right at this particular corner. Then the sloping hill would curve around and the sidewalk would happily meet the main avenue. *Almost there,* she thought.

Clio rounded the corner, then stopped short as adrenaline exploded in her chest.

At the top of the gentle hill, two figures pulled a chain-link fence across the walkway. They were only silhouettes to her, but she heard the deep timbre of their voices rumble down toward her.

They called out--not to each other, but to others who must have been nearby. Clio suddenly doubted they were workers. There was something in the sound of those voices, perhaps a kind of ready glee that seemed troubling and unfriendly, that combined with the fading light and encroaching walls to send Clio back into the shadows of the alley. Answering calls seemed to come from all directions, youthful and wild.

Calling herself irrational had little effect on her pounding heart. She knew she should just walk up the hill. They were just locals, maybe getting ready for a street festival or something; whatever reason they had for closing off the neighborhood, surely they would let her out. But the sound of their laughter made her take another step back.

It would be just as easy to retrace her steps. Five minutes' time would return her to the safety--no, to the *familiarity*, she reassured herself--of the well-traveled streets.

Clio's fingers slid around the straps of her backpack as she rushed back the way she'd come. All she wanted was to escape the close walls of this alley. Clio wished herself back on the open lawns of the gardens, free of the cloistering effects of these ugly buildings that were really *much* too close together. Their claustrophobic proximity seemed to constrict her lungs as well as her way.

Her breath exhaled in one long rush when she found herself in the small square again. She sucked in more air and continued, not looking into corners this time as she barely kept herself from an outright run. Dread clenched her belly when she noticed a gate drawn across the sidewalk she had used only minutes before.

A padlock hung in thick, ugly reality from the latch. Clio's eyes traveled up the path, hoping to catch sight of the street vendor who had sold her the water--but he and the stand were gone, as if they'd never been there. Even the sounds from the workers had ceased.

Think.

A nervous look around revealed a couple of side alleys. The street those little boys had gone down offered the only spark of comfort. That was the one she would follow. Despite her resolve, the tension in her neck and shoulders tightened.

Hugging the right wall, she went on. Her head jerked up

when she thought she caught sight of movement in a narrow window above her. *Nothing there.* Her gaze wrenched forward again when a door slammed nearby. Spooked, she walked faster.

The alley branched. The sky was a deep, dark purple now. Clio took another right turn, hoping it would lead her out of this maze and not further in. She thought herself a fool to have ever found quiet, crooked lanes appealing. She'd give anything for a broad and busy avenue to open up in front of her.

Instead, she emerged into a large, wedge-shaped courtyard of sorts, formed by the intersection of three buildings and a high wall. Walkways branched off between them. Her heart sank at the thought of having to choose again, but then she received another jolt when she noticed two boys--young men, really--sitting on that high wall. They hunkered beneath a wavering streetlamp that cast a washed-out yellow circle around them and their dangling legs.

One of the boys whistled at her. Clio watched, her heart in her throat, as he jumped easily to the ground.

"What are you doing here?" he asked.

His voice held honest shock, and no aggression. Clio's breath came back to her a little.

"I was just-- I've been trying to reach the station at--"

"The station?" The boy still seated on the wall scoffed. "Got turned around, did you?"

"Yes, I think so. The way through...it was blocked off." Gathering the shreds of her courage, Clio took two measured steps forward. "Could you tell me how to get there from here, please?"

She turned her attention back to the boy who stood twenty feet in front of her. The lamp's light allowed her to make out his messy shock of red hair and the mass of freckles that covered his face. He glanced up at the boy on the wall, and they both looked at the sky.

"They're out and about a bit early today, I guess."

The boy on the wall nodded. "You shouldn't be worried

about getting *there*," he told Clio. "You should be worried about getting *out*."

Clio's pulse began to race faster. "What do you mean?" she spluttered. "There *is* a way through, isn't there? I mean, not all the streets are blocked, are they?"

Her voice came out high and breathless on the last question, and her arms crept around herself. She gripped her elbows as she stared at them. She wouldn't panic. She *wouldn't*.

"Maybe not yet," the red-haired one answered.

Not yet. She suppressed the urge to whimper.

"But soon, if they've been busy." The boy on the wall pulled one leg beneath his chin and regarded her with interest.

"You could," the red-haired boy called her attention back, "stay."

"Stay?" The pitch of her voice rose again.

"Yes, stay with us." The boy on the wall jumped down. Side by side, he stood with his companion. His tan complexion and dark hair contrasted with his friend.

They grinned at her.

"Well," the dark-haired one offered. "If you get inside and stay until morning, you'll probably be fine."

"But I--" Clio took a shuddering breath. "I just want to go home. *Please.* Please, show me the way out."

"What's your name?"

"Cl-Claudia." Clio faltered as she hid her real name in an utterly futile display of caution.

The red-haired boy grinned knowingly. "I'm Jack."

"Hi."

The dark-haired boy laughed, not unkindly, and Clio felt a hot flush spread over her cheeks. "Don't you want to know mine?" he asked.

Anxious and a little angry, but not wanting to antagonize her best chance of finding a way out, Clio nodded.

"I'm Jack, too, Cl-Cl-Claudia. You can call us Red Jack and Black Jack to keep us straight."

His smirk made her angrier, and she scowled, knowing

that he was only making fun of her.

"Thanks, *Jack.* Can you show me the way or not?"

Red Jack shrugged. "It may be too late already."

Clio could feel the tears prick her eyes. She fought to keep them from falling, though her distress finally seemed to faze the two boys. Black Jack sighed, and he exchanged a look with his companion.

"Maybe if we take her through the night market..."

"Yeah," Red Jack agreed. "Not a bad idea."

"Put this on."

Clio stared at the jacket Black Jack had removed. He held it toward her and raised his eyebrows.

"Do you want them to notice you?" he asked.

She didn't even know who *they* were, but she shivered to think of the shouting men and the long shadows that had stretched down the hill. She put the black jacket on and zipped it up, partially covering the white beacon of her dress.

"The hood, too."

With trembling fingers, she pulled the hood up around her face. It felt strange and uncomfortable. The unfamiliar warmth of another person's body enveloped her. His scent surrounded her, but Clio remembered herself enough to rouse a moment's politeness.

"Thank you," she murmured. She unconsciously thrust her hands deep into the jacket's pockets.

"Don't thank us yet," Red Jack replied with a grin.

"Come on." Black Jack slipped off like a shadow against the wall. Red Jack followed, not looking to see if Clio did the same.

She had no choice but to follow them, walking rapidly in the greater fear that she would lose sight of them and be left alone. Even worse, it was turning full dark.

For several minutes Clio trailed after them, occasionally hearing a voice or two from nearby. The Jacks made so many twists and turns that her sense of direction was hopelessly confounded. Finally, the sounds of life and activity grew louder.

They emerged onto a bustling enclave of shops and stalls. People dressed for the night strolled along the sidewalks on either side of the enclosed, exuberant market. Despite her earlier explorations of the city, this place was nothing like the markets she knew.

People laughed and chattered, and vendors hawked their wares...but it was different, somehow. The heels on the women's shoes seemed so tall and sharp, as if they were walking on pointed needles. Their lipstick was too bright, their voices too shrill. The men were loud and boisterous and seemed to lurk in every doorway, watching everything that passed in front of them with knowing leers. Even the scents of the foods seemed strange and unsettling.

Under different circumstances, Clio might have been charmed. But she had no desire now to linger, or to find out what went on past the long row of tantalizing doorways that opened onto the street.

"Don't think you're home free yet." Dark humor laced the voice in her ear.

On Clio's other side, an equally amused murmur made her shiver. "Not even close."

The Jacks tugged her arms and carried her between them, past the long line of doors and stalls and people. Just before they pulled her around a corner into a much quieter street, Clio looked over her shoulder.

Down at the far end of the market, where they had entered moments before, a single silhouette stained the shadow of the alleyway. There was something compelling and terrible about that one figure, stirring a deep intuition that she should escape its notice. But still, she looked, resisting the pull of the boys.

With horrified fascination, Clio watched the figure detach itself from the shadows and turn its head in her direction.

Her lips parted in a gasp, but her guides dragged her away. The Jacks whisked her down the street so quickly that she had to nearly run to match their strides.

"Oh, you really shouldn't have done that," Red Jack said

in grim mirth.

"Did he see us?" she whispered. "Is he...is he coming after *me*?"

"I'd say so, yeah. *They* are," the boy replied with malicious significance.

"But *why?*" Clio hated herself for uttering the useless question, and for dropping to a plaintive whine.

"She's feeling sorry for herself now," Black Jack commented.

"I think you're right."

"I'm not!" Clio exclaimed. "I'm just--"

"Just a lost little girl who came to play when she didn't know the rules?"

"I'm not..." *Lost.* Clio was well and truly lost. "...little."

Clio's anger flared at the mocking amusement she saw in their faces. "And this isn't a game," she added sharply.

The boys laughed, dragging her through a quick turn and then another. She was beginning to feel dizzy, and nausea made her stomach roll.

"Are we almost there?" she asked in desperation.

"That's an interesting question, isn't it?"

"Very. But I think what she means to ask is--are we almost *out*?"

"You *know* that's what I mean!" Clio cried in frustration.

"Shh. Voices carry around here."

Indeed, a smattering of hoots and calls broke out, sounding like the youthful, wild voices she'd heard earlier. She couldn't pinpoint the direction of the sound--it echoed so oddly within the walls here. But it was much too close for comfort.

They ducked into a cramped alley, and Clio clutched Black Jack's arm as they huddled against the wall. His face creased in something that may have been pity or just amused disgust. Then he jumped up to the fire escape that clung to the cement wall.

He reached for her. After a moment's hesitation, she took his hand and allowed the redhead to boost her up.

They all climbed as silently as possible to the roof of the

building. It was flat and empty, but the Jacks motioned for her to crouch down when those awful calls rose again. It sounded like a pack of petulant boys who'd outgrown innocent pastimes and gone feral.

"What now?" Clio whispered. She was growing more suspicious that this impromptu hide-and-seek was just a dark joke, but she had no choice other than to cling to her companions.

"Too bad," Red Jack murmured.

"*What?*" She gripped the boy's arm.

Black Jack shook his head. "It's a lost cause, after all."

Clio's muted panic finally erupted, and her vision brightened and tunneled to an alarming degree. "What do you mean?" she breathed.

"They're really on the move tonight."

"It was a good try," Red Jack offered. "Any other night, maybe..."

"Oh, God." Clio swayed in her unsteady crouch and dropped to her knees. "Don't let them find me. Please, you can't!"

"They'll find you soon enough."

She shook her head, incapable of further speech.

Black Jack pursed his lips. "There is *one* thing you could try."

Clio snapped her head back. "What? *What?!*"

Red Jack frowned at his friend. Clio dug her blunt nails deep into his arm.

"Tell me!" she begged.

The redhead didn't even look at her. His gaze stayed locked on his friend.

"But which is worse, Black?" he murmured.

"That's her choice to make, Red."

"*What* choice, dammit?! What are you talking about?!"

Both boys looked at her, all traces of amusement wiped from their expressions. An underlying excitement crackled below the surface.

"You could..." Red Jack began.

"...try your luck in *The Building,*" Black Jack finished.

"The building? You mean this one?"

"No," the Jacks answered in unison. "That one."

Clio's gaze followed their fingers to the opposite end of the roof. An imposing gray building lined with many dark windows dominated the view. Clio crept closer to the roof's edge.

The gray building's façade was done in some indeterminable style and gave no clue to its purpose. Graffiti tagged the gray stone, and some of the windows were covered or broken. The building looked as if it had been left unused for ages.

Clio knew it could be almost anything--an abandoned school, a factory, or even a grand, old apartment house. Marble steps led up to the front entrance, but the back of the building disappeared in the darkness behind a high stone wall topped with wrought-iron spikes. Whatever the building was or had been, it seemed out of place in the midst of the ugly, squat structures that surrounded it.

"What is it?" Clio whispered. She looked back at the boys, a wave of dizziness spinning the world for a moment. The boys' faces seemed to float in front of her.

"The way out." Brown freckles and white teeth loomed close. "*Maybe,*" Red Jack amended.

"Maybe," Black Jack agreed.

"Stop playing games," Clio hissed. "Can we get out that way or not? Does the other side come out on the avenue?"

Identical wicked grins split the faces of the two Jacks. Their eyes appeared black as they stared at her, pupils huge in the dark.

"Silly Claudia," Red Jack scolded lightly. "All work and no play makes Jack a dull boy."

"The game's the thing," Black Jack agreed.

Clio stared at them.

Were these boys stringing her along, or were they actually *crazy?*

Her dismay grew as the voices crowed from below. She heard more slapping footsteps along the alley. The blood drained from her face.

The two smiling Jacks watched Clio expectantly.

"Running out of time," Red Jack whispered. "You'd better hurry."

"You're not...coming with me?" Clio breathed. Her hands trembled, and she latched onto her backpack straps like they were a lifeline.

"Can't." Black Jack's eyes glimmered. "We belong here."

Clio bit down into the flesh of her lower lip. The fire escape behind them began to rattle.

"Oh..." Her gasp turned into a half-sob. "What if it's locked?"

"Only one way to find out."

Rough hands pushed her toward the roof's edge. She felt a moment of pure terror until she saw the metal stairs leading down, a mirror to the one she'd just climbed.

"Hellooo," an unfamiliar voice cackled. "Anybody up there?"

The insincere cheer of the voice made Clio shudder. She climbed onto the metal cage and looked at the Jacks, her gaze moving from one boy to the other.

"Good luck, Cl-Cl-Claudia."

She flushed suddenly with guilt. "My real name is Clio," she murmured.

"Tricky girl, isn't she?" A constellation of freckles twisted into new configurations.

"Keeps a few cards up her sleeve. Some might be offended."

"I-I'm sorry," Clio stuttered. "Thank you for helping me."

They ignored her gratitude, but Black Jack leaned down until his nose was inches from hers.

"Better run, Clio," he breathed. "And don't look back. They won't follow once you reach the steps. They won't *dare*."

"But be careful, all the same." Red Jack nodded sagely. "It's *The Building*, you know. A person might go in, but will he--"

"Or she."

"Or she," amended Red Jack, "come out the other side?"

The boys laughed again, sending Clio into a mad rush down the rusty stairs. The fire escape on the other side of the building clattered violently as her pursuers clambered to the top.

Focus, Clio ordered herself. *Hold onto the rail, drop to the ground.* Clio's knee skinned on the rough concrete, but she ignored the pain and the red drops that welled between the grit that lodged there. It was forty, fifty feet to that marble stairway.

Don't look back. She pushed up from her crouch and ran.

This was insane. She knew it, but she couldn't stop her feet from pounding toward the hulking beast of a structure. If only there was time to *think*--but the voices surrounded her. Shadows seemed to slip from the suffocating blackness and lope behind her, just out of reach.

Her legs pumped harder. Something seemed to brush her flying hair. *Fingers?* An oddly high-pitched laugh made her sob. It was so *close.*

She slammed against the bottom steps gracelessly and scrambled, using her hands as she lurched forward against the cold stone. Uncaring of her dignity, she threw herself onto the wide landing and heaved great, sobbing breaths. She waited for them to follow...but only hoots and catcalls reached her.

"Cliiiiooooo..."

Her skin crawled in revulsion as the syllables of her name echoed in the square.

How did they--?

She felt sick, that little betrayal clenching her heart. Had the Jacks told? They couldn't have. They had *helped* her! Or had they?

Her eyes rose to the red double doors that guarded the entrance. There was no lock that she could see, but that meant nothing. She would just have to find out for herself--if she chose to go in.

"Cliiiooo..." the voices taunted and teased. "Come out and play."

"We'll show you *lots* of games."

Catcalls and sniggered laughter assaulted her, but no one came closer. The Jacks hadn't lied about that, at least.

Don't look back.

Above the red door, large letters carved in old Roman font--the kind where the *u* looked like a *v*--spelled out two words: *Gauntlet, Unlimited.* Beneath that, on the curved arch that overspread the grand landing, was the inscription *Alea iacta est.* She was sure she'd heard that phrase before, though she couldn't remember where or what the words meant.

Caught between the terrible choices, Clio's fear faded for the barest moment into an eerie calm.

She could probably figure it out later. It would come to her; things usually did. Gallows humor pulled a thin smile to her lips. At least it didn't say, *Abandon all hope, ye who enter here.*

And then the fear came slamming back. Nothing could stop the trembling in her hands, but Clio stepped forward and wrapped her fingers around the ornate, iron bar and pushed. With startling ease, it swung open and a hush descended on the dark square.

Okay, then. One step over the threshold, a half-step sideways, and she released the ponderous door and waited for the inevitable closing thud. It slipped back into place with nothing but a deceptively gentle click.

All sound from outside was instantly cut off. She was left in a profound and heavy stillness that seemed to force the air from her lungs.

Yellowish, washed-out light from the lampposts in the square filtered through the grime of the high windows of the lobby. It was enough to allow Clio to make out the dimensions of the large room without illuminating the far corners. Across the way, curved staircases twisted up into the gloom, bracketing another imposing door.

She sagged back against the door, knees weak from the fading adrenaline. A thick silence seemed to fill the space until furtive scuffling sounds disturbed it. Clio grimaced.

Rats, no doubt. They were common enough, and rats she could handle.

It was harder--much harder--to think of moving away from the solid door. This abandoned building hardly seemed a sanctuary or the way out that she needed. She feared the Jacks had sent her on an even wilder goose chase, and Clio was tempted to turn and run back out into the square she'd just escaped.

But the possibility of facing the wild, pursuing men filled her with a greater dread. And she stopped at the disquieting thought that she would find the door locked. It would be worse to know that the decision had been taken from her.

I could wait until morning.

The thought of huddling in discomfort and anxiety for the entire night revolted her. She had only the Jacks' word that no one else would enter the building. She didn't want to wait here to test the truth of it.

She would have to take her chances in the building.

It was creepy, but she could deal with that one step at a time. She was too old to be afraid of the dark. A strap of her backpack had fallen down to her elbow, and she slid it back up as she squared her shoulders.

"Ready or not," Clio whispered in false bravado, "here I come."

With a steadying breath, Clio made her way through scattered debris, trying to mute the sound of her leather sandals on the marble. Despite her efforts, her right foot went skidding out from under her. She flailed gracelessly and landed on her butt with a bruising jolt. A sibilant curse escaped her and echoed around the four walls.

The offending item seemed to be a worn and creased brochure. Clio reached for it, squinting at the photo on the cover. It was a building--this building--but the text was small and fine, rendered in a font that would strain her eyes even under proper light. She folded it and slid it into the pocket of her jacket.

Black Jack's black jacket.

A laugh huffed out unexpectedly, and Clio pushed to her feet, barely aware of the stretched grin on her face. More skittering sounds came from the side of the room. Shadows seemed to dance in her peripheral vision, and she realized the danger of allowing her imagination to get the better of her.

"Get a grip, Clio," she murmured firmly.

She started again, picking a careful path through overturned remnants of furniture and assorted mess. The lobby was huge, and, even in the gloom, she could make out some of the architectural details that hinted at its past elegance. It must have been something in its day.

A troubled frown creased her forehead. It was odd that a place like this lay empty and abandoned in this part of the city. Unease bloomed at the thought that maybe the building wasn't abandoned at all.

She finally reached a closed door that stretched several feet above her head. It didn't seem like a door one could enter quietly, and she wanted nothing more than to slip unnoticed through all doorways and halls until she reached the exit on the other side.

Her gaze flickered from the darkened stairwell on the left to the one on her right, and Clio shuddered. The stairwells seemed like gaping mouths...long tongues let down to catch what they could. She had absolutely no desire to ascend in the dark to explore the upper reaches of the building. Nor did she want to stay in this room.

"It won't open by itself, you know."

Clio shrieked, jerking back as if burnt. She snapped her head around.

From the shadows, hoarse laughter wheezed from what seemed like a mound of rubble. "At least," the voice croaked, "it never has before."

Clio's eyes finally made out a huddled figure against the wall--one that was undeniably human and too small to be threatening. Clio expelled a long, shaky breath and hunched over the hand she'd unthinkingly pressed against her heart.

"Sorry," Clio gasped. "I didn't see you there."

"No harm done, girl. I was just having a little nap. But you won't tell them, will you?" The voice--*a woman's?*--held a hint of conspiratorial mirth.

"Tell who?" Clio asked cautiously.

The person sat up in a production of grunts and groans. The sound of scraping metal preceded a glowing flame that illuminated a creased, worn face. Thin lips clamped a slender cigarette between them, but surprisingly elegant fingers cupped the lighter. The jagged, dirty fingernails were a stark contrast to the smooth hands.

Wrinkles deepened as the old woman grinned. The lit cigarette swayed, its glowing orange tip capturing Clio's attention until the sharp click of the closing lighter snapped her out of it.

The woman didn't speak, and her expression was impossible to make out without the flame. Clio was gripped by the helpless awkwardness that always came when she was in the presence of someone homeless. Then the thought struck her that this *was* the woman's home, and Clio was an intruder.

"I'm sorry, do you...live here?"

A mucus-filled laugh coughed out harshly and Clio colored, embarrassed.

"Here and there," the woman croaked.

"I-I'm just... I mean, I was told that I could go through the building. That it would take me back to the main avenue. So I'm...passing through..." Clio's halting speech trailed off.

"Yes, you'll pass through. Everyone does." The tip of the cigarette glowed brightly again and a little bout of coughing ensued before the rough voice continued. "Except me. You could stay and keep me company. What do you say, girl?"

"I…thank you-- " Clio shifted uncomfortably, trying to suppress a shiver. "But I really want to go home."

"To market, to market, to buy a fat pig. Home again, home again, jiggety-jig."

Clio couldn't help but smile at the childish humor in the woman's voice. It evoked an image of the woman as a young girl, perhaps reciting the rhyme as she played. A deeper thrust of empathy sent Clio closer.

"I didn't buy a pig today," Clio answered.

With a sudden lurch that made Clio jump, the old woman cast something hard and small into the corner. It connected with a solid thud; a loud squeak and the scurrying of little feet accompanied a fleeing shadow.

"They try and steal my food when I'm not paying attention." A deep inhale finished off the last of the cigarette. The old woman stubbed it out on the floor. "Didn't buy any pigs, but I bet you saw some. The kind that walk on two legs."

A lewd gesture accompanied the conjecture. Clio gave a nervous laugh, startled by the abrupt turn of thought and its crudity, but the awkwardness fell away when the woman erupted into dry coughs. Alarm brought Clio to her knees, and she reached into her bag for the bottle of water.

"Here, drink this." Clio placed one hand on the woman's arm and lifted the bottle to her lips, helping to hold it steady as the woman's trembling hand came up to grasp it. A few mouthfuls made it down the woman's throat, and Clio pulled her hands away when the fit seemed to pass.

This close, the woman's stench hit Clio's nostrils with pungent force. Clio's compassion rose again.

"Are...are you hungry?" Clio asked. The bread she'd purchased earlier had cooled, but its fresh smell drifted from the open backpack. That simple interlude felt like it had taken place a hundred years before. "I have some rolls I bought a little while ago."

Clio offered the small bag tentatively, not wanting to offend, but the woman snatched it. She peered into the bag to sniff at the contents.

The woman reached out to pat Clio's hand. Clio flushed, embarrassed by the gratitude, until the strangely smooth fingers wrapped around her wrist and yanked her closer.

"You're a good girl." Clio struggled not to gag from the damp breath that washed over her face. It reeked of rotten food and bile and stale tobacco. "So I'll give you something in return."

"You don't have to," Clio protested, trying to regain possession of her arm without giving offense--but the woman's grip tightened, and Clio felt the beat of panic in her chest again. The woman's fingers were stronger than expected.

The woman fumbled in the deep folds of the many layers she wore. She pulled out a small object with a cackle of discovery.

"It's yours now," the woman said.

Her grip on Clio was suddenly replaced by a bracelet that dangled tiny charms. It jingled as Clio lifted her arm.

"Oh, but I can't take--"

"Tch. Tit for tat. You'll thank me later if not now."

The subtle rebuke made Clio flush again. "I--*thank you,*" Clio corrected. "It's very nice of you, I just meant it's not necessary."

"Of course it's not *necessary.*" The woman's tone was scornful. "It's a *gift.*"

Clio bit her lip. "I'm sorry."

The old woman grunted. "Better be on your way, girl," she said with a shade of spite. "You may be inside now, but it isn't safe to stay in one place too long." She sniggered and settled back against the wall, tearing into one of the rolls Clio had given her. "Unless you want to stay here with me forever, after all."

Dirty fingers suddenly snatched at Clio's arm, and Clio lurched back to evade the woman's grasp. She scrambled to her feet and stepped away; the woman made no attempt to follow. Mocking laughter made Clio's eyes prick with humiliation, and she snatched up her backpack in a fit of anger.

The old woman was singing now--a crooning song in her broken voice. As she sang, something small scuffled in the rubbish piled against the walls. Clio watched in horror as a large rat crawled into the woman's lap to take the piece of bread from her fingers. The woman spoke to the creature in cooing tones.

The numbing shock finally broke the last thread of Clio's composure. A sob of revulsion wrenched from deep within her as she turned and ran for the door. Blind instinct pushed her on; she only knew she couldn't stay there for one second longer.

Clio flung herself at the door, but it opened with unexpected ease. She stumbled into the utter blackness that waited beyond it.

Oh, God. Not good--not good at all.

Clio threw her hands out in front of her and felt for the wall. Her chest ached from the pounding of her heart as she shuffled along. There had to be a door, a *window* that would give her a way out. She reached a corner and twisted to follow the wall.

Her hands hit cold metal. She felt it cautiously, finding the long vertical seam of an elevator door. She shuffled sideways, her fingertips skimming the wall until she felt the control panel, the buttons. She moved past them in unreasoning fear of those doors opening in front of her to reveal a deep, dark shaft or something worse.

She continued her blind journey and bumped into something bulky. It was fronted by glass and a panel of buttons. *A vending machine?* she wondered.

She envisioned moldering candy bars. She shuddered and moved on, her hands sliding over nothing but peeling paint. Her fingertips eventually discovered a smooth plate that held a row of three switches, all in the down position.

Surely...surely it wouldn't work. But one by one she flicked them up and held her breath. One second, then two, then three passed before a low thrum reverberated around her. The sound resolved into buzzing, dirty fluorescent lighting that wavered above her head and illuminated the small elevator bank. A moment later, the hallway branching off the alcove lit up with its own hum of ancient bulbs.

Oh, great, she thought. A hysterical bubble welled up in her throat. *More doors.*

The corridor was long and wide, ending in a pair of industrial metal doors. She hoped that one was an exit--or if not, that it would take her away from all the insanity behind her. She forced her feet to move forward, ignoring the ranks of doors on either side, and sped up until she was running.

She sighed with relief when she saw the two doors weren't chained shut. The relief was short-lived.

They weren't chained, but locked. *Locked.*

A sudden and violent hatred for the two boys who had sent her here burned through Clio. Her fist slammed against the metal door with a muted boom.

What now? she thought miserably.

Clio took a shuddering breath. To her right, the open stairwell offered two choices--up or down. To go down, to descend to an even deeper level, wasn't something she thought she could do. It also seemed blatantly stupid.

To go up was marginally less terrifying, but it would also take her farther from a quick exit. She turned, looking back down the long hallway at the doorway to the lobby. Going back wasn't an option--the old woman's warning rang clear in her mind.

Clio's breath came fast and harsh through her nose, punctuating the quiet as she fought back tears. Before her fear could paralyze her, she forced herself to approach the closest door. The knob was cold in her hand, and she twisted it slowly, her pulse speeding up with the motion.

Her eyes closed in defeat. It was locked, too.

Clio inhaled shakily and took a few steps forward. She tried another door and the knob turned easily, but when she pushed open the door to an empty room, it was almost a letdown.

Desperate, Clio rushed to the window that had been covered in a wooden plank. She pulled at the board, scraping her hands as she furiously tried to pry it away. It didn't budge. There wasn't even a crack to peek through. Clio sobbed out a curse, resting her forehead against the rough wood.

After a moment, she lifted her head and numbly walked out. She closed the door behind her.

A third of the way down the hallway, another door finally opened to her touch. Her eyes widened as the light from the hallway spilled into a small bedroom. It looked like a dormitory room, but it stank of stale air. A metal bedframe rested along one wall, and a desk, chair, and small dresser made up the rest of the furniture.

She found a switch that snapped on the dingy, bare bulb overhead. Clio's heart sank. The window was also boarded here, though a sheer yellow curtain had been hung in front of it, as if in some ghastly effort to provide warmth to the gloomy room. A layer of grime coated all visible surfaces, and rumpled, gray sheets covered the bed. Her throat tightened with pity at the thought of anyone actually sleeping there.

A smaller door stood in the wall across from the bed. Clio made herself walk to it.

"Please," she whispered. If this didn't provide a way out then she'd have to find something to pry open the window. *But please,* she begged again, silently this time.

Before her hand closed around the door handle, a hushed sound made her freeze.

It had come from behind the door, soft and stealthy--like the shuffle of a footstep or a sharp intake of breath. Or had she imagined it? Excruciatingly slow, she turned her head and put her ear as close to the door as she dared. She held her breath and counted to ten. Nothing. A few more beats and her pulse began to even out.

Just as she reached again for the handle, warm, moist air blew across her toes. It was only a moment of pure shock that sealed her lips and kept her from shrieking.

A draft? Just a warm draft? Clio stared down at the slight gap between the bottom of the door and the floor.

Then comprehension slammed into her. Someone--or some *thing,* her mind morbidly supplied--could be down on that dirty floor on the other side of the door. *Slithering on the cold ground like a snake.* Clio shuddered, envisioning a long, rough tongue flicking out to lick her bare toes.

If she crouched down, would she find something peering at her, its eyes black with blown pupils to see in the dim light? She could feel disconnect slipping back, threatening to whiten her vision.

She couldn't faint. She *couldn't.* Who knew what would happen then?

Her fingers curled, nails digging into her palms. She focused on the pain and slid her feet backward in carefully measured steps. Halfway across the room, she turned--and her hands flew up to crush against her mouth.

In the thick dust of the mirror that hung over the dresser someone had recently dragged their fingers, leaving a brighter gleam of the reflective surface in the tracks.

Her chest hitched once. Clio slowly looked over her shoulder at the door behind her.

Get out. The beat of her heart drummed the rhythm. *Get out. Get out. Get out. Get out.*

Survival pangs moved her limbs. Out in the hall, she closed the door with trembling hands.

She couldn't stay here. She was done. She'd go back outside--right through the lobby. Maybe the Jacks would hide her, or she could hide herself and wait until morning. Whatever happened, happened. She was *done.* Warring instincts slowed her feet, but she took a step forward, then another one.

A loud ding came from the elevators in the bank around the corner. Clio froze. In a second, she knew she would hear the smooth rumble of doors gliding open.

It wasn't fair. What was she supposed to do? She couldn't move. She couldn't think...

"Are you crazy?!" a voice suddenly hissed in her ear.

Clio was jerked around to face a tall, dark-skinned girl with cropped hair. The girl glared at Clio in fear and disgust.

Clio's throat constricted in shock. Their faces were so close, Clio could see that the eyes she stared into were different colors--one blue and one brown.

The girl snarled quietly. "You turned the lights on?!" she whispered furiously.

She began to drag Clio down the hallway, away from the lobby. The pneumatic slide of the doors echoed in the corridor. Someone down there said something, garbled words Clio couldn't make out.

"We've got to get out of here *now,*" the girl whispered. Her fingers bruised Clio's upper arm.

Down the hallway, muffled laughter broke out. Clio looked into those strange eyes and then back down the hallway, feeling as if the world had slowed and now wavered, like a dream. Shadows tangled and moved in the alcove at the end.

A vicious jerk snapped Clio's neck back around. "Get a grip!" the girl hissed. "Go to the fourth floor, second door on the right at the far end. Lock it and wait there." She shoved Clio at the stairs just as a shout burst from the end of the hall. "*Run.*"

The floating sense of numbness deserted Clio in one fell rush, draining the blood from her face. A hit of adrenaline propelled her up the stairs as fast as she could go. Behind her, she heard the girl yell--a taunt--before pounding up behind Clio. Loud catcalls pursued them with the sound of so many feet.

Clio stumbled, passed a landing and another. How many was that? The shouts grew muted as Clio reached what she thought was the fourth floor. It was pitch-black up there, completely devoid of light.

The girl hadn't followed. Had she led their chasers away? Clio ran blindly to the end of the hallway, one hand on the wall, trying to remember what the girl had said. *Second door on the right from the end.* She fumbled to what she thought was the right one.

It opened. She ran in and shut it with a sob, her fingers finding the lock and turning it until it clicked. Only then did her fingers search the wall for a switch. She didn't care if it was stupid. She didn't care what the girl would say...if she ever saw her again.

The light snapped on, which was when Clio realized her eyes were squeezed shut. She opened them and blinked. As her eyes adjusted to the dim light, she took in the ugly, gray bathroom and its dirty tile floor.

Clio dropped herself into a corner. She hugged her knees and rocked slowly, her gaze never leaving the locked door.

♦ ♣ ♠ ♥

Chapter 2

♦ ♣ ♠ ♥

Clio woke with a start and froze.

Her ears strained to hear the stealthy sounds that had seemed so close a moment ago--a faint whisper of breath; an insidious slide of creeping footsteps; the faint, careful scrape of metal in a turning lock. But the silence remained unbroken. She quietly sat up and took surveillance of the small, utilitarian bathroom where she had gone to ground.

The harsh brightness from the overhead light made her squint. The sink, the toilet stall, the dull mirror, the mop and bucket--it was all just as it had been when she'd curled up on the cold tiles and finally fallen asleep. Her eyes went to the still-locked door, and the erratic pounding of her heart began to slow.

The breath she'd been holding released in a long sigh. She used her knuckles to brush the dried residue of sleep from the corners of her eyes.

She hadn't dreamt her chase through the city. This was real. She'd been herded into the building by those awful voices calling her name. The Jacks had been part of it--pretending to help her--but they must have known. The crazy lady from the lobby. The unseen people crowding around her in the dark...and that girl.

That girl had *helped* her. Where was she now?

Clio pulled her knees beneath her chin, her back against the wall, and ignored for a moment the dull ache of a full bladder. Her dirty, scraped knee throbbed as the blood-flecked skin stretched tight. Gingerly, she stretched her legs out again, and catalogued her other aches: sore muscles from a night spent on the hard floor, a slight twinge from a rolled ankle, an empty stomach, and the promise of a headache brewing at the base of her skull.

All things considered, she was in pretty good shape. Clio slowly stood.

The bathroom held no window, but a small, slatted vent near the upper edge of the wall allowed some natural light into the room. She could see the pattern of light and shadow on the floor. *Daylight, then.* It wasn't a particularly reassuring thought, but anything was better than the dark.

As quietly as she could, she retrieved the bucket and overturned it beneath the vent, before climbing on top. Even with the added height, she couldn't do more than graze the bottom half of the metal vent with her fingertips. No sounds of traffic or people or pigeons reached her. The unnatural silence was almost more chilling than anything she'd experienced so far. How could it be possible that a neighborhood in the middle of the city could sound so...abandoned? She shivered at the thought.

She could yell for help, and maybe no one would hear her--or maybe they *would,* only not from outside. The last thing she wanted was to hear a voice on the other side of the bathroom door, or worse, to see the handle turning back as someone slowly turned it.

She stepped off the bucket and entered the stall. A roll of toilet paper still hung in its place; she pulled off two long strips to lay on either side of the toilet seat. The absurdity of her fastidiousness struck her, and a humorless grin twisted her lips as she sat down to relieve her aching bladder. *One day, when you've been trapped here long enough, you'll be just like that old woman in the lobby.* The voice inside her head sounded darkly amused and strange, as if it didn't belong to her at all. *You won't be so choosy about where and how you go.*

Clio clenched her jaw in denial as she rose and adjusted her clothing. *That will never happen.* She flushed the toilet without thinking and winced at the loud rush of water.

Stupid, she chastised herself. *You have to be more careful!*

She needed to drink, though, even if the sink would make its own noise. It would fill her empty stomach, at least. The sink was stained, but the water came out clear and cold. Clio filled her cupped hands and drank, repeating the process until the front of the borrowed jacket she wore was damp from the water that had trickled down her chin.

She wiped the remaining moisture from her face with her sleeve and finally dared to look in the spotted mirror. A tension she hadn't been fully aware of eased when she met the gaze of her own reflection. Her eyes were puffy and dark-shadowed, her face creased from the grain of the backpack she'd used as a pillow. But it was still her.

What were you expecting, anyway?

Her reflection didn't answer the unspoken question. Clio reached up and slowly used her fingers to comb through the tangles in her hair.

She turned away, her hands slipping into the pockets of the jacket. She frowned as her fingers touched something; she pulled out the pamphlet she had picked up in the lobby. The gloss had worn away, taking part of the text with it, but she could still see the picture of the building's entrance with its grand, red doors.

Gauntlet, Unlimited. The motto *Alea iacta est*--carved above the door--was written in pretty script beneath the picture. A translation lay below it:

The die is cast.

What's that supposed to mean? Clio opened the brochure and skimmed over the contents of the inner flaps.

Its location in the city center makes it a desirable, beautiful, and interesting place of residence...

Clio snorted.

Gauntlet is designed to provide all the comforts of a quiet, pleasant home, combined with special care and curriculum tailored to each individual candidate.

"Candidate?" Her brow creased. "Candidate for what?"

She still wasn't sure what kind of place it was. From the odd phrases that caught her eye, it could be anything--a school, a research center, or even some kind of weird religious institution.

Under the heading *Tenets* was a bulleted list:

Experimental Philosophy. Ambient Rhetoric. Improvisational Theology. Karmic Theater. Practical Psychosomatics.

Her eyebrows rose.

The back of the pamphlet was stained by water or some other substance, so Clio could only make out snatches of descriptions and blotched photos. Whatever this place used to be, it had seen better days. Now it was nothing more than a dump and a trap, full of squatters and creeps and--

"I see you followed my advice."

Clio screamed. In what seemed a feat of remarkable physics, she threw her back against the far wall in a split second. Her heart beat wildly as she stared at the tall, unsmiling girl who had helped her the night before.

"H-how did you get in here?" Clio gasped. She hadn't come in through the door, Clio was sure of that.

The girl studied her closely for a moment, then reached into a deep pocket of her pants. "You look hungry."

Clio reflexively caught the can tossed to her. Peaches. Her mouth began to water in anticipation of the sweet juice of the fruit. Her stomach churned, a soundless rumble awakening her hunger.

Still, Clio watched the girl carefully. "Who are you?" she finally asked.

The girl's eyes narrowed, but after a moment, her shoulders shrugged. She stepped nearer to Clio, ignoring the way Clio tensed.

"My name's Britt." The girl folded her legs and sat on the floor, pulling out another can and lifting the tab to roll the lid open. "What's yours?"

Clio bit her lip. The question brought back unpleasant thoughts, but it wasn't like giving her name could hurt her now. "Clio," she offered reluctantly, sliding down the wall to sit. She scooted her knees up as a psychological barrier.

Britt pulled out a slice of peach with her fingers and sucked the juices off it before popping it into her mouth. "Just get here last night?"

Clio nodded. "Yeah...are you...I mean...have you been here long?"

Britt shrugged. "Long enough."

"What *is* this place?" The question came out as something of a whine, but Clio didn't care. A rush of questions spilled out of her mouth before she could wait for an answer.

"How did you get here? Were you chased, too? Do you know the Jacks?"

"The Jacks?" Britt repeated.

"The boys from outside. One had red hair, and the other black. And...well, they said they were both called Jack."

Britt's eyes flickered, but she looked away as her face closed over. "Never heard of them."

"Oh..." Disappointment flooded Clio. She had hoped this girl might know what was going on.

"Are you..." Clio tried to think of a way to phrase it tactfully. "Are you living here? I mean, did you come here...on purpose?"

Britt's gaze returned with incredulous disgust. "Right." The sarcasm was thick. "Because my dream in life is to be constantly chased by prowlers and eat breakfast, lunch, and dinner out of a can." She dug into the peaches again and waved a slice around. "And to save your clueless, ungrateful ass after a really fun day of scavenging through shit in real-life survival horror mode. Only here, there's no walk-through guide, and I'm pretty sure we only get the one life."

Shocked by the sudden heat of Britt's reply, Clio shrank back. "I'm sorry."

"Don't be." Britt chewed the fruit and licked her lips. "It's not your fault we're here."

"Then whose fault is it?" Clio asked. "You make it sound like this is some big game." Clio sat forward and looked at

Britt intently. "What's really going on? And...and *why me?"*

"Why you?" Britt's mouth twisted, but she regarded Clio with something like pity. "Why me? Who knows? We're just the playing pieces, I think. Or windup toys. Revved up and let loose to bounce around this madhouse." She shrugged. "Maybe we're in control, or maybe someone else is."

"But--"

"As for what this is," Britt interrupted, "it's the Gauntlet. Says so right on the box, doesn't it? And there's only one goal when you're running a gauntlet."

Clio could figure out that one for herself. "Make it to the other side."

Britt nodded. "Yeah. Preferably in one piece."

"You haven't found a way out?" Clio asked weakly.

A sour look crossed Britt's face. "Would I be here now?"

"How long *have* you been here?"

"You ask a lot of questions," Britt murmured. Her fingers strayed up to the necklace that rested against her collarbone. It was a simple silver chain, adorned with a small pendant--a single metal die. Even in the dim light, Clio could see that the piece was beautifully rendered.

"Look," Britt went on. "Just because I saved your ass last night and I'm taking pity on you *now* doesn't mean we're best friends, or that I trust you." She didn't sound angry, but she wore a scowl. "Because we're not, and I don't. That's the first rule you should learn. Don't trust anyone around here. Got it?"

Clio nodded. Embarrassment sent her fiddling with the can of peaches. She opened it and the scent of the sweet syrup made her stomach rumble. Clio quickly glanced at Britt before mumbling her thanks and slipping a slice into her mouth.

Oh, it was better than she'd expected--the hit of sugar shocked her system and eased the shaky tension of her body that she hadn't even acknowledged. She made quick work of the rest of the can and licked her fingers clean.

"Thank you," she said again, offering Britt a tentative smile.

She received a grunt in return, but Britt seemed to soften a little. Clio watched Britt play with her necklace again--obviously an unconscious habit. Clio lifted a finger toward the die-shaped pendant, only meaning to point.

"That's an unusual--"

But before Clio could finish, Britt grabbed her wrist in an unforgiving grip. "Don't touch it," Britt snapped.

Clio stared in shock as her arm was held aloft. Britt's cold words were punctuated by a hard, steady squeeze to Clio's wrist, and her oddly colored eyes narrowed.

"I wasn't going to," Clio said tightly, somewhat afraid, but returning the glare. She tried to jerk her arm away, but Britt held firm. Clio's forgotten charm bracelet jingled on her captured arm.

Britt's gaze moved lower, and her eyes widened. Her other hand came up to push Clio's sleeve away. As she peered at the dangling charms, Clio suddenly noticed something she hadn't the night before.

Five charms hung there: the four symbols from a deck of playing cards--a spade, a heart, a diamond, and a club--and a little foolscap complete with tiny bells. The charms were simple, an odd design choice for an older woman.

But Britt seemed rapt.

"Hey," Clio said as she gave a tentative tug of her arm. Britt's sudden obsession was freaking her out.

Britt's mismatched eyes fixed on hers. "Where did you get this?" she demanded.

"From an old woman in the lobby. She was crazy. Well, she was okay at first, but then things got *seriously*--"

"Shut up," Britt snapped. Her grip grew tighter. "Listen. Don't lose this."

"Ow! What are you--"

Britt jerked Clio's arm. "I *mean* it. Don't lose it, and don't flash it around if you can help it."

"*Okay!*" Clio blurted. "Whatever. I wasn't planning to."

Britt finally released her wrist. Clio rubbed it sulkily, wondering if Britt wasn't completely loony herself.

"I know you think I'm out of my mind," Britt replied.

Clio flushed, hating how easily Britt read her. Britt seemed to ignore it.

"But trust me," Britt continued. "It's important. It's your best chance of finding a way out."

Clio stared doubtfully at the bracelet. "How?"

"You'll have to figure that out, but it was given to you. It's yours, so it'll mark your path. A way only *you* can find."

"My path..." Clio repeated slowly. "Is that what your necklace does for you?"

A brief silence filled the air between them before Britt nodded. "Yes."

Clio felt like Britt was lying, or not telling the whole truth, but she couldn't say why. "But couldn't we...join up?" Clio asked. "Work together?"

Britt scoffed. "Like I need someone to babysit on top of everything else."

Clio's crestfallen expression seemed to elicit a sigh from Britt. The girl added grudgingly, "We'll see. I'm *not* making any promises."

Clio grinned.

♦♣♠♥

Several hours later, Clio's optimism had vanished. Britt led her upstairs and down, through corridors and black hallways that stretched endlessly. The Gauntlet was much larger than anything Clio had first envisioned.

It didn't make *sense.* Clio had never heard of a building this size in the city--but even if it *did* exist, how could something like that be kept a secret?

"I don't understand why we're doing this," Clio complained at last. "Why can't we just keep looking for a way out?"

She was tired and hungry and filthy, and the last thing she wanted to do was follow Britt any longer through the bewildering maze of halls. If Britt left her now, she wasn't sure she could even find her way back to the front door--although Britt had assured her that they could never get out that way.

"You're right," Britt exclaimed. "Let's head straight to the exit we have the exact directions to. Hey, why don't you lead the way?"

Britt sounded irritated beneath her sarcasm, and it gave Clio a perverse sense of pleasure to have finally gotten under the girl's skin. Even so, she wasn't about to alienate the only other normal person she'd encountered, and one who seemed willing to help her.

"Sorry," Clio muttered. "I'm just--"

"Tired. Hungry. I know," Britt said flatly. "*That's* why we're doing this. We can't just call for takeout or run down to the corner store for supplies. Think of this as an elaborate dumpster dive. If you want to survive, you've got to keep your eyes open for anything that will help you."

Clio was silent a moment. "But...won't it all run out at some point?" she asked. "This place is enormous, but there are other people looking for supplies, too, right?"

"You keep thinking this place is normal. It's not. Things can...change."

"What do you mean?"

"I think..." Britt hesitated. "I think stuff is planted sometimes. Never obviously, but in ways that make it seem natural. Like finding a hidden stash of food that someone may have left at a safe point. I do that--set up a cache here and there. You never know when you might get cornered or have to run away from your current base." She let out a breath. "And the Gauntlet is much bigger than you think."

Clio thought about that unpleasant truth for a while.

"I hate this place," Clio murmured at last.

Britt snorted. "Get used to it. Anyway, lucky for you, foraging was the only reason I was that close to the main lobby. Haven't been back in ages, so I figured I'd give it a quick look." She shook her head in disgust. "There you were, just waiting for the prowlers like a deer in headlights."

"The prowlers," Clio repeated. "You said that before. Who

are they?"

"People you want to stay far away from." Britt flicked the flashlight beam in Clio's eyes, making Clio wince. "*Never* go to the subbasements. Stay clear of the lower levels if you can help it. They usually don't go too high, and they only come out at night."

"What difference does it make?" Clio pushed the flashlight away. "It's always dark in here."

"Who knows?" Britt bounced the light around the intersection of four hallways. "Just be glad that's how it works."

"Yippee," Clio deadpanned.

"Cheer up." Britt walked away, and a moment later the lights in the left-hand corridor flickered to life. Blinking away the discomfort, Clio met Britt's amused gaze.

"Let's go shopping," Britt announced.

Clio watched Britt jiggle the handle of the first door. When it didn't open, she pulled thin tools out of one of her pockets and bent to pick the lock.

"You take one side of the hall," Britt said, "and I'll take the other. If it's locked, just move down. Most of them won't be." When Clio hesitated, Britt raised an eyebrow.

"It's not rocket science," Britt added. "Just search the room for anything useful. This wing is a dormitory, so you might find some toiletries and things like that. Oh..." Britt looked almost wistful. "If you find any cigarettes, grab them."

Britt disappeared inside the room before Clio could work up the nerve to try her own door. Clio had to fight the urge to follow after her like a little duckling.

It was broad daylight outside, right? Even if Clio couldn't see it or prove it. Britt said it was so, and Clio's only choice was to believe her.

"Prowlers," Clio muttered. They were probably all delusional--vampire wannabes or something. That made sense, actually. Maybe she had wandered into some huge live-action role-playing game. LARPers who had gone overboard were freaky, but if that were true, then she'd be able to just tell them that she'd accidentally wandered in. They'd probably be happy to get her out of here. She was messing up their script, for all she knew, and that was why they'd chased her.

Despite her theories, her hand remained still on the handle in front of her. *Don't be a wimp,* she ordered herself.

Clio opened the door.

It was a dorm room, just like Britt had said, but Clio had a hard time imagining anyone wanting to live there. It was stark, cold, and uncomfortable. This blank institutional décor pervaded everything Clio had seen in the Gauntlet so far, except for that grand lobby. That, at least, must have been beautiful once.

To lure people in.

Clio jumped when Britt called from across the hall. "You'll have better luck finding stuff if you actually go inside," Britt said dryly.

Clio's cheeks burned as she rushed inside. There wasn't much to explore. The dresser drawers smelled musty; they held neatly rolled socks and a stack of white underwear that had seen better days. No way was Clio desperate enough to wear someone else's used underwear, even if it had been laundered a billion years ago.

The second row of drawers held personal items: a monogrammed brush and mirror set, makeup, and a faded pulp fiction paperback book that looked decades old. It was strange how such everyday items seemed like mysterious, ancient artifacts in this situation.

Who had owned these? More importantly, why were these things still *here?* What had happened to the owner?

Clio frowned, shaking herself out of those thoughts. "As if I care," she murmured. "I just want out of here."

On impulse, she grabbed the book and put it in her bag. The rest of the drawers yielded nothing helpful, so she moved to the closet. Two shapeless garments that looked like hospital gowns hung on hooks inside, a pair of slippers neatly lined up beneath them.

She turned to the only other door in the room. Clio opened it to find a bathroom with an identical door on the other side of the sink.

What a surprise. A dirty gray room.

When she turned on the light, her reflection stared back at her from the spotty mirror. Clio made a face and then went in. The medicine cabinet yielded a decent haul. Clio took a bottle of aspirin, a pair of small scissors, and rolls of bandages and tape, but left the half-used tube of hardened toothpaste.

A pillbox caught her eye, and she looked at it curiously. Through the semiopaque plastic, she could see the vague shapes of pills in pink, blue, and yellow candy shades. The box had no label, so she put it back and closed the cabinet.

The mirror showed her a dusty smudge on the bridge of her nose. She rubbed it away before turning on the faucet out of habit, but the pipes only gave a creaky groan. That was worrisome. The water didn't work everywhere, apparently. She was glad of the comforting weight of the bottle she carried in her pack.

A black spider crawled out of the sink's drain. Clio shuddered and backed away. "It's all yours," she muttered.

She left the dry basin and opened the door to an adjoining room. It was a mirror image of the first, with the twin bed flush against the far wall and the dresser by the door. She squatted to go through it. A few snapshots were scattered in the bottom drawer--Clio picked one up and looked at the unsmiling face of a girl not much older than she.

The other pictures were of the same girl, all in a similar pose, but her face changed subtly in each shot, running the gambit between a fresh-faced, subtle smile and an expressionless mask. They were mixed together, so Clio had no way of knowing the evolution of the shots. She couldn't help being curious about which had come first, the smile or the mask, and if it was the Gauntlet that had prompted the transformation.

Out in the hall, a door opened and closed; she knew Britt was getting ahead of her and would probably be annoyed if she took too long. She closed the drawer and reached for the next one, but the slow creak of rusty hinges froze her in mid-motion.

"Britt?" Clio's voice wavered.

Britt didn't answer, but a door swung open and bumped against the wall behind her. Slowly, Clio looked over her shoulder.

The closet door gaped open, and a pale leg drew back inside. Clio heard a clatter and a thump, and then a thin, stooped figure shambled out from the darkness.

Clio screamed.

The shaggy head rose and turned in her direction. Clio's stomach plummeted to her feet at the sight of the blank, slack-jawed face. The woman began to shuffle toward Clio; Clio scrambled back and banged her hip painfully on the edge of the dresser.

The woman kept coming. Clio couldn't see her eyes because her bangs were so overgrown, but she seemed to have Clio in her sights. Clio ran for the door to the hallway, yanked it open, and rushed right into Britt.

Britt grunted and staggered back from the impact, but she managed to keep both of them on their feet. Clio jerked away and pointed at the room. "There's someone in there!" she cried.

Clio screamed again as the woman appeared in the doorway. But before the woman could come after them, Britt strode forward and gave the woman a hard shove. She calmly reached around the door, turned the lock on the knob, and shut the door to the room.

Clio stared at her, her heart galloping in her chest.

"I..." Clio's voice skewed high and shaky. "I thought you said the prowlers don't come out during the day!"

Britt gave a humorless laugh. "That's not a prowler."

Confused by Britt's attitude, Clio struggled to control the flight instinct raging through her. "Then who--*what* is she?!"

"There's something wrong with them," Britt offered, "but that's all I know. Brain damage, maybe."

"Brain damage?!" Clio cried. "How?!"

Another shrug from Britt ratcheted up Clio's frustration,

but Britt seemed unconcerned. "You'll see them around," Britt added. "Ignore them unless they get too close, but they're easy to avoid. They won't hurt you."

Britt moved on to another door and went in. Clio ran after her.

"But--"

"Look, I wouldn't obsess over things that don't matter right now. If you want to try and figure out more about how some drooler got the way she is, be my guest." Britt pushed a toppled table out of her way with her foot. She didn't bother looking back at Clio.

"But first you need to learn how to take care of yourself," Britt said evenly. "That's the only chance you've got."

♦♣♠♥

"Come on."

Clio stopped searching through the drawer and looked up. The tone of the casual command made it clear that sticking around would be a bad idea. "Did you hear something?"

Britt walked out without answering or waiting to see if Clio followed. Clio did, shutting the door behind her.

Ever since Britt had let her tag along, Clio had learned to trust the girl's instincts, even if she didn't fully trust the girl herself. The past several days had given her a better understanding of the vastness of the building and its bewildering layout, as well as the hierarchy of its so-called residents. She'd gotten much more efficient at scavenging the rooms and even finding her way around the place, though being separated from Britt for longer than a half hour made her *extremely* anxious.

The fresh chemical smell of a marker made her wrinkle her nose. Britt had already penned the rough, small symbol on the inner doorframe to indicate they'd explored the room. It was adorned with the additional flourish that marked it as a potential safe spot. Clio knew all too well that you could never assume it *stayed* safe.

The hallway was still empty, but Clio didn't relax. Britt tucked the purple marker into one of the deep pockets of her cargo pants and jerked her chin. Again, Clio followed.

"Where are we going?" Clio asked.

"This way."

Clio rolled her eyes behind Britt's back, then caught up to shoot her a pointed look. "Any place in particular?"

"You stink," Britt declared.

Clio gaped a moment, earning a smirk from Britt. It certainly wasn't a lie, but Clio defensively shoved her hands deep into the pockets of her jacket.

"I haven't exactly had time for a luxurious bubble bath lately," Clio replied with a scowl. "And you don't smell any better."

Britt actually laughed at that--it was more of a snort, really, but Clio was happy to see a glimpse of humor. "Exactly."

"Exactly, what?"

Without breaking stride, Britt easily maneuvered the pile of debris that partially blocked the entrance to another wing. The heavy doors hung askew, pulled off their hinges in some way that Clio didn't want to consider. Clio followed a little less gracefully, hanging onto the doorframe with one hand as she climbed over the rubble.

"We need a bath," Britt explained. She pointed to a door that looked like a maintenance closet.

"In there?" Clio asked. She was skeptical, but the idea was tempting. Several days without washing or brushing her hair had left it lank and stringy. Clio ran a hand through it, making a moue of disgust at the greasy feel of the strands.

Britt smirked again and bent to pick the lock. She'd taught Clio and given her one of her spare lock pick sets, though Clio still wasn't as good at it. Britt had shown her that it didn't work on all locks, but it was worth it if you could lock a room you wanted to have safe access to later.

"Through here."

Britt wrenched the lock open with a click. The room beyond held a fuse box, a bucket and mop, and a shelf that suspended a bottle of bleach. A pair of long, blue overalls hung from a peg on the far wall. Britt tugged at a dangling chain to turn on the closet's lone lightbulb before closing and locking the door behind them.

"Charming." Clio hoped she'd get used to the depressing drabness of the building. "You take me to the nicest places."

"If you don't like it," Britt folded her arms across her chest and raised an eyebrow in challenge, "do something about it."

Clio sighed and surveyed the compact closet. A small metal access panel was fastened under the shelving. It popped off easily to reveal some pipes and a shutoff valve.

Too obvious. She cast a quick look at Britt, who seemed to watch her with faint amusement. Clio's ears went pink, and she turned and pulled aside the hanging overalls. Nothing there, but Clio pressed along the wall. Finally, she looked up.

A corner of the ceiling just above the shelving had a faint seam. She brightened. She quickly overturned the bucket, climbed onto it, and rose up on her toes to prod at the seam. A hard lunge popped the access panel out of its snug fit, and Clio pushed it open.

"Yes!"

The sound of slow clapping interrupted her concentration. She turned to see Britt's slanted grin.

"Of course, with the time you took, the prowlers would've already had you."

Clio didn't like the reminder. A prickle traveled down her spine. "I thought this was just for practice," she argued.

Britt's smile evaporated. "It's never just for practice around here," she replied coldly. "You'd better remember that."

They stared at each other for an uncomfortable moment, then Clio nodded curtly. "Are we going up, then?"

Britt laced her hands together and braced herself near Clio. Clio held onto the shelf with one hand and stepped into the stirrup of Britt's hands. The muscles in Britt's arms corded when she heaved Clio toward the ceiling. Clio grabbed the edges of the opening and pulled herself through as Britt pushed her from below.

A dark shaft greeted her, and she struggled to contain her claustrophobic response. Tight spaces were the stuff of nightmares. She'd prefer spiders or rats or just about *anything* to another crawl through the dark. Except nothing was worse than a run-in with the prowlers, from what Britt implied.

There was just enough light to see down the shaft stretching before her. It was pretty big; at least the walls wouldn't touch her. *It could be worse,* she told herself. *A lot worse.*

"Here." Britt passed her a pencil flashlight. Clio clicked it on right before the light in the closet snapped off.

Cover your tracks was one of the first rules Britt had taught her. Using the bucket and the shelving, Britt boosted herself up with an ease that Clio envied. Clio scrambled backward on her hands and knees, the flashlight pointed at the floor of the tunnel.

"Stay close," Britt warned.

Britt flipped the cover back down before edging past Clio. She reached back for the flashlight, and Clio passed it to her with some reluctance. The narrow passage went straight ahead before branching off in two directions.

Britt flicked the light up to the roof of the shaft, illuminating the purple symbol that marked the right-hand path. When she tipped the flashlight under her chin, the yellow light turned her grin ghoulish.

"After you," Britt drawled.

"What's in the other direction?" Clio asked.

"Don't know. Haven't had a chance to find out. Do you want to explore?"

Clio shook her head violently, and Britt snorted.

"Then get going," Britt ordered. "It's getting late."

"Right," Clio said without enthusiasm. She crawled past Britt, the beam of the flashlight providing tight illumination over her shoulder. Her knees were beginning to hurt, and the close quarters were getting to her. She struggled to keep her breathing even. It seemed loud in her own ears.

The walls ***aren't*** *closing in,* Clio reassured herself, but her mind still spat out terrible fantasies. She envisioned the shaft narrowing to brush up against her back and arms...until she was forced to wriggle forward on her belly. She'd end up trapped like a specimen in a test tube, unable to turn around or move or breathe--

"Hey!"

The sharp word from behind echoed down the shaft. Clio looked back, and Britt squinted at her.

"It's just about a hundred more feet," Britt called evenly. The light wavered and dimmed as Britt caught up, before going out altogether. She cursed and shook the light, but it didn't brighten.

"We're almost there," Britt huffed. "Just keep moving."

In the utter dark, Britt's breathing *also* seemed abnormally loud. Clio found that sound behind her unsettling. After several moments of blind crawling, Clio could almost imagine that it wasn't Britt behind her--that maybe she'd sent Clio ahead so she could slip back and take the other turn, abandoning Clio in the dark. Maybe the breathing she heard wasn't Britt's at all anymore. Any moment she might feel hot breath on the back of her neck--

"*Go.*"

"Sorry," Clio blurted. She realized she'd come to a complete stop; she began crawling again, her backpack a deadweight on her back. "What am I looking f--"

Clio gasped, a huge intake of air rushing into her lungs as her groping hands found nothing where she expected solid floor. She overbalanced, lunging forward gracelessly and colliding with the now sloping plane of the shaft. The incline was steep and slippery, and she rushed down on her stomach in the utter darkness.

Her heart lodged in her throat, blocking off her scream. Another of Britt's rules rang in her head--*never scream, even when you need to.*

Had Britt set her up? As Clio slid helplessly into the blackness, her eyes went round with horror. She was headed *down.* Oh, God. To the subbasements. Had Britt sold her out to the prowlers?!

Clio slid out into free fall for one heart-stopping moment, then smacked down onto a pile of something relatively soft. She was too winded to move, but her eyes adjusted to a new glow. A soft, diffuse light seemed to ripple in front of her.

She moved slightly, winced, and bit her lip to keep from groaning. The effort was wasted when Britt landed on top of her a second later. Clio cried out, then whimpered as Britt rolled off and flopped on her back next to her.

"Why the hell didn't you move?"

Clio unpeeled her face from what she now realized was a gym mat. "I thought you'd tricked me," she gasped.

"I did," Britt said with a laugh. "I wish I could've seen your face when you first started down." Her hand rose up and made a violent sweep. "Whooosh!" She chuckled again, and Clio stared in disbelief, wondering what had happened to Britt's usual reserve.

"I thought you were sending me to them!" Clio blurted.

The laughter stopped abruptly, and Britt sat up. "I would never do that. Not even if..."

Britt looked away and shrugged. "I just wouldn't," she said with finality. "Besides, it's not so bad having you around, even if you do slow me down." She slanted a tight grin toward Clio. "It's good to have someone to watch your back."

The unexpected warmth drew a smile from Clio. She was pleased, despite the backhanded nature of the compliment.

"I thought you said rule number one is not to trust anybody," Clio said.

"I did. And it's good advice, but...well..." Britt spread her hands. "I've brought you to one of my secret places, so it's all *water* under the bridge now."

The emphasis Britt put on the word brought Clio's new surroundings into focus. Now she could identify the strong, familiar smell in the air. The odd play of light on the wall came from the reflection of water rippling in a pool. Clio turned her head and inhaled softly in delight.

The pool was huge and the water clear. It lay shortly past their pile of gym mats, filling the rest of the vast room. The air smelled like chlorine--so the water was too well-maintained for this place to be abandoned.

"How is this here?" Clio breathed. "Who takes care of this?"

"Maybe a housecleaning service comes in twice a week to tidy up the place."

"Right."

"You think it's a trap?" Britt asked. She leaned down to murmur in Clio's ear, "*Come into my parlor?* said the spider to the fly."

Clio elbowed her. "That's not funny."

"Look, I don't know." Britt jumped to the ground and kicked off her sneakers. "It's been like this since I first found it. I've never seen anyone else here. There's only one way in." She pointed up. "And one way out. You can't get back in through the door down here. It locks automatically, but the doors are smooth on the other side. Nothing to pick."

Clio slid off the pile of mats and walked to the edge of the pool, looking into it as if she expected to see circling sharks.

Britt smirked. "I haven't seen you this jumpy since that drooler came out of the closet."

"Shut up. And don't call them that." Clio shuddered. "I hate them worse than the prowlers."

"You shouldn't. The prowlers are just like us--smart and fast. The droolers aren't much of a threat."

"*They're* the ones that give me the creeps," Clio insisted. "It's like their eyes don't even see. They just come at you with that slow, blind shuffle."

"Better than a fast sprint."

Clio frowned. "What do you think happened to them? Drugs? Lobotomies? That brochure makes it sound like this place could've been some treatment facility. Do you think the...the owners did this to them?"

"Who knows?" Britt tossed as she started unfastening her pants. She was single-minded when she'd set out to do something. "Maybe they were conducting experiments. Maybe we'll come across their secret laboratories one day--find jars of mutant rats and disembodied human brains."

Clio gave a grudging laugh. "You really aren't helping."

"*Maybe* they're what we'll turn into if we can't found a way out."

Any trace of humor within Clio evaporated, and a sick feeling settled in the pit of her stomach. "That won't happen to me," she said shakily. "I'm getting out of here."

"You do that." Britt's pants fell to the floor with a soft rustle. "But first--I'm going for a swim."

Clio nodded and stepped back. She dropped her backpack on the smooth cement floor.

"This just seems too good to be true," Clio murmured. "Something this nice...none of it makes sense. Are you sure it's safe here?"

"First you complain about the supply closet," Britt said with a grunt. "And now this, when I finally take you someplace nice. Really?" Britt pulled off her tank top. "It's not safe anywhere. Would you rather be *not safe* in some ratty hole upstairs, or down here having a swim?" She lifted one ankle to tug off a sock. "There are showers, too."

"Really?" Clio looked at her with undisguised hope.

"*Hot* showers." Standing in just her bra and underwear, Britt grinned. "Swim first, though." She went to unfasten her bra, and Clio blushed and turned away.

A moment later, Britt dove into the pool; Clio jumped in surprise as a splash soaked her. An unwilling grin tugged her lips when Britt came up out of the water and laughed, unrepentant.

"Come on," Britt coaxed. "All work and no play..."

Makes Jack a dull boy. Goosebumps rose up on Clio's arms, and for an instant she looked at Britt with distrust.

What's really going on here?

"Don't make me throw you in," Britt called. She made as if to hoist herself up, and Clio took a couple of hasty steps back.

"Okay, okay!" She took off her jacket and sandals, then somewhat shyly slid the straps of her sundress off her shoulders. The dress fell down to her hips; she pushed it the rest of the way off and stepped out of it.

She rubbed at the hair standing up on her arms and stared doubtfully at the water, where Britt was floating on her back with her eyes closed. Quickly, ignoring her self-consciousness, Clio unclasped her bra and let it fall.

Instead of diving, she sat down on the edge of the pool and lowered herself into the water. She sucked in a breath as the cool water eddied around her shoulders; she sank a little lower, hugging herself.

She finally slid her head beneath the surface and stroked forward underwater, the tension bleeding out of her body. She emerged halfway down the pool and gasped for air.

Hands landed on her shoulders and pushed her under again. Clio thrashed and came up sputtering. Britt's teeth flashed as she laughed and kicked away backward, sending a volley of water in Clio's direction.

Clio heard their voices echo against the wall as they raced and played, for once not cautious about being heard. Since Britt didn't seem worried, Clio was happy to relax. It was wonderful. The heavy weight of fear and captivity gave way to freedom, almost like the waters had the power to cleanse more than grime.

But it was only temporary. Much too soon, Britt lifted herself out of the pool. The sheen of water made her skin look like deep brown lacquer, highlighting her long-limbed form. With perfect ease she strode naked to the pile of her clothes and picked them up. Clio bobbed in the water, reluctant to leave behind the moments of pleasure.

"Ready for that hot shower?" Without waiting for a reply, Britt walked through a pair of swinging doors, leaving Clio alone in the large room--which suddenly seemed to hold more shadows. Staying where she was became much less appealing.

Clio swam quickly to the ladder and climbed out. She glanced once more at the quiet water before grabbing her things and running to the showers.

Britt was already under the spray in one stall. Clio dumped

her things and climbed eagerly into the next.

When the first stream of hot water hit her, Clio moaned in pleasure. She rotated under the spray to let it hit every part of her. She finally met Britt's gaze, and they grinned at each other.

Britt's close-cropped hair was sudsy with shampoo, and Clio's eyes widened. "You have shampoo?" she squeaked.

"Here." A small bottle arced over the partition, and Clio made a fumbling catch.

Clio portioned out a dollop. "Oh, God," she moaned as she massaged it into her scalp. "That feels so good."

"You sound like you're auditioning for a porno," Britt quipped.

"Sex couldn't possibly feel this good."

Britt snickered. "Well," she said dryly, "that all depends."

"If you say so." Clio was too blissful to think about it. She peeled off the underwear she hadn't removed in the pool and spread the rich lather all over her body, reveling in the slightly fruity scent. Another happy moan escaped her, followed by a giggle. She *did* sound like a porn star wannabe.

"Don't take too long," Britt warned, although she had the grace to sound regretful that she was cutting their time short.

Clio lifted her petulant scowl into the hot needles of the spray. She began to scrub harder, washing away the accumulated filth of the past several days. White foam swirled around her feet, and she bent to retrieve her underwear, giving them a good rinse before sadly shutting off the water.

After she'd wrung them as dry as she could get them, Clio put her underwear back on and went out to stare morosely at her dress, which could hardly be called white anymore. She was beginning to hate the sight of it. Older stains had mixed with the latest dingy streaks from the vent slide.

Pragmatic as always, Britt threw on her green-brown cargo pants and white tank top. Clio looked at her enviously. Britt's clothes were dirty, but they didn't show it nearly as much, and they were so much more practical than her stupid dress and sandals.

"No time to clean our clothes today." Britt eyed Clio critically as she stepped into the dress. "You need new ones, anyway. Those are crap for getting around in here."

"Yeah?" Clio snapped. "Well, maybe we can go to the mall tomorrow." She regretted her tone instantly, but Britt just looked amused.

"There's a wing I've been wanting to check out," Britt offered. "Maybe we can find something there."

"Okay." Clio tucked her wet hair behind her ears and smiled apologetically. "Thanks for bringing me here."

Britt gave a light shrug of one shoulder. "No big deal."

"It *is,*" Clio said quietly.

The sincerity in Clio's voice seemed to surprise Britt. She looked up, her eyes searching Clio's. After a moment, Britt smiled widely, and Clio felt her own lips curve in response.

Britt ducked away and made a show of checking her pockets. "All right," she said at last. "Let's go."

The gruff order sent warmth to bloom in Clio's chest--something she hadn't felt since coming to this place. She put on her jacket and backpack, strangely excited for another foray into the bowels of this endless building.

"Quiet from here on out," Britt said, all cool practicality again. "Just because I haven't run into trouble here before doesn't mean we won't today."

Clio's positivity vanished as quickly as it had come.

♦♣♠♥

"This sucks," Clio hissed. The dropped water bottle leaked at her feet, but the growing puddle was the least of her concerns.

She gripped Britt's arm tightly as they backed further into the large auditorium. The slow tide of vacant-faced shufflers advanced on them, silent but for the flat-footed swish of their soles on the floor.

"I've never seen so many of them at once," Britt murmured, and she actually sounded worried.

Sheer panic was Clio's first inclination. "You said they don't hurt people, right?" The slender beam of her flashlight swept back and forth while she and Britt backpedaled down the central aisle of metal chairs.

The uncanny military precision of the ranks of shambling droolers was disturbed when the first of the herd began to stumble into those chairs. The screech of metal on floor made Clio's skin crawl.

"*Britt,*" Clio repeated. "*You said they don't hurt people.*"

"I don't think so," Britt replied at last. "I told you, some of them don't even move. It's like their brains are so fried they can't function at all. Sometimes you'll find them curled up in the weirdest places."

"But what about these?" Clio wheezed. "Are you sure we're not going to be zombie chow in a minute?!"

"I've never seen them bite anyone. It's more like they just...cling." Britt dug through one of her innumerable pockets. "And we can move faster than them."

"Oh, *that's* reassuring." Clio tugged at Britt as she eyed the closest of the shambling creatures; the flashlight lit up her pale and papery skin. "A group hug that never ends."

Pity welled up in Clio, but it couldn't drown out her revulsion. It was so hard to think of the droolers as human, with their slack faces and empty eyes that wiped them of all personality. Whoever had done this to them was *truly* inhuman.

"What are you even doing?" Clio demanded.

Britt held up a small spray can as she continued to step back.

"Pepper spray?" Clio's fingers dug into Britt. "Seriously?"

"Just covering my bases."

Clio and Britt edged quickly to a door on the far side of the room, listening to the shuffling figures blunder through the rows of chairs. Britt grabbed the door handle.

"...It's locked."

A spike of adrenaline burned Clio's chest. *Don't panic. Breathe.*

"Can you pick it?" Clio whispered.

Britt passed her the flashlight, and Clio shone it at the door where they'd entered the room. A few stragglers were still coming through. Clio figured they could probably go back that way if they needed to, assuming more droolers wouldn't show up out of nowhere. She pointed the light back at the lock, though she knew Britt didn't really need to see to do the job.

"Yeah." Britt was already down on the floor, coolly inserting her tiny hook and wrench into the lock.

Clio bit her tongue. She didn't need to tell Britt to hurry, so she just tried to keep her knees from shaking. The screech of chairs was evidence of the droolers' progress.

Britt cursed, tossed down her pick, and grabbed another one from her pocket.

Clio swept the flashlight beam around again. The female drooler from before was barely twenty feet away now--and the others weren't far behind.

"*Britt,*" she warned.

"I *got* it. Just shut up and let me concentrate."

"Okay." Clio took a deep breath. Even if she was deadweight most of the time, she could at least buy Britt some time. "Be right back."

Clio ran as close to the woman as she dared, flashing the light in her face and letting out a resounding yell. She veered off to the right.

"Hey, zombies! Over here! Pay no attention to the bossy girl by the door!"

She didn't need to look to know that Britt's middle finger had popped up in a quick salute. Clio grabbed a chair and jogged along the wall, scraping the metal legs against the concrete.

She knew that if she ran along the length of the entire crowd, they could change course to reach her and cut off her exit. *Don't go too far,* she warned herself. Clio dropped the chair and sprinted toward the back of the room, letting one hand on the wall guide her.

"It's open!" Britt called. "Come on!"

Clio cut around the stragglers at the back of the group to race down the center aisle to Britt. But then she slipped on the water that had pooled in the middle of the aisle.

She went down hard. The rough landing jarred the flashlight from her grip, and she helplessly watched it roll down the aisle.

"Clio!"

Her knee flamed to life from the impact, but she grabbed onto the back of a chair and heaved herself up. Her leg didn't buckle; she sighed in relief that her knee wasn't twisted. "I'm okay!"

The light bobbed as Britt snatched up the flashlight and ran toward her. As Clio stumbled from the bodies that closed in, Britt came up through the chairs, kicking them into the droolers until she could loop Clio's arm over her shoulder. She half-dragged Clio back toward the door.

"I'm fine," Clio gasped, twisting forward as grasping hands caught at her arms and hair. The throbbing of her knee barely registered.

Britt hauled her forward, ignoring everything but getting them to the door. When the two of them finally rushed through, Clio slammed the door shut.

As they stared down the new dark hallway, Britt didn't give them time to catch their breath. Her usually steady hand shook as she shone the light down the corridor.

It was empty--uncharted territory.

Her mouth brushed Clio's ear in the barest whisper. "Let's go."

Clio wanted nothing more than to leave the auditorium behind, so she grabbed Britt's hand and squeezed. They almost made it to the end of the corridor before the lights burst on.

Clio blinked wildly against the painful intrusion of the unaccustomed brightness. She stumbled, disoriented, as she tried to focus on the figures heading rapidly toward them.

They were dressed in black, wearing some kind of mask--no, those were goggles--that obscured their faces. They looked

like bulbous-eyed subterranean creatures.

Clio recoiled as Britt hissed out one word:

"Prowlers."

Male laughter rang out. *That* sounded human.

It was only when Britt's hand was ripped away that Clio came to life. She kicked and struggled, but strong hands her pulled back. Britt had already sent one of the masked figures to his knees, clutching at his balls. Clio reached for her as more men flooded in from nowhere.

Clio stomped down hard on the foot of whoever was holding her. He cursed loudly as his grip loosened. She twisted out of his hold and ran toward Britt, who was being violently dragged back the way they'd come.

Clio threw herself forward, but her way was blocked by two of the masked prowlers. They pushed her back easily to fall against the hard body behind her.

"Britt!" she screamed, thrashing wildly against the hold on her arms. She was hoisted to her feet.

"Six!" Britt yelled as Clio was dragged in the opposite direction. "Remember number six!"

The hallway plunged back into darkness.

♦ ♣ ♠ ♥

Chapter 3

♦ ♣ ♠ ♥

"Watch out--she kicks."

Clio heard muffled voices behind black masks, their laughter punctuated by a quick sting at the curve of her throat. The laughter faded into a surreal, staccato echo that swirled around her in a soupy fog. Her dress was suddenly too clammy against her skin, too heavy for her body. She was weary, fighting the drag.

Her vision darkened as her head lolled.

Only tiny pinpoints of red light bobbed and wove around her, leaving glowing tails in the dark. She tried to track the pretty crimson swirls, but her eyelids drooped.

The rhythm of a quick stride was hypnotic; snatches of voices became nothing but a low drone in the back of her mind. The cold surface of a table registered through her numb skin, then faded back into insignificance. Something turned her onto her back.

Sudden, painful light exploded in front of her. She couldn't blink--she couldn't move at all. An unmasked face hovered over her. Her eyes couldn't focus.

"A cute one."

More laughter, subdued this time, eddied in the currents around her.

The cool voice spoke again, but sharply. Everything else fell into silence.

The blurred face loomed closer. "Listen, Clio."

Her leaden body didn't react, but the voice pierced through her. Heavy breath caught in her throat.

They knew her *name*. The fear that she wasn't here by *accident* sharpened her thoughts for a moment. Then the prickle of terror faded, like every other sensation.

"Look at the light and listen." The smooth voice whispered into her ear until the white light consumed everything.

Voices asked her questions, though she couldn't always understand them. Sometimes they sped up to high-pitched warbles, and she thought she mumbled something about chipmunks through her thick, stupid tongue because they laughed as fingers brushed her hair from her face. She felt another sting, this time in the crease of her elbow.

The voices mellowed...a dark head swam in her vision...a pretty smile, white teeth. They laughed again.

Had she said that out loud? Clio floated, and the deep, soothing voice that went with the smile soothed her. *Come with me,* it said.

She did.

♦♣♠♥

An age later--maybe eons--Clio's eyes opened.

She wanted to blink, but her eyelids were slow. They sluggishly closed off the intense overhead light.

Her unresponsive body wouldn't obey her commands, but her nerves were alive again. They sent sensory details that had been numbed for so long--the snug clamp of straps across her wrists and ankles, the faint odor of unknown chemicals, a whirr of machinery. Chill air stirred over her clammy skin.

Snatches of her impossible journey remained, though each time she tried to remember her smiling guide her thoughts grasped uselessly at fragmented details. She ceased thinking of it at all.

Instead of being distressed, Clio remained in a cocoon of calm...even when her wrists were unbound and strong, warm fingers pressed against her pulse. She felt her eyelids being lifted, gently, but the action let in a flood of painful light.

A sound of protest must have made it past her lips, because a new voice spoke above her. This one was close enough that she felt the flutter of the words against her face.

"I'm sorry," it rumbled. "Bear with it just a little longer."

Oh, this voice was even nicer. Resonant and solemn, but respectful and soft...maybe even kind.

Why did that make her chest contract? He was probably a doctor--he sounded like one.

She parted her lips, but all she managed was a croak. Before she could try again, a straw was placed against her lips. A hand cradled the back of her skull, and she weakly took a sip of deliciously cool water.

"I'm sorry," he said again. "I didn't have much time. I couldn't remove all the triggers, or restore..."

The words faded in and out, but Clio was content to just listen.

"...might not remember until..." Her eyelids fluttered. She wanted to see the owner of the voice. "...possible flashes of..."

The light was still bright above her, but she could see a shadowed blur, splintered and spinning in her vision. She squinted, trying to resolve the images into one, but a greater urgency entered his voice, and she struggled to really listen. She fought the fatigue that was seeping back into her limbs and consciousness.

"...outside...the gray..." His voice turned stern. "...stay away...city...remember, Clio."

"What's...your...name?" Clio finally managed to breathe.

Soft laughter made her warm. Before she could hear his final word, Clio slipped into unconsciousness.

♦♣♠♥

Water dripped from something. Clio listened for the tiny sound that came at regular intervals.

One, two, three, *plink*. One, two, three, *plink*.

She sighed.

Clio was already tired of the dank, subbasement room that was apparently her prison. She'd woken up to find one of her wrists handcuffed to the metal headboard of a narrow bed. Her other hand was free, but she had given up her frantic attempts to break loose some time ago; it had only made her head ache. When no other threat had materialized, she'd gradually sunk back into the bed to think about her options.

There weren't many.

The room was bare and industrial, with rough walls and exposed piping. Clio had become intimately familiar with the shape and color of the faded water spots above her head. She hadn't been awake that long, probably less than an hour or two, though the maddening drip made her captivity feel longer. Enough time had passed that, despite her fear, a little boredom had crept in.

Another heavy sigh escaped her, and this one was unintentional. She closed her eyes.

The coppery smell of rust filtered through her nostrils. At least there was no mildew or mold--her lungs would be constricting if that were the case, and she couldn't very well run to the drugstore for a packet of antihistamines.

Her brain felt a little fuzzy still, but her thoughts were clearing. A hazy recollection sent a tendril of apprehension down her spine. Had they drugged her? She couldn't quite remember past the moment she'd seen the prowlers drag Britt away.

"...Clio..."

She remembered voices murmuring her name, but she had no idea why. Had she been dreaming while unconscious? That made sense. All she had was an impression of swirling images that wouldn't focus. She couldn't recall any details, but a vague anxiety clung to her like the residue of a fading nightmare.

She tried to focus on the fact that, as far as she could tell, the worst the prowlers had done was handcuff her in a creepy room. They'd even left the light on, though the dim glow of the bare bulb barely reached the corners of the room. Clio shifted, trying to bring her legs into a more comfortable position, and wondered with a pang if Britt was in similar straits somewhere.

The wait wouldn't end. Clio dozed off again, or at least went into some sort of dazed trance, because she wasn't aware of anything else until a warm puff of air stirred the hair over her ear.

"Cl-Cl-Clio..."

Clio gasped. Her eyes flew open.

"Red Jack!"

A finger lightly touched her lips as the bed dipped. She jerked her head to the side; sure enough, the teenaged redhead slid his chin over the edge of the bed.

"Shh. Speak softly unless you want unwelcome company."

Clio awkwardly struggled up onto her side. Her elbow dug into the thin mattress.

"What are you doing here?" she whispered.

"Oh, just observing what a knack you have for getting yourself into trouble."

"Thanks to you," Clio hissed. "I *wouldn't* be here if it wasn't for you!"

"That hurts, Clio," Red Jack drawled. His wounded tone made Clio grit her teeth. "*You* were the one who asked us for help, remember?"

"Yes, and you were just playing with me. You *knew* what you were sending me into."

He shrugged. "Of course we knew. We had to play our part."

His casual acknowledgment infuriated her. She wanted to smack the smile off his face.

"Your part in *what*?" she demanded.

"You know that already, don't you?" rumbled a new voice behind her. Clio gasped again.

Black Jack. The bed creaked as he crept up over the edge of the mattress behind her.

She felt him trace his fingers over the arm that stretched

over her head. Clio stiffened, but he only danced his fingertips to the dangling cuff. He tugged at it playfully.

"It's just a little game," he said. "We didn't lie. If you're clever enough--"

"And brave enough," Red Jack interjected.

"--then you can win your way through."

"Your way *out*." Red Jack laughed. "If that's still what you want."

Clio's neck strained as she looked over her shoulder into Black Jack's dark eyes. He raised his eyebrows at her.

"But Clio..." His fingers tapped at the handcuff. "Winning means so much *more* than that. More than you can imagine."

"But..." A question welled in Clio's throat. She was almost afraid to ask it.

"What if I'm not clever or brave enough?" she breathed. "What happens if I *lose*?"

Red Jack chuckled softly, and her gaze turned to him. There was suddenly nothing amused in his expression.

"That all depends. You've seen what happens to some already."

"Clio won't let that happen to her." Black Jack's murmur was almost soothing. "I'd put my money on *that*."

"I'm not so sure, Black. She's already in deep trouble."

"But we can help her out this one last time, can't we?"

"We *could*," Red Jack mocked. "But it doesn't look like she wants our help."

Clio glared. "You got me into this. Of course I'm not going to believe you really want to help me."

"What choice do you have?" Black Jack asked. "Do you want to find out what happens when they come back for you?"

"Maybe she likes it down here in the dark."

"Shut up," Clio flared. "Don't talk about me like I'm not here."

"Shh," Red Jack hissed. "I told you to keep your voice down. You may not appreciate it, but you're not the only one at risk here."

That made Clio stop for a second. Were they...were they disobeying something by coming to her?

She seized on the opportunity in a desperate gamble. "If you really want to help me," she whispered viciously, "then do it. Get me out of these cuffs."

Muffled laughter teased her hair, and she heard a light jingle beside her ear. She turned to see Black Jack dangle a key ring. His grin widened as their eyes met.

"That's the spirit," he murmured.

The metal briefly cut into her skin as he positioned the key in the lock. When the cuff sprang open, she jerked her hand down and automatically rubbed her wrist. She unsteadily pushed herself off the bed and backed away from the boys who rose to stand to either side of it.

The Jacks didn't move. Clio looked from one to the other to find both their gazes on her wrist, peculiar matching expressions twisting their faces. She was thrown off enough that she didn't protest when Red Jack came to life. He moved forward quickly and took her wrist. His thumb stroked over the red mark left by the handcuff.

Black Jack moved behind her just as swiftly.

Red Jack drew her closer, his fingers tightening around the narrow bones of her wrist. Her charm bracelet, once again forgotten, jingled softly beneath his grip.

"With *this*," Red Jack brushed the dangling charms, "we could do more than help you escape this room." He looked up at her, his disarming grin back in place. "Give it to me and I'll have you on your way home before you can blink."

Clio tried to shift away, but Black Jack loomed behind her. His hands settled on her shoulders, making her stomach flutter.

"But...I thought...isn't it only meant for me?" She tried to pull her wrist away, but Red Jack clutched her tighter.

"It's meant for whoever knows how to use it. Do *you*?"

"I...I know it can help me find a way through," Clio said haltingly.

"Had much luck with that?" Red Jack's sarcastic question

ignited a spark of anger.

"It's not really any of your business, is it?"

Red Jack's eyes narrowed, but Black Jack snorted in amusement.

"What you need to realize, little Clio, is that not everybody is playing the same game."

"Then how do you tell who wins?"

A laugh met her question. "That's easy." Red Jack tilted his head. "The one who's holding all the cards at the end."

"Then I shouldn't give up mine, right?"

She was startled when Black Jack's fingers gave her shoulders a tiny squeeze, but Red Jack's scowl drew her attention back to him.

"That all depends," Red Jack said lowly.

"On what?"

"Winning for you is getting out of here, isn't it? I'm offering you that. A way out of the Gauntlet." Red Jack leaned closer. "I can put you back on the streets and send you on your way home. No harm, no foul."

Black Jack's fingers dug into her shoulders again, harder and longer this time before they released. It felt almost like...a warning.

Against what? she wondered. *Red Jack? They practically finish each other's sentences!*

Was this another trick?

She mulled over Red Jack's offer. If she could trust him to do what he said, then she could go home...but why *should* she believe him? Either one of them? They'd fooled her once.

And there was something else.

"What about Britt?"

Red Jack loosened his hold a little, as if surprised. "What?"

"My friend. They took her, too." Clio steeled herself. "If I agree to give you my bracelet, then you have to get *both* of us out of here."

Black Jack's fingers flexed, but it felt more like an involuntary reaction this time.

"That's impossible," Red Jack said flatly.

Clio jerked her arm away and stared him down. "Why?"

"She's gone," Black Jack murmured. "She escaped before they could lock her up. They've been trying to round her up for ages, but she's very...resourceful."

Unlike me. Clio's surge of relief was tempered by the depressing awareness of her own weaknesses.

"She didn't come to help you, did she?" Red Jack pointed out. "*We* did."

She tried to ignore the faint hurt that snaked itself into her thoughts. Just because Britt hadn't come yet didn't mean she never would. Clio frowned into Red Jack's obnoxious, freckled face.

"You don't know anything about her," she snapped. "And I don't need your help. We have our own plans."

"Do you?" Red Jack asked. "And what would those be?"

"I already told you--it's none of your business what I do."

"You won't even tell me what 'number six' means?" Red Jack murmured.

Clio stiffened.

"I'll bet it's some kind of code, right? Clever little girls. Hm..." Red Jack overtly tapped his finger against his chin. "A rendezvous point, maybe?"

"So you *were* there," Clio hissed. "You're one of the prowlers, aren't you? This really *is* just a sick game to you. You want to use me to get Britt!"

"The prowlers?" Red Jack smirked. "No. We told you from the beginning--we're the Jacks. And I don't care about your friend. She can handle herself much better than *you* can, don't forget. And you're a fool to trust her, anyway."

Clio clenched her fists. Britt had told her not to trust anybody. Now Red Jack was saying Clio shouldn't trust *Britt.* With the logic in this place, Clio wasn't surprised.

"But I should trust *you?*" Clio asked Red Jack.

"I give you my word that I'll get you out."

"And if I say no thanks?"

Red Jack's grin stretched wider. "Not everyone will ask as nicely as I have."

Her stomach fluttered again.

"You can't *take* it from me," Clio protested, trying not to sound as uncertain as she felt. "I know that much."

"Who told you that? Your *friend*?"

Clio's chin tilted up. "Yes. I know it's one of the rules."

"Oh, but Clio..." Red Jack flashed his teeth. "No one ever said we aren't allowed to cheat."

Her eyes widened, and she swayed back from Red Jack's gloating face. Black Jack's hands steadied her; she jerked away from him, too. She suddenly couldn't bear the proximity of these two near-strangers. She backed away.

Her eyes darted around the room, looking for the things Britt had taught her to notice. She curled her hand protectively around her wrist, hiding the bracelet in the cradle of her palm.

"I won't give it to you," she warned.

"Are you sure?" Red Jack's voice sounded almost teasing now. "It's true--I can't take it from you. That one rule is...strictly enforced. But there are others in here who can be very...persuasive." He leaned against the pipe and watched her casually, as if they had all the time in the world. "They can make you *desperate* to give it to them. Wouldn't it be better to give it to me now? At least I'll see that you get what you say you want...a shower, a good meal, a warm bed. Home."

Strangely enough, it was the list of things she'd been craving since the very first night that struck a chord within her. Were those mundane things really so important? True, she missed them, but...but...she didn't want them badly enough to abandon Britt, who had helped her from the beginning.

It didn't hurt that a large part of her was pissed at being toyed with--she was being treated like a playing piece in a game she didn't understand. Nothing would be better than actually beating them. If she took the easy way out, she would just be...nothing. A loser.

A more sinister thought intruded. If she stayed and didn't win, she didn't know what would happen. The thought of being turned into a vacant shell--like the droolers--terrified her.

Her entire being revolted against that fate.

"You...you promise to get me out of here?" Clio looked at the door, then back at Red Jack.

He waved a hand. "Just say the word."

Clio's gaze flicked to Black Jack; she couldn't read his expression. She forced herself to take a step closer as she slid the bracelet off her wrist. She watched Red Jack's ill-concealed excitement from beneath her lashes.

She filled her lungs in a deep breath.

Then she leapt, swinging at the bare bulb over her head. The brittle globe fractured instantly, dropping the room into darkness. Red Jack cursed as bodies stumbled around the room.

The metal legs of the bed screeched across the concrete floor. Red Jack cursed again. Whether he was looking for her or the door, she didn't know.

Clio dove toward a corner of the room, where a fat pipe along the wall bent toward the ceiling. Praying she was right, she climbed onto it and pushed where she thought she'd seen the outline of a panel.

The piece of ceiling swung open.

A jolt of primal triumph made her tremble. She pulled herself up, her arms shaking with the effort, as her foot tried to make purchase against the pipe. For an instant, her strength held, and her heart leapt.

And then the slick sole of her sandal slipped. Her arms gave out, and she slid all the way down.

No!

She reached again, poised to leap, but hands on her hips stopped her in mid-motion. The anguished denial froze on her lips.

"Games are often won by luck," Black Jack whispered into her hair. His lips curved against her ear. "When all else fails, trust in yours."

Then his hands were pushing her up, and she scrambled into the shaft. She felt the black hole shutting behind her.

Her fingers found the ladder bolted to the wall. She began

to climb into the black--not thinking, just moving her arms and legs over and over until her calves burned. She climbed so long that she lost all sense of time and space.

She began seeing things. Pale, white spots floated in her vision--tiny pinpricks, like when she rubbed her eyes too hard. But gradually, the white glow grew and brightened. Through the blur of grateful tears, she saw beams of soft light that shone through a grate.

She punched through. On the other side of the grate was a small room, flooded with natural light that streamed through a partially boarded window. The rotting boards had mostly fallen away; she climbed easily through the gap, blinking her eyes against the light.

She found herself in a small and narrow courtyard, enclosed by gray walls on four sides. The walls towered up several stories, with no apparent footholds to climb higher--but Clio was barely disappointed. She was outside.

She was outside. She could see the sun and the sky.

Clio started laughing. The colors seemed unreal--impossibly bright blue and yellow, like a child's drawing. The rough concrete of the yard was warm as she lay on her back. She rested her head and stared straight up, her hands curled around her eyes, so that all her vision was filled with vibrant color.

♦♣♠♥

Clio didn't know how much time had passed. Like a worshipper, she'd stripped off her jacket to lay supine beneath the sun, allowing herself to indulge in the heat on her limbs and face.

Surely, if anyone was coming after her, they would have already caught up. Black Jack must have kept her secret. She mulled that--and his almost playful words--over for a moment before deliberating on the prowlers who had confined her in the first place.

Maybe they didn't even know she was gone yet. Judging by the placement of the sun, she guessed it was one o'clock in the afternoon. Perhaps all the prowlers were fast asleep. She didn't have much faith in the "rules" now, but she still hoped the prowlers would stick to form and stay below.

She needed to figure out exactly where she was, and if she would be able to find her way back to Britt. She assumed she was on the ground floor, which was too close to prowler territory for comfort. And just how far below ground did the Gauntlet extend? Her climb seemed to indicate several levels.

The Gauntlet was far from the single building she'd first thought it to be. It had to be enormous, hidden in plain sight in the midst of a metropolis. It still mystified her. How much did she miss in everyday life because she wasn't looking closely enough?

The thought made her search the courtyard again, but her exploration revealed nothing but weeds growing thickly in the broken surface of the concrete yard, and a window on each austere wall. It was a crossroads of sorts; she took a closer look, shielding her eyes from the glare of the sky. It looked like this was the intersection of four different wings or structures. She had no idea which way to go.

The way she'd come was her last choice. She wanted distance from *them*. On the other hand, she didn't want to end up farther away from Britt. She growled in frustration.

"Just pick one and commit," Clio said out loud. "That's what Britt would do." Anyway, she could retrace her steps if necessary.

She took another turn around the courtyard, peering through the open holes of the arched windows. The rooms they revealed were similar--empty and dusty from exposure to the elements, and seemed to breathe out dank air. Moisture rings discolored the floor and walls, and identical doors provided the only possible exits.

"Trust my luck?" Clio gave a short laugh. "I could flip a coin if I had one."

She climbed up onto the nearest window ledge and jumped into the room. A closer inspection revealed nothing useful, so she tried the door. She was almost surprised that it was unlocked. It opened smoothly onto a shockingly clean, modern-looking service corridor that stretched a hundred yards before ending in another door.

The lights were on. A wave of cooler air from the hallway raised goose bumps on her arms. Clio waited and watched, but nothing happened. She finally shut the door.

She went back out to the courtyard and into each of the other rooms, but ended up with the same results. She eventually returned to the room she'd first emerged from and picked up the grate she'd left lying on the wall, belatedly following Britt's advice to cover her tracks.

When she settled it back into place, she noticed a faint, ridged footprint left in the grit underneath it. It couldn't have come from her flat sandal. She bent and looked at the strange footprint as her heart began to pound.

It could have been Britt's. The size was right, and it had to be fairly fresh or the wind would have disturbed it.

Or it could've been planted to look like Britt's, a sly voice in her head suggested.

You're a fool to trust her, Red Jack's voice added.

Clio frowned. She turned and looked carefully around the room.

There. Another partial mark had left waves in the dirt beneath the window that faced the grate. Clio knelt closer, but she found no other evidence that someone had been there.

"If Britt was here, she would've left some sign," she said slowly to herself.

Clio brightened, but a thorough inspection of the doorframe revealed no secret mark in purple. It was possible that Britt hadn't had time to follow her standard procedure, or she'd simply been too agitated to think of it.

If it wasn't Britt who had passed through, then *should* she try this route? She deliberated on the question, and grudgingly realized that if someone was trying to manipulate her--herd her in a certain direction--then ultimately she might not have a choice. Going a different way might only prolong the game, or she might run into something unplanned and unpleasant.

"You want me to go this way?" she asked aloud. "Fine, then." If they expected her to run away and hide, she'd show them not to underestimate her. She hoped she wasn't *that* naïve any longer.

Britt would probably disagree. One corner of her mouth twisted up, and Clio squared her shoulders.

She missed the weight of her backpack; it had held at least a bottle of water and a small portion of food. On cue with that thought, her stomach growled. She tallied another grudge to hold against the jerks behind the scenes.

She opened the door, and the chilled air made her shiver again. Reluctantly, she pulled on her jacket. She couldn't afford to lose anything else, and it gave her a bit of comfort, honestly. Regardless of his part in tricking her into this, Black Jack had helped her get away from that basement. She wanted to believe he was sincere...but she acknowledged this could be just another trick. She couldn't be sure of anything.

Clio pushed her hands into her pockets. Her eyes widened when her right hand curled around something.

She withdrew a plastic card.

"Black Jack..." Clio whispered.

It was white, with a black magnetic stripe that ran the length of it. Something that looked like a serial number was printed on the other side.

JS19IE03. A key card?

Her lips pursed as she turned it over in her fingers; she eyed the door at the end of the hallway. The narrow corridor was the brightest and cleanest she'd seen inside the Gauntlet, certainly without the usual air of abandonment. It was a jarring change, as if she had moved abruptly from one stage setting to another with wildly different scenery.

Her sandals slapped on the polished floor, taking her to the solitary door at the end of the hall. Its silver handle gleamed; when it turned smoothly under her hand, she released the breath she'd held in a soft laugh. The heavy scrape of metal hinges echoed as she stepped into a foyer.

The walls were painted in a pleasing, warm, butter yellow

hue, and the floor was springy with a plush carpet. Low, comfortable-looking chairs and sofas were arranged against the walls. It looked like an extremely cozy waiting room--something a therapist's office might have, designed to put the nervous patient at ease.

Clio supposed she should be nervous, and she *was*. But after the minimal amenities of the Gauntlet so far, the pretty room made her a bit giddy.

She sat in one of the fat armchairs and bounced a little. Oh, yes, it was as comfortable as it looked. Clio let herself sink back into the cushions with a soft moan.

She chuckled. How pathetic was it when sitting in a chair--albeit a fantastic one--became a near orgasmic experience? Her curiosity soon drew her from its comforts, and Clio leaned forward to examine the books on a low table in front of her.

The first was a huge coffee-table book full of gorgeous photographs. At first glance, the pictures were of natural or architectural landscapes that looked perfectly ordinary. But upon closer inspection, they revealed surreal elements, such as a house too impossibly proportioned to exist. In one image, a waterfall flowed uphill. In another, a pristine fountain sparkled with cyan water in the midst of a barren wasteland.

Within the second book, *Flora and Fauna,* she did find plants and animals in abundance, only the animals were the human kind. Clio flushed in surprise. The nature shots showed men and women naked and reclining on tree trunks, grassy lawns, and in the midst of flower gardens. They were erotic, but not overly sexual.

That didn't stop her from hastily setting the book aside. Without thinking, she folded her hands primly on her lap and waited. After a moment, she realized the absurdity of the situation and laughed at herself.

Clio *was* almost surprised that a receptionist didn't eventually appear to greet her. She got up and made her way to a short hallway that led to an imposing mahogany door. Feeling a little ridiculous, Clio knocked.

Of course no one answered. She pushed open the door and entered another elegant but lightly furnished room with sedate lighting and neutral, calming colors. It contained a long reclining chair, a simpler chair with a straight back, and a small table and lamp between them. It looked exactly like her idea of a psychotherapist's office. The air seemed heavier here--almost hushed.

She was drawn to the striking artwork on the walls. The first one she recognized as a print, though she couldn't remember the painter's name. She read the nameplate: *The Treachery of Images. René Magritte.*

The picture was an old-fashioned smoking pipe painted on a yellow background, with a sentence in French beneath it: *Ceci n'est pas une pipe.* Her rusty high school French was good enough to translate the simple sentence, but shockingly, someone had neatly scripted the translation in ballpoint pen beneath it.

This is not a pipe.

On impulse, she touched the blue ink, dragging a fingertip across the words. The writing smeared easily, and her heart sped up. It was fresh.

She tried to calm down as she rubbed at the blue stain on her finger. Someone had just been here. Very, very recently.

Her eyes rose back to the wall. Beside the painting was a framed pamphlet, titled *The Cave of Trophonius.* A picture of a woodcut depicted a man descending into the black mouth of a cave. Another showed his exit: his mouth open, a look of ecstasy on his face, a group of men listening at his feet.

Clio read aloud, "Those who wished to consult the oracle were required to fast and sacrifice and descend into the cave. Most were so frightened that they forgot all they experienced in the depths. Each one was taken and placed on the oracular seat, where the priests of the cave would record his utterances and thereby reveal the oracular message within."

Oracular message? Clio's confusion grew. What did any of this have to do with the Gauntlet?

The last artwork was a framed triptych of photographs

of frescoes, taken at the ruins of an ancient Roman villa. The scenes seemed to depict a variety of religious rites. The piece was titled *Villa of the Mysteries*.

Clio was intrigued. She turned away from the wall and examined the room more carefully. Her eyes caught on a small pad lying facedown on the table.

A pen was tucked into the spiral loop at the top. Clio picked up the pad and turned it over. A single sentence was written in the same neat, blue script that marred the painting: *There is no meaning to be found in the world but what meaning we give it.*

She raised an eyebrow. She glanced at the reclining chair, halfway tempted to see what would happen if she lay down and closed her eyes. She clicked the pen a few times and smiled wryly. She wasn't interesting enough for psychoanalysis at this point. But by the time *they* finished with her, she might very well be.

The smile slid off her face.

Another door opened onto a long hallway that looked like a wing of a medical facility. Clio sighed. A short, intersecting corridor with a series of doors offered her a number of choices.

She shrugged and started with the first. It was labeled *Administration* and adorned with a key card reader.

She took the card out of her pocket, then held her breath as she slid it through. The device rewarded her with a beep and a click. She pulled the door open.

"Thank you, Jack."

The room beyond was a personal office, with a standard desk and metal filing cabinets. She immediately went to the desk. A daily calendar sat on the corner, turned to the current date as far as Clio could guess. The daily quote was from Benjamin Franklin: *"Games lubricate the body and the mind."*

"What does he know?" was Clio's sardonic response. But it was the scrawled quote beneath it, in the now familiar blue script, that made her laugh.

"Your focus determines your reality." –Qui-Gon Jinn

Whoever this recent tagger was, she liked them. At least they had a cute sense of humor.

Her eyes traveled across the desk until she stopped abruptly. There was a file folder labeled with *her name* on the tab.

She gasped and picked it up. Her stomach plummeted when she saw pages inside that outlined her life and interests. It included chilling details, down to the brand of toothpaste she preferred.

A series of photographs were clipped to the back flap, mostly focusing on her brief time in the city. Several had been taken of her where she worked, where she ate, the parks and squares she liked to visit, even the lobby of her apartment building. Most disturbing was the photo of her the day she'd left for the city. She remembered that day well--smiling excitedly, teary, and waving goodbye to her friends and family.

They had known her even then. They had *chosen* her even then. This wasn't some awful, random mistake.

If this was all...*deliberate*...then what? Why did they want *her*?

A sudden, sharp pain lanced through her head. She winced and a flash of memory--or what seemed like memory--hit her.

"Clio," someone had said. *"We've known about you for quite a while, so let's be friends, shall we?"*

She had no idea where the thought came from. She closed her eyes, fingers pressed hard against her temples as incoherent flashes of memories teased her. She remembered voices, though, talking to her in a haze. There was a soothing voice at the end...and a pretty smile.

Clio shuddered and opened her eyes. Her hands trembled a little as she picked up the dossier again; she flipped to the front. A serial number was linked to her name, like the one on the security card. *WW22IC01.* She couldn't decipher any meaning from it.

She looked more closely at the chart that was labeled *Therapy.*

Phase 1: Candidate Observation
Phase 2: Initiate Status/Induction
Phase 3: Strange Loop/Subjectivity and Escape
Phase 4: Greater Mysteries/Things Done, Things Shown, Things Said
Phase 5: Reduction of Name/Form and Detox
Phase 6: Initiate Elect/Reentry
Phase 7: Aggregate Relinquishment
Phase 8: Hierophant/Ascendancy

"Hierophant," Clio whispered. She knew vaguely what that was: an old word for something like a priest. It was one of the major tarot cards, too. But she could only guess at its symbolism, and how it related to her.

Maybe whoever was behind the Gauntlet was part of some weird, modern cult. She looked up, almost expecting a troop of tambourine-playing supplicants to dance into the office with chants on their lips. If they thought she'd be into that, they'd be sorely disappointed.

She let the folder drop and wondered again why anyone would want her for this. How had they ever found her? Chosen her? It was clear now that she probably couldn't avoid whatever they were trying to do--scare her, teach her, use her, it was all the same. She was trapped in a cage someone had elaborately prepared.

But if she was a victim, she'd go out fighting. If she was a lab rat, she'd surprise them. If she *really* was some kind of initiate, then she had to admit, she wanted to find out *why*. And under whose order?

An even deeper truth pushed its way into her awareness. Something that had been poking at her subconscious for days.

She'd been terrified more than once in this place--scared for her life, even. But some of it, especially the times with Britt, had been...exhilarating. Her fear had been tempered by a dark sense of curiosity.

She'd come to the city because she'd wanted something more than an average existence. She'd wanted a challenge--something new, something *special*. She had the strange feeling that the same desire was tied to this, somehow.

There was only one way to find out. Clio stood up.

Her determination was foiled when the door labeled *Labs* failed to open to her security card. It was the smaller writing on the door that really piqued her interest: *Experimental Philosophy, Practical Psychosomatics, Psychotropic Mentalism*. She recognized some of the names--from the pamphlet she'd found in the lobby at the very beginning of the Gauntlet.

A sudden thought struck her. Had that been her induction? The Jacks? The lobby?

She swiped the card again, but the door beeped in angry warning. The display flashed: *Access level J denied.*

Her disappointment was punctuated by the biohazard symbol beneath the placard. Somehow, it made her desire to see what was inside even stronger. She had a feeling it was *meant* to tease her. She rattled the door and sulked a little.

But the next door was intriguing enough to make up for it. Who could possibly resist something called *Karmic Theater*? She held her breath, but this time the door clicked open. She stepped into a velvet jewelry box of a hallway, lined with dark red walls and carpeting. It ended in an archway covered by a shiny black curtain that draped gracefully to the floor.

Anticipation sent a little thrill to the depths of her belly. She quickly drew the curtain aside and emerged into a room that fulfilled the promise of the lush hallway. It was intimate--a theater in the round--but decadent with colored fabrics, enveloping her with a rich, plush ambience that managed to be both comforting and exotic.

She sank into one of the chairs that ringed the stage, disappearing into its depths. She stared up at the proscenium arch that loomed in front of her. A soft, amber spotlight shone just beneath it.

No show began. No actors waiting in the wings appeared.

Perhaps *she* was the show.

Clio couldn't stop the smile that tugged at the corners of her mouth. She'd always hated being the center of attention.

She didn't sing or dance particularly well, and she certainly had no desire to perform in front of an audience, even an invisible one.

But she found herself climbing the steps to the stage and pirouetting in the spotlight--just because *they* might think she wouldn't. Then she made a deep bow, letting her hair fall forward, and dramatically flung it back as she rose again.

It was only then, in the suddenly oppressive and obvious silence, did self-consciousness make her face flush. She turned abruptly and exited stage left, passing through another black curtain. She entered a new room that made her gasp with unexpected delight.

If the theater was amazing, this room was a *dream*. Racks upon racks of costumes lined the walls of the round room and ringed the edges of the center dais. It was a color wheel of fabrics and periods and styles, ranging from the mundane to the fantastic. It filled Clio with childish glee.

The sunken center of the room was circled by a ring of low, cushioned benches. Inside stood three ornate cheval mirrors, positioned to allow the viewer to see herself from all angles.

At first, a reluctance to make a spectacle of herself *here* held her back...but it was quickly overcome by her desire to try on the fantastic outfits. Soon, a pile of silk, tulle, satin, leather, and polyester grew around her as she tried and discarded costume after costume.

She quickly tired of the more elaborate getups; they were almost impossible to do up properly without help, and once they were on, they were a nightmare to walk around in. Struggling to breathe counteracted any grand romance she felt sweeping around in enormous skirts and tight bodices. But she admired herself dutifully and then moved on.

She adored the superhero section. The tight leotards and knee-high boots were much more to her liking, though she sadly noted that she didn't fill out the tops the way comic heroines did. She jumped experimentally in front of the long mirrors, eyeing herself.

"Anyway," she said aloud. "I can probably run faster

without having to worry about a good support bra."

She grinned at herself and snapped the golden rope in her hand. It trailed behind her as she walked along the curved racks.

If she was playing right into some cliché, or whatever it was they expected from her, she'd stopped caring. She just wished Britt was there to join her.

She giggled a little, imagining Britt's expression if Clio showed up out of the blue wearing a *costume*. She laughed even harder at the thought of Britt stuffed into one of the enormous dresses.

As much as Clio was enjoying herself, she needed to move on, and there was no way she would wander the Gauntlet in a star-spangled leotard. A solution presented itself a moment later, when she turned into a little alcove that held a hidden treasure of clothing and accessories.

Clio sucked in a breath as her hands flew to her mouth. She stared avidly at the display of leather and brocade, buckles, knobs, gears, and, most of all, *beautiful* boots. It was a steampunk aficionado's dream.

An excited squeak escaped her lips, and Clio abruptly lunged at a pair of flat, knee-high boots with an abundance of hardware. The supple brown leather felt buttery smooth beneath her fingers as she explored them with a fetishist's enthusiasm.

She released the last of her inhibitions to the wind, and soon strutted in front of the looking glass with an admiring gaze for her own image. She pleasingly filled out a pair of black leather shorts with triple flaps that buckled on the sides of her legs. The snug vest cinched her waist and made her look curvier than usual. The knee-high boots--the crowning glory--were quite simply kick-ass.

She rotated, admiring herself from all sides. In *this*, she felt powerful. Even sexy.

The thought made her blush a little. She probably couldn't walk around in this outfit without feeling self-conscious.

"But I'm keeping the boots!"

They would still be in stark contrast to her white sundress, which was little more than a dust rag at that point. She went back to the alcove to make a few alterations. Happily, Clio found a pair of narrow denim pants decorated with an abundance of loose straps--some swung from hip to hip, some looped and buckled around each thigh. The straps were probably more decorative than functional, but she still looked badass in them, and they went great with the boots.

She added a soft gray camisole with crisscrossing black straps, studded with silver rivets. Clio also took a rich leather belt and bag combination that lay low around her hips; they buckled around her thigh at the bottom, keeping the bag snug against her hip. A last-minute impulse made her snatch up the shorts and tuck them into the bag.

The prowlers had taken her backpack. Whoever was behind dumping her in the Gauntlet was responsible, so the way she saw it, she had every right to help herself. She *was* disturbed at the possibility that this was all some weird psychological test, and that they would be analyzing her every move, but that wasn't enough to deter her from this tiny win.

Besides, she felt better equipped to *fight* now: these boots could do some damage. She smirked into the mirror, raising her knee up and executing a slow front kick.

She gladly left the dirty heap of her old dress, but after some thought, she retrieved Black Jack's jacket. Somehow, it felt like a piece of reality--something to hang on to, anyway. *And it's warm,* she further justified.

She slung it over her shoulder and took one last look at herself in the mirror. With her new clothes, and her hair pulled back tightly with a makeshift tie torn from her dress, she looked older. Tougher. Britt wouldn't look at her with exasperated pity now.

Not as often, anyway.

Clio *was* tougher, and she'd discovered a lot in this expedition. She had so much to tell Britt when she found her again. And she *would* find her.

When Clio retraced her steps and discovered the door

with the key card was a one-way trip, she took it in stride. She went back to the stage...where a true surprise waited for her back in the wings.

It was a door marked with a star--and each of the five points was graced with a symbol from her bracelet. As Clio's heart began to race, she turned the handle. *No lock.*

The door opened to a snugly appointed room. The warm shade of the paint, the thick carpet, and the cozy, quirky furnishings all waited to cocoon her within a personal and intimate world. It was the antithesis of the sad, ugly dorms of the abandoned hallways; this room was perfection, clean and inviting, as if prepared with everything that could possibly entice her.

And of course, it probably had been. But she stopped caring if it was a reward, or a trap, or anything else. She gave in to the inevitable. This one day, she would allow herself to eat, to bathe, and to sleep in comfort.

Before her eyes closed that night, she admitted to herself, all snuggled up in the safety of the soft sheets, that she was almost looking forward to whatever came next.

♦ ♣ ♠ ♥

The scent of something heavenly brought Clio out of the depths of a satisfying sleep. For a brief, muddled moment, she was back home, waking up in her childhood bed and straining to hear the sounds of her mother in the kitchen. On cue, her stomach rumbled. Clio smiled.

She rolled from her side to arch her back in a deep stretch. Something jingled as her arms spread above her head. Clio froze.

The mild hunger pains in her stomach twisted into bitter disappointment.

Clio blinked her eyes open, but the windowless room was utterly dark. Her fingers fumbled for the lamp next to her. The warm light glowed around her, illuminating a tray next to her bed.

A small basket of fresh blueberry muffins sat next to a pot of tea and creamer--her favorite breakfast. Clio frowned as she considered how *they* had discovered that. She only briefly acknowledged that the food itself could be dangerous--if someone were out to hurt her, they would have done so while she slept.

And she was *hungry*. Britt had never had enough canned goods for Clio to feel full, and there was no knowing when another meal would come along. Her stomach growled louder this time, prompting Clio to grab a muffin.

They were still warm. Clio moaned as she barely chewed the first bite. The buttery sweetness spread over her tongue, and she swallowed only to take another large bite. She wolfed the muffin down in the space of a minute.

She paused to pour herself some tea before consuming another of the treats. They were delicious, and as the minutes passed and she didn't start puking or dying, she relaxed a little more. She allowed herself to slow down and enjoy her third muffin at leisure.

When she was too stuffed to do anything but lean back against the pillows and sip tea, Clio laughed a little. She never would have expected breakfast in bed after spending so many nights on cold, dirty floors.

Maybe, though...maybe it meant that she was getting closer to the end. The excitement of that thought was too much to smother completely.

Don't get your hopes up, she warned herself. *And what about Britt?*

"Britt."

Clio chewed at her lip worriedly, and a rush of guilt swamped her. Here she was, lying around and gorging on muffins while Britt could be in trouble. Even if she wasn't, Clio knew very well that Britt wouldn't be distracted by *breakfast*. No, Britt would be out looking for Clio.

That got Clio out of bed--a sacrifice that wasn't easy to make. She shuffled over to the main light switch and snapped it on. When the room lit up, she recoiled in surprise.

In place of a mirror from the night before, a large, recessed monitor now took up a good portion of the wall. The split-screen display showed various locations--empty rooms and hallways, dark shafts, bathrooms, and supply closets. Clio gasped when she saw the pool where Britt had taken her. Occasionally, the pictures faded out to be replaced by new scenes.

Clio watched in fascination. Her breath caught when two people sitting on overturned crates flashed in the upper corner of the display.

"Britt!"

Britt's face on the monitor turned up briefly, almost as if she'd heard Clio's voice. But even more shockingly, Britt was laughing. Clio couldn't hear what was being said, but the two girls--and she was almost sure the other person was a girl, despite the grainy video feed--were definitely laughing.

Clio had seen Britt laugh...a little before, but never with such gusto and with her head thrown back. Clio wondered what could be so funny.

Something in her chest twisted. Who was that other girl? Where had she come from?

Clio moved closer to the screen and noticed a small console with controls. With a bit of trial and error, she figured out how to zoom in on the feed.

The girls were eating, too. A nice little stash of food was scattered next to them.

"Where did all that come from?" Clio's voice sounded thin and high-pitched in her ears. She suddenly felt a lot less guilty about her muffins.

Her eyes focused on the other girl. It was hard to pick up details, but the girl was pale, as if she hadn't seen the sun in ages, and she was shorter and heavier than Britt. Her hair was a little wild and shaved on one side. She gesticulated broadly as she talked, which seemed to entertain Britt.

Whatever Clio struggled with was forgotten when her eyes fell on something at the girl's feet. The zoom wouldn't go any closer, so Clio rose on her toes and peered at the grainy picture.

An unpleasant frisson of shock ran down her spine. The puddle of dark cloth was a prowler mask. The bug-eyed shape of the goggles was unmistakable.

"Who *is* she?"

Questions tumbled in Clio's thoughts, mainly focused on what relationship Britt had with this person. And for how long.

"Did Britt take the mask when she got away?"

Clio bit her lip. Maybe this girl had helped her. Or maybe...the girl was a prowler herself.

No.

It didn't have to mean anything bad. Clio tried to quiet the thumping of her heart, but she couldn't completely quell her fear. How *had* Britt managed to get away? The Jacks had told her not to trust Britt. Red Jack, anyway. And Britt *herself* had said not to trust anyone.

"But...Britt's not like that," Clio whispered.

Britt wouldn't string someone along just to betray her later. Clio believed that. It *felt* true.

As far as the other girl's loyalties went, Clio couldn't say.

"I've got to get back to Britt."

Clio pulled back the zoom until she could see the whole room the girls sat in. It looked like every other room in the Gauntlet. Nothing distinguished it. Clio scowled in frustration.

She played with the controls until she figured out how to switch feeds. She kept an eye on Britt as she cycled through location after location. Britt and the girl were smoking now. Britt had been out of her own smokes for days.

The sudden appearance of two prowlers in the middle of the display frightened Clio, but they passed through a hallway and disappeared again. She flipped rapidly between feeds to find them again, but had no luck.

A brighter location popped up, lit with natural light.

Outside!

Her breath caught. It was a rooftop garden with high walls, but Clio could see the sky and the tips of taller buildings in the distance. If she could figure out how to get there, maybe she could climb down the side of the building.

The exhilaration quickly faded. These disconnected locations didn't help at all--she had no idea how to reach any one in particular. She cycled through the feeds until another familiar room caught her eye.

It was the theater. The stage was dark except for a small spotlight that beamed beneath the arch. A wooden easel stood there, holding a poster printed with a flourished vaudeville font. Clio zoomed in.

Act II ~ Deus ex Machina

~

Ace in the hole!

~

Fight or Flight?

At the bottom of the poster, a fat king sat on a bicycle and held up an ace of spades card. But what caught Clio's eye was the rolled paper dangling from a ribbon tied to one of the easel's wooden supports. Her name was written on a paper heart threaded through the ribbon.

Clio flew out of the room.

Her feet squeaked against the boards of the stage until she skidded to a halt in front of the easel; she winced as she landed on her knees. Her hands were shaky when she reached for the scrolled paper.

She untied the ribbon and spread the scroll. It was a blueprint--a map. A doorway had been circled in red ink in the bottom left, with the word *EXIT* printed next to it and underlined twice. Her heart began to pound.

EXIT.

Clio's eyes traced the lines of the map. She picked out the route that led from that tantalizing *EXIT* all the way back to the theater. There it was: a hidden door that would get her out of here. The mechanism to reveal it was clearly marked.

A trick--it had to be a trick. But it wasn't. Somehow Clio knew that. This was a true chance, a way out, and all she had to do was follow the map.

That was when she saw the two black dots in a small room on the far side of the blueprints. Arrows pointed to each one, labeled with small, neat letters.

Britt. Lilah.

Fight or flight.

♦ ♣ ♠ ♥

It took Clio longer than expected to get there. She had to backtrack once when she found a hallway blocked by a pile of concrete rubble, and to work around it, she had to crawl through a tight service shaft.

That wasn't blocked, luckily. Clio emerged into the wider hallway with relief. A quick scan of the map confirmed that her destination was through the door ahead.

Clio tightened up her ponytail and brushed off her knees. Her nerves burned as she walked to the door.

"At least I'm dressed for my big return," Clio whispered to herself. A little defiantly, she threw open the door.

The girls inside leapt to their feet.

Clio felt a slight, wicked flicker of satisfaction at the shock on their faces. Then Britt's face lit up.

"Clio!"

Clio's chest warmed at Britt's response, and her defensive resolve softened. She walked through the door and beamed.

Before she could greet Britt, the other girl stepped between them and eyed Clio up and down. Clio stared at the short, plump girl with rainbow-colored hair that fell over one eye. The other side of her head had been shaved to stubble and dyed bright yellow.

The girl smirked and cocked her head. Her heart-shaped paperclip earring jingled.

"*This* is her?" the girl drawled. One surprisingly nondescript eyebrow rose, and her smirk grew. “I thought you said she was a princess.”

♦ ♣ ♠ ♥

Chapter 4

♦ ♣ ♠ ♥

Clio could feel the weight of their stares. Heat began to creep up the back of her neck.

"This *is* the right place." She clenched her jaw in frustration and peered at the map again.

But the thick, featureless, steel door still loomed before them. Its silence seemed to mock them as it blocked their path.

The silence stretched out for a moment, and Clio's imagination conjured a picture of them pulling faces behind her back. She turned quickly, but Britt looked serious, her eyebrows pinched together. Lilah was the opposite--she yawned and scratched the back of her neck.

"Are you sure it was this corridor?" Britt asked.

"You can see the map for yourself!" Clio flung her hand out toward Britt and flapped the paper in front of her.

What bothered Clio more than anything was that the door hadn't been there *a few hours earlier*. The depressing slab of metal had sprung from nothing in the short period since she'd left the theater.

"Maybe we got turned around in the service tunnel," Britt offered.

"I didn't get turned around. *This* hallway led to the passage with the trapdoor up to the theater. This door wasn't here before."

"But it looks like it's been here for ages, doesn't it?" Britt asked.

"And you were just here, right?" Lilah pointed out. "Supposedly?"

"*Yes,*" Clio snapped. "I'm *telling* you, this is the right place." Her fingernails dug into her palms.

"We believe you." Britt held her hands up in a placating gesture. "Just calm down."

"I *am* calm." Clio made an effort not to talk through gritted teeth. "And I'm not crazy."

Lilah snorted; Britt shot her a warning look. Lilah rolled her eyes, walked up to the door, and pushed at it again.

"Well, there's a door here now, without a doorknob, and it's not opening unless you know some magic words." Lilah shot Clio a sarcastic grin. "So what's the plan?"

Shoving you into the nearest broom closet and barring the door.

Clio's thoughts must have shown in her face, because Britt placed a hand on her shoulder and tugged the map from her grasp.

"We could try and find a way around this. Come at it from a different direction."

Lilah muttered something under her breath about wild-goose chases.

Britt gave an exasperated sigh. "Lilah--"

"She's right," Clio interrupted. "I should have known they wouldn't make it so easy. They gave me a choice. I knew that, but..."

"Who?"

"Whoever is behind all of this," Clio muttered. "I still thought we should try, anyway."

Lilah snorted. "Right. Can we go back now?"

Britt hesitated.

"Fine." Clio rolled up the map and shoved it in her bag. "Let's go back."

The long walk back was mostly filled with awkward silence, frigid and resentful on Clio's part. She knew it was unfair, but that didn't stop her. She didn't *want* to talk to Britt. The stinging disappointment was too great. Aside from the exchange of a few more words on Britt's action-packed escape from the prowlers, silence reigned.

When they'd finally made it back to their safe room--and Clio was unhappily aware that it was *theirs*, not *hers and theirs*--Britt and Lilah huddled together in a corner and spoke in whispers. Clio pretended to ignore them by poking around the rest of the room.

Eventually, Clio slid down against the wall and stared at her knees. It was still early in the day, but she felt exhausted. The disappointment weighed down her shoulders, and the whispering, which they weren't doing very well because Clio heard her own name quite clearly, made her wither inside. She let her forehead slump to her knees.

"Clio."

Britt's shadow fell over her. Clio quickly busied herself with going through the leather bag she'd taken from the theater.

"Yeah?" She was proud of how nonchalant she sounded.

"I'm going to make a run to fill up the bottles. Want to come?"

Clio didn't want to go with her. The awkward tension between them would be *worse* if they were alone. But anything was better than staying with just snarky Rainbow Fright for company.

"Sure."

"Lilah's going out in a bit to scout the west hallway."

Damn. Clio could have stayed behind, after all. Her gaze flicked over to the other girl, who seemed totally at home in her surroundings. Lilah's high-top sneakers were propped up on a small crate as she lolled on the floor, with her tattered leather vest--which suited her raggedy plaid pants--rolled up beneath her head. She fed herself from a can of fruit salad. A bright red cherry disappeared into her cupid bow mouth.

Lilah caught Clio's gaze; her mouth lifted on one side as she raised an eyebrow. Clio flushed and turned back to Britt.

"I'm ready when you are."

Clio followed Britt out. They rounded the first turn and were halfway down the second hall before the silence got to be too much.

"I'm gl--"

"I didn't--"

Clio exchanged glances with Britt, then puffed out a laugh. Some of the awkward tension faded.

"Go ahead." Britt inclined her head.

"No, you."

Britt hesitated. She flashed Clio a quick, sidelong glance.

"I didn't call you a princess," Britt said at last.

"Oh." Clio tried to keep her face neutral as she shrugged. "It's no big deal."

Britt stopped. "Really," she said shortly. "I didn't say that."

Clio turned to face her, a bit offended that Britt was acting annoyed with *her*. "Then why did she say you did?"

"Because..." In a rare turn, Britt looked a little sheepish. "She *was* asking about you. What you were like. I *didn't* call you that. But...well, I may have said you were a little bit..."

"A little what?" Clio tried to ask the question lightly, but her nerves were on edge. She cared about Britt's answer more than she wanted to admit. She closed her arms over her chest in an unconsciously defensive stance.

"Well, a bit...prissy." Britt winced a little, but Clio didn't respond, so Britt went on hastily. "But that's it. It was no big deal. You shouldn't get so worked up over it."

Oh, that was it. Clio heard the slight air of condescension now. Her eyes narrowed.

"Gee, Britt," she said darkly. "I'm so glad you're here to tell me how I should feel."

Now Britt frowned. "See, I knew you'd react like this."

"Really?" Clio snapped back. "All prissy, you mean?"

"What I *said* was that you *used* to be like that. But that was only in the beginning--you've mostly gotten over it. But maybe I was wrong."

"Maybe you were!"

Clio sighed angrily and started walking again at a jagged clip. Britt fell in step with her. They didn't speak again for a good minute, until Clio realized how ridiculous they probably looked marching stiffly though the hallways in sync.

Clio bit her lip to hold in a smile. She glanced at Britt; the helplessly irritated and baffled expression on Britt's face made it even worse.

A little snort escaped Clio. Britt's social skills sucked, but she tried, sort of. Britt looked at her curiously, and Clio tried to remold her expression into "pissed."

"*Mostly* not prissy now?" Clio clarified.

They stared at each other again until Clio's expression broke. She grinned, then so did Britt.

And that was it. The humor of the situation reduced them to actual laughter. Britt bumped her shoulder.

"Mostly not prissy now," she agreed. "Wear it with pride, Clio."

The bathroom was around the corner, which meant fresh water. Britt let the water run a bit to clear out the pipes.

Clio waited for a second, shifting her weight from one leg to the next. "So why was Lilah asking about me?" she asked at last.

Britt threw her a look that implied *don't be stupid.*

"Because she wanted to know why I was going back into prowler territory to look for you."

Sudden warmth spread through Clio. She had to duck her head and fumble with one of the bottles at the tap to hide her pleased grin.

"You were going to look for me?"

A hand slapped the back of her head, and she dropped the bottle in the sink. "Ow!"

"Don't ask dumb questions," Britt said thinly. "I'm not gonna abandon you, even if you *are* a pain in the ass."

Clio's smile turned goofy. "Thanks."

Britt looked a little embarrassed. She grabbed another bottle and went to the next sink.

"Whatever. You did the same."

"Yeah," Clio hummed as she went back to filling bottles.

She knew she'd been right to trust Britt. The mind games

weren't going to mess with her. Britt *was* her friend.

"I believe you, you know."

Clio looked up. "About what?" she asked.

"That you took us to the right place. What you said you saw. But this place always screws with you--don't beat yourself up over it."

"Oh." Clio nodded. "Thanks. But...I'm sorry I got your hopes up."

Britt shrugged. "I never get my hopes up. Life is much easier to take that way."

Clio snorted. "Easier said than done."

Britt smirked. "I *thought* you'd toughened up. Your look sure has."

"Shut up," Clio laughed, a little self-consciously. "Um, what do you think?"

"Cool boots."

Clio beamed. "I know, right? I wish you could see the costume room. It was amazing!"

"I wish I could've seen the room with the files or the video feeds."

Clio deflated a little. "Yeah, I should've searched the files more, but I was just so shocked about mine. I didn't think..."

"Don't worry about it," Britt said with a wave of her hand. "You found out a lot. They must have something special planned for you."

"You think so?" Clio asked. "But why?"

"You tell me. What's your secret?"

"Like I have any!" Clio scoffed. "There's absolutely nothing special about me."

"Then maybe that's it," Britt deadpanned. "Maybe they found the most boring person they could, just to play with her and see what happens."

Clio's outraged gasp made Britt chuckle. She ducked as Clio flung a stream of water from one of her bottles.

"Thanks a lot. You really know how to flatter a person." Clio stuck out her tongue. "And what's so special about you, then?"

"Isn't it obvious? Beauty, brains, brawn..." Britt smirked and flexed her muscles. "And super ninja skills."

♦♣♠♥

The red rubber ball bounced off the floor, hit the far wall, and bounced back toward Lilah, who caught it with one hand. Floor, wall, hand. The sequence had been going on for half an hour.

Clio made every effort to ignore it. She pretended to nap, her eyes squeezed shut, and wished Britt would hurry up and come back.

They'd all briefly split up to cover more territory. Clio had taken the route back toward the special wing she'd found--she still hadn't completely given up on getting back in. Lilah's unsubtle scoffing hadn't discouraged her, and Britt had said it wouldn't hurt for her to cover that ground.

Clio had found an untouched supply closet, so at least she hadn't returned empty-handed. She kicked herself for not going farther, though. Now she was trapped with the sanity-rattling sound of Lilah and her stupid ball.

"You don't like me much, do you?"

Clio's eyes snapped open before she caught herself. Lilah was watching her with a knowing grin.

Crap.

Clio slowly sat up and crossed her legs. She went for a diplomatic answer.

"I don't even know you," Clio said.

"But you have a problem with me."

The ball hit the wall again. The loud crack made Clio's eyebrows pinch together.

"Do you have to keep doing that?" Clio murmured.

Thwack!

Lilah smirked. "I'm bored. Why don't you get whatever it is off your chest--maybe *that* will keep me entertained instead."

Thwack!

"Fine," Clio said through her teeth. She flicked her bangs out of her eyes and fixed Lilah with a pointed look. "Where did that prowler mask come from?"

"What mask?" Lilah asked indifferently.

"I saw it on the feeds. Don't pretend like you don't know what I'm talking about."

Lilah laughed. "You mean this mask?" She reached into the beat-up duffle bag at her feet and pulled out the limp, black fabric.

Clio stared in morbid fascination. The bulbous goggles were sewn into the fabric and looked just as creepy as she remembered.

"Where did you find it?" Clio demanded.

Lilah twirled the mask on one finger. "What makes you think it isn't mine?"

Before Clio could respond, Lilah pulled the mask over her head. The blank face turned toward Clio; Clio couldn't stop the shiver that tickled down her spine. Lilah stood up and loomed over Clio.

Clio gave a loud sniff. "It wouldn't surprise me, actually."

The expressionless face of the mask showed nothing, but Lilah's body language spoke volumes. Clio had no problem imagining a malicious grin across Lilah's pert features.

Suddenly, Lilah crossed over to the wall and flipped the switch. The room went dark.

Clio tensed. A pair of red dots began to glow a few feet away from her. Clio scrambled to her feet.

"Cliiiiooo..." Lilah advanced.

"You're not funny," Clio said with as much bravado as she could muster. Still, she took a step back and promptly tripped over a pile of cans.

She bit out a curse as she fell on her butt. The red dots danced closer until they were right before her eyes.

Lilah laughed. "Ooh," she drawled. "I didn't think Princess Clio was capable of such language."

Pissed off, Clio reached forward and tugged the mask off Lilah's head. Now there was nothing but the dark...and

Lilah's warm breath washing over Clio's face.

"Y-you're too short to be a prowler." It was a petty slam, but Clio still enjoyed dishing it out.

"You don't really think you saw *all* of them, do you?" Lilah chuckled. "You only ran into a few."

"How do you know that? Are you admitting that you *are* one?"

This time, Lilah breathed right into her ear. "Wouldn't you like to know?" She tweaked Clio's ponytail. Clio grabbed Lilah's wrist and yanked it away.

That was when the door opened. A second later, the light snapped on.

Britt scowled from the doorway. She rested her fists against her hips, her wary gaze running over Lilah's bizarrely intimate position above Clio.

"What the hell is going on?" she demanded.

Lilah sat back on her heels and grinned. "We're just getting to know each other better."

"What are you doing with that damn mask?" Britt closed the door behind her.

Clio tossed it aside in distaste. "I was asking *her* where she got it. She, of course, just made a joke of it."

"Can I help it if she doesn't have a sense of humor?" Lilah appealed to Britt. "She thinks I'm a prowler."

"I didn't say that!" Clio snapped, loud enough that she flushed. "I just...said it wouldn't surprise me if you were!"

Britt frowned. "She's not a prowler," she said with finality. She sat down and began to pick through the pile of cans.

"How do you know?" Clio asked sharply.

"She's been around awhile. She's helped me. We've helped each other."

Clio's indignation deflated. She awkwardly scooted out from under Lilah, avoiding eye contact.

So Britt had known Lilah longer. Clio's chest tightened as a feeling of resentment swelled up inside her. Britt had never mentioned Lilah to her. Why not? Were there other acquaintances in the Gauntlet who might show up one day?

Clio ducked her chin, taking a quick peek at Lilah under the pretense of tucking hair behind her ears. Lilah watched Britt, a small smile playing about her lips. Britt threw Lilah an exasperated look, but the hint of a smile was there, too.

Some sort of communication seemed to pass between them. Lilah sighed and slid her eyes to Clio.

"Sorry. I was just messing around."

The jealousy she'd been trying to suppress surged up strong in Clio.

"So where *did* you get it?" Clio snapped.

Lilah reclined back on her elbows. "It was a gift."

"A *gift?* From who?"

"Let's just say, I...have friends in unusual places."

Clio glanced at Britt, but her expression was impassive. Clio frowned.

"Are you saying you're friends with the prowlers?" Clio asked defensively.

"No." The heart-shaped earring twirled when Lilah shook her head. "I'm saying I have a mutually...beneficial relationship...with *one* of them." A grin full of innuendo spread across her face, and she leaned closer to add a conspiratorial air.

It took a moment for Clio to digest that. And when did, she grimaced. An image of Lilah and a black-masked figure writhing together in some dark cell flashed into her mind with horrifying clarity. Clio banished it as quickly as she could, trying to scrub the evidence from her brain.

As much as Lilah got on her nerves, she couldn't imagine anyone willing to put themselves in prowler hands. It seemed so...so *insane*...and kind of sick. Hopefully, they used a bed, at least? A clean one. Even Lilah deserved that much.

It suddenly struck Clio that there were real people under those masks, and she wondered for the first time how prowlers ended up in their positions.

Lilah's self-satisfied expression seemed to indicate that she didn't find her...liaisons distasteful. Clio grimaced again.

"How did you even meet?" she asked in horrified fascination.

"Ran into him when I was caught out late once." Lilah shrugged. "He was alone. And lonely. I helped him out with that."

Clio's blush seemed to amuse her. "Don't worry--he's really cute. The next time I see him, I could ask if he has a friend for you."

Not deigning to respond to that, Clio turned to Britt. "This doesn't bother you?" Clio asked. "Did you know about it?"

Britt didn't reply for a moment, but she exchanged another look with Lilah. The feeling of being left out hit Clio again.

"Everyone deals with this place in their own way," Britt said carefully.

"What's the big deal, anyway?" Lilah rolled up to a sitting position. "Are you that big of a prude?"

"It's not that!" Clio cried angrily. "How can we trust you if--"

For the first time, Lilah didn't look amused. "I don't care if you trust me or not, Princess. I've done what I had to--to keep myself fed, to get protection and information. Plus, I'm getting laid on a regular basis. Are *you?*"

"Stop teasing Clio," Britt interjected. She tried to sound stern, but Clio could hear the amusement underneath it.

How could Britt take this so lightly?

"Are you really sure you can trust her?" Clio demanded. "She's actually bragging about knowing one of those creeps who grabbed us!"

As Britt began to respond, Lilah's needling voice overrode her.

"Let's turn that around. How trustworthy are *you,* Princess?"

Clio stared, taken aback by the question. She finally mustered a bit of indignation. "I haven't done anything to show I'm not!"

"Oh, really?" Lilah sneered. "Then why are you getting all this special treatment? You get fancy new clothes, a real bed, fresh food, a map with a way marked on it, and, from what you say, all wrapped in a pretty bow just for you. How do we know *you* aren't playing *us*?"

Clio was speechless. She stared at Lilah for several seconds.

"But I'm not." Finally, Clio looked to Britt. "Britt," she entreated. "You don't believe that, do you?"

Lilah leaned forward, her eyes gleaming. "Think about it. She's asking all these questions. Maybe she's trying to get information to use against us, or against my friend. He'd be in big trouble if someone found out he was helping me."

"I'm not doing that!" Clio's fists clenched. A hot flush of helplessness and anger made her tremble. She didn't know how to defend herself from this. She had no way of proving anything she said.

Lilah scoffed. Clio felt hot tears prick at the corners of her eyes.

"That's enough." Britt's voice was sharp. "You're both acting like idiots, and you're driving me crazy."

"But--"

"I *know* you're not some secret agent, Clio." Britt rolled her eyes. "Seriously, you're probably a horrible liar. You wear your feelings all over your face."

Clio frowned. That stung a little.

"*Lilah* knows you're not, too," Britt continued. "She's just yanking your chain."

"Yeah, I was just messing with you, Clio." Lilah's plump cheeks dimpled as she offered Clio a fake smile. "You should be used to that."

"What's that supposed to mean?"

"How long did the prowlers have you?"

"Not...not that long," Clio replied, her voice wavering.

"But long enough." Round shoulders rose in a sympathetic shrug, and Lilah relaxed back into her lounging pose. "So they probably fucked with you a little."

A sick feeling twisted Clio's stomach. "What are you saying?"

"Oh, don't worry. I'm just talking about a quick little mindfuck. That's what all this is, isn't it? One big mental fuckfest?"

"That's *enough,* Lilah." Britt shot Lilah a warning glare.

"No, I want to know what she means." Clio's voice sounded high-pitched to her own ears, even through the thick blood that surged behind her eardrums.

The voices... Clio already knew, didn't she? She already knew what Lilah meant. She'd forgotten most of it, and pushed the rest deep down so she wouldn't have to think about it. But she knew.

Her hand crept up to the curve of her neck and shoulder. Fingertips pressed into flesh that had been tender for days, but had only bloomed with a colorful purple bruise that morning.

Oh, Clio *tried* to tell herself it was just a bruise from being manhandled, but she knew. The tiny sting as they'd dragged her away from Britt. And there was a matching bruise on her arm, with a tiny red dot in the center. She couldn't remember as clearly how she got that one, but she couldn't pretend anymore. They were from injections.

They *had* done things to her mind.

The blood in her face rushed downward, chilling her momentarily. *What* had they done? Not knowing was unbearable, but knowing might be worse. She already felt deeply tainted. Her vision tunneled as a rising sense of hysteria and vulnerability bubbled up within her.

Distantly, she watched Lilah's face change from amusement to something like alarm. Clio wasn't sure why. Britt was saying her name urgently. Lilah shot up to her knees, her brightly colored bangs flopping over one eye.

Clio felt a muted pain in her arms when Britt grabbed her and shook her, eclipsing her view of Lilah. Clio stared into Britt's mismatched eyes. A shudder wracked her body; the blinding light faded to a more bearable intensity.

Blue and brown, Clio thought. *No, it's actually more of a hazel.* This close, she could see the flecks of green and gray mixed into those eyes. It was kind of cool.

"Clio!"

Clio blinked. An awareness of her body and her surroundings hit with sudden force. She sucked in a breath and stiffened in Britt's grip.

Oh, God. She'd almost fainted. The blood flooded her cheeks this time, and she pulled away from Britt's hands with an embarrassed mutter.

"I-I'm fine."

"Are you sure?" Britt demanded.

Clio nodded, folding her shaky arms around her body. She closed her eyes and tried to reach past the fuzzed-out patches that blocked shadowy faces and words. But she still came up with nothing...just the pricks of the injections and the fleeting, fading sound of soft laughter.

She exhaled and looked up at Britt and Lilah. "Am I going to end up like one of those...those walking lobotomies?" she whispered.

"No." Britt released her. "That won't happen to you."

Clio ignored Britt and focused on Lilah. "*You've* got the connections, right?" she asked bitterly. "Is that what they're going to do to me?"

Lilah had the grace to look a little chagrined. She sounded much less confident when she answered. "I...no...I don't think so."

"Calm down and think about it." Britt squeezed Clio's shoulder. "You're still you. You don't feel any different from when you first got here, right? You're not having crazy thoughts, are you?"

After a moment, Clio gave a hesitant nod.

"I don't *feel* any different," she murmured. "But what if--"

Britt shook her head. "No 'what ifs.' Just think about what you can see and feel for yourself. Besides, you haven't started drooling yet, have you? You're not shuffling through the halls like a zombie flick refugee."

An unwilling smile tugged at the corners of Clio's lips. But it swiftly faded as heaviness settled in her gut.

"Sometimes I think it's only a matter of time," Clio said quietly.

To Clio's surprise, Lilah sighed. "Look," she muttered. "I didn't mean to freak you out."

"Right," Clio said flatly. Britt's expression also implied complete disbelief, which made Clio feel a bit better.

"Well, maybe a little, but that was just because you were being such a snotty--"

"*Lilah.*" This time a line of steel ran through the exasperation in Britt's voice. Lilah threw up her hands.

"I'm just saying," Lilah insisted. "I'm willing to get over this if she is."

"Fine," Clio said quickly, surprising even herself. "I just want to get out of this in one piece, so I...I hope we can get along and figure out how to get out of here together."

She stuck her hand out, enjoying the stunned looks on both their faces. Lilah shook her hand, uncharacteristically silent.

Then Clio withdrew from the conversation. She wanted to think about the missing chunk of time before she woke up cuffed to the bed. If she could make sense of the swirl of impressions she had, it might tell her something. Her fingers absently fiddled with the charms of her bracelet.

And regardless of what they thought, she wasn't giving up on getting back to the theater wing. It was the only place she had found any sort of real answers. It was the only place that had given her *hope.*

♦ ♣ ♠ ♥

The uneasy truce held for a few days. Lilah had mellowed, or maybe Clio had, and Clio began to relax a little in her company. She even occasionally *enjoyed* the girl's perverse sense of humor. In any case, Lilah took off for long periods of the day, doing who knew what, so Clio spent a lot of time with only Britt for company.

That suited her just fine. Britt agreed that they should push forward, deeper into the Gauntlet than they'd ever been before--even if it meant losing access to familiar waypoints and the few irreplaceable luxuries, like the pool. Britt admitted that she'd gotten complacent. She'd needed the push from Clio.

What made Clio happiest was Britt's decision to explore what Clio thought of as *her* wing. They hadn't convinced Lilah yet, but Britt didn't seem worried. She was more concerned with the logistics of moving her supply caches to new locations.

That project had taken up most of the day. Lilah had disappeared soon after waking up, which irked Clio a little, but she and Britt made good progress alone. In one more day, Clio could say goodbye to those drab hallways. The new territory looked similar, but at least Clio was moving forward. And the idea of that elusive exit she'd glimpsed hung like an invisible carrot over her head.

While returning to their safe room that day, Clio heard hushed voices before she even touched the door. Britt and Lilah had returned before her. In the quiet murmurs that drifted through the slightly open doorway, the sound of Clio's own name gave her pause.

She couldn't resist the temptation to eavesdrop. She quietly pressed up against the wall and peeked through the crack in the door.

Britt and Lilah were crouched down furtively, looking at something Clio couldn't see. Clio only made out brief snatches of words.

"...humor her..."

"...trigger again..."

A hot flush raged against Clio's cheeks.

Lilah laughed, and to Clio's ear, it sounded mocking. Her gut twisted a little when Britt chuckled, too.

Clio tried to harden her expression. She pushed the door open and entered with a fake grin. She pretended she didn't notice when they stood up and moved away from each other a little too quickly.

"Guess what I found in the pocket of some old overalls?" Clio announced.

The women practically attacked her for the pack that held only a few stale cigarettes. If not for the scene she'd just observed, Clio would have been amused by their excitement and pleased to be providing the coveted treats. Now it was just a good excuse to send them away until they'd smoked them.

Clio curled up and pretended to be asleep before they returned. Given the awkward state of her feelings, she just hoped things sorted themselves out in the morning.

She really should have known better.

♦♣♠♥

"It's gone."

Clio stared at the few contents of her bag, strewn on the floor around her knees. Her mind raced through the last few days.

No, she thought. *I put it back.* She was sure of it.

"What's gone?" Britt asked from across the room.

Clio felt her eyes blaze furiously as she looked up at Lilah.

"The map," Clio snapped. "It was in here and now it's gone."

"Clio..." Britt warned.

"Give it back," Clio interrupted. Her gaze didn't waver from Lilah. "I know you took it, so give it back."

Lilah laughed in a scornful little huff. "What would I want with it?" she drawled. "It's useless. Except as some weird security blanket for you."

Hot anger surged through Clio. She was beyond pissed off. She felt almost incandescent with rage, but a strange sort of calm before the storm kept her voice even.

"Give it back," she said one more time.

Lilah's pale, round face mocked her, her eyes wide with overdone innocence. "I told you--I don't have it."

Clio rose in one smooth movement. For once, Lilah's brash presence seemed diminished, and Clio relished the charge her anger was building. Surprise flickered across Lilah's face, wiping away the smirk that taunted Clio.

The satisfaction kept Clio from exploding.

"What did you do with it?"

"Nothing! I haven't seen it since the last time you dragged

it out to obsess over."

Britt stepped in quickly. "Are you sure you didn't leave it somewhere?"

"Yes!" Clio snapped.

"Whatever. I don't have it." Lilah shrugged, which made Clio seethe.

Clio shrugged off Britt's hand and glowered down at Lilah. "I know you're lying!" she shouted. "It didn't just disappear! You took it because..."

"It's a *useless piece of trash,*" Lilah shot with a sneer.

"You...you never even *cared* that it showed a way out, did you? You probably just threw it out because there's something really freaking *wrong* with you!" Clio's fists trembled with fury. "Your little *romance* with a *prowler* proves that."

"Poor Clio," Lilah mocked. "Now your jealousy's screwing with your brain. Maybe if you lightened up a little, a stupid piece of paper wouldn't matter so much to you."

"Lighten up?" Clio cried. "It was a *map!* For this *prison!* It's almost like you want to--"

Clio's eyes widened abruptly, and her mouth hung open. After a moment, Clio expelled a harsh breath and fixed Lilah with an incredulous glare.

"You *don't* want to get out," Clio accused shakily.

Instead of defending herself, as Clio had hoped she would, Lilah shrugged.

"So what?"

Icy dread clawed Clio's heart. Her vision blurred as blood flooded her face.

"So what? So *what?* You're out of your mind!" Clio swallowed bile. "And even if you...you *like* it in here, doesn't mean we all want to be stuck here forever!"

Lilah laughed in her face. "Why not? Would you rather be working at some dull job all day? Living some average, boring little life? I *do* like it here. I'm not ashamed of it."

"How..." Clio shook her head in disgust.

"Because *I'm* not afraid. Because I *like* the thrill--not knowing what's around the corner, having to live by my wits. No one to tell me what to do or how to be. There's food, a roof over my head, and even a little *romance*." Lilah accompanied that barb with a mocking arch of her brow. "*If* you have the guts to chase it down."

Clio sucked in a harsh breath. For a moment, a tiny piece of her could almost sympathize.

But the rest of her, the *vast majority* of her, smothered that thought. The Gauntlet revolted every reasonable sense in her body.

"You...you have no right to make that choice for *me*," she hissed at last.

"Right. Because Princess Clio is *so* special."

"Don't call me that!"

"Enough!" Britt stepped in again. "This is going nowhere. Clio, I don't think Lilah took the map. Whatever happened to it, it's not important now--"

Clio turned away, cutting Britt off mid-sentence. Her eyes searched the room until she found Lilah's tattered bag; she made a beeline for it. She ignored Lilah's outraged cry as she flipped the bag upside down.

Nail polish bottles in a variety of wild shades clattered on the floor. One bottle of neon green rolled across the floor and hit the baseboard. Clio sorted through the pile, much larger than what her own bag yielded: a lighter, cosmetics, a comb, a foil packet of potato chips, and other odds and ends.

There was no map.

Clio's chin dropped to her chest, and she stifled a dry sob.

"Clio." Britt's cautious voice drifted from the other side of the room.

Lilah, on the other hand, stomped over to the mess. She dropped to her knees beside Clio and sneered.

"Find what you were looking for?"

Clio flushed. "You know I didn't, but that doesn't mean anything."

"You're really an assho--"

"***Stop it!***" Britt's roar made them both jump. "Lay off, Lilah!"

Lilah's face screwed up, but she didn't say anything else. Clio felt a surge of validation.

Until Britt went on. "And Clio," Britt added. "You're being unfair."

Indignation flared in Clio's chest. "*I* am?" she cried. "Why *wouldn't* I think she took it? We all know she's constantly screwing with me!"

Britt shook her head in weary irritation. "You need to get over it," she murmured. "If the map's gone, it's gone. Making a big production won't change anything."

"Fine!" Clio lashed out, an unbearable tightness in her chest and throat. "Maybe you don't really want to get out of here, either!"

"That's not true. You're being ridiculous."

"You both act like I'm the crazy one for wanting to find a way out! Well...well..." Clio's shrill stammer wavered. "Then I'll go off on my own. I'm sure I can remember most of the map, anyway. *I'm* not giving up. This place sucks!"

And so do the both of you!

Ignoring Britt's stricken expression, Clio shoved her things together and stormed out. Britt didn't come after her.

That fact kept Clio moving, even when the indignation had fizzled and she'd calmed down. She obviously hadn't expected *Lilah* to chase after her, but Britt? She'd hoped Britt would try to talk her out of storming off.

Maybe Britt didn't really *want* Clio around now that she had Lilah. Maybe Britt was happy Clio had made it so easy on them by leaving on her own.

Clio was too angry to focus on her surroundings, but her feet took her back toward the blocked wing. Her thoughts were filled with wild plans to fall back on if she couldn't get through. She could take the prowler mask from Lilah and sneak back into the basement, passing herself off as one of them. If she found the room she'd been chained in, she could climb the shaft again and get back to the new wing that way.

Unfortunately, she had no idea *how* to get back to the basement room. Britt would. Lilah probably did. Clio sniffed. That little snake probably knew all about prowler territory.

Clio entertained herself with the fantasy of sneaking around in disguise, navigating enemy territory with bold daring. A vision of herself emerging triumphant again into the light of the sun and the choice of the four hallways was intensely gratifying. As far-fetched as it was, it did make her feel better.

So much so that she barely hesitated when she was forced to navigate the dark service shaft on hands and knees. She didn't have a flashlight, because she'd stupidly left behind the one Britt had given her. But Clio had been through the small shaft a few times--she knew the length of it. Her residual anger helped cage her instinctual fear of the narrow space.

She was making good time, fueled by adrenaline and purpose, until about halfway through. She stopped abruptly.

What?

Clio looked over her shoulder, though it was utterly black in the shaft. She strained to hear...whatever it was she thought she'd just heard.

A whisper? A glide of fabric on rough metal? The muted slap of scrambling hands?

Was Britt following her, after all?

Clio waited for several long seconds. The silence was as complete as the darkness.

Her lips pursed to form Britt's name, but something stopped her. The idea of speaking into the black void made her shiver.

A dialogue began to play out in Clio's thoughts. One that required she crawl forward again with careful nonchalance.

There was nothing in there with her. That was what the steady, sober voice in her mind said. She had heard an echo of her own making, or had just imagined the sound.

Don't panic.

Another voice, insidious and sly, whispered that *of course she wasn't alone.* What did she think happened to girls who went off on their own in a place like this?

No. She wouldn't think like that--she was spooking herself. There wasn't anyone following her. Nothing would come out of the dark and grab her trailing ankle. She wouldn't be dragged away like some spider's prey.

Just keep moving.

Not too fast, the sly voice whispered again. *Don't give away that you heard them, because then...then they might really come after you. They might catch you.*

Clio started to move faster--not an outright scramble, but fast enough that she stirred up the stifled air. The scuffing of her boots and the slap of her hands disguised anything else that might be heard in the shaft behind her.

Her imagination provided more than enough to fill in the possibilities. And then she was scrambling, soft whimpers slipping in short bursts from her tightly pressed lips when she parted them for air. She was certain now that she heard the sounds of someone following her. It had to be the frantic scuffle of crawling pursuers.

The heels of her hands burned, scraping on the rough floor of the shaft. Her knees screamed from the impact of the hard surface. But she ignored everything as she choked out breaths.

She finally reached the end. She shoved open the covering and spilled out onto the floor of the corridor.

The crashing sound of metal accompanied her graceless exit. She twisted, scrambling backwards and crab-like away from the mouth of the shaft. *Run!* the sane voice cried, but she was beyond hearing it. Her spine hit the wall, and she stared wild-eyed.

She waited.

After a full minute, she slumped onto her knees. Her hitched breathing finally started to even out.

She'd just freaked herself out. It wasn't the first time. A weak chuckle forced itself out, sounding a bit too close to a sob.

Britt would make her laugh about it. Britt would definitely laugh *at* her, but somehow the thought of that didn't sound unappealing. For the first time since she stormed off, Clio began to regret her impulsive actions. She'd give anything to have Britt with her in that moment.

But the whole length of the service shaft--not to mention several derelict wings--now stood between her and Britt.

Clio groaned. How stupid could she be?

She stood slowly, her knees complaining as she unfolded them. Returning was beginning to sound pretty good, but the shaft was like a dark, blank eye pinning her to the spot.

There was no sense pretending--she didn't think she could make herself crawl back into it yet. *Or ever.*

"Anyway," she breathed, trying to console her pride. "I've come all this way." As long as she was there, she had to try one more time.

Even without the map, it was easy enough to retrace her steps to the point where she'd brought Britt and Lilah. Half an hour later, she stood in front of the metal door that had thwarted them.

Her stomach plummeted. A knocker had been added to the once unadorned facade. The heart-shaped brass fixture had an aged patina...and looked as if it had been in place forever.

Her fingers trembled as she lifted the heavy metal and, with breathless anticipation, banged it three times against the door. The sound echoed in the empty hallway.

Nothing happened.

On the sweep of disappointment, she took up the knocker and pounded it against the door again and again. Her other fist pummeled the door in tandem until she collapsed, angry and spent, against the unyielding surface.

A curse died on her lips when she saw the small depression in the center of the heart. The heart shape was mirrored there, a smaller version, just about the size of...

Clio gasped and lifted her wrist. The heart-shaped charm would fit perfectly in the groove of the knocker's surface. She fumbled with the bracelet, clumsy fingers working the small charm off the link.

Oh, God. Could it be that easy? It had to be a trick, just like everything else.

Except it wasn't.

The charm slid smoothly into place. For a moment, disappointment threatened to crash through her when the door remained closed. Then she held her breath and briskly knocked again.

The heavy metal door swung inward. Tears sprang to Clio's eyes.

This was it. The short corridor that led to the theater's secret entrance and the way out.

Clio bit her lip. Britt would probably come looking for her. If Clio left the door like this, then Britt could find her way out, too. She'd seen the map. Clio barely considered Lilah, except to wonder if the woman would *truly* choose to stay if an exit was staring her in the face.

Clio stepped across the threshold, one hand resting on the door, the other on the frame.

But...she knew the door might *not* stay open, whether she left her charm or not. It *probably* wouldn't, if she was being honest with herself.

Britt would never know what happened to her. Britt might never come close to another exit like this.

A sick feeling pooled in Clio's belly. If she didn't take her *own* chance now...well, she'd already seen what happened in that situation.

"Shit," Clio hissed, the unaccustomed vulgarity coming out flat.

Clio *almost* went on, but one of the voices in her head came back. This time, it sounded like Britt.

I'm not gonna abandon you.

Clio heaved a sigh. It felt angry in her chest.

"Fine," she told the knocker as she pried the charm out of its core. "I'm going to get her. We're going to be *right back.* And you'll be right here waiting."

The charm popped out. Clio caught it in her palm as the door swung toward her with inexorable force, pushing her rudely into the hallway.

She looked at the door for a moment longer, then dropped her gaze to the miniature heart in her hand. Her fingers curled slowly around it until it was hidden from view.

Clio ran.

Her side ached with a slight stich before she got all the way back to the service shaft. She slowed to a jog as she turned a corner.

And collided with Britt. They both hit the floor hard.

"Clio?!"

Clio didn't spare a breath for her excited surprise. She sprang up right away, barely noticing Lilah--who stood, mouth open, a few feet away.

"Get up!" Clio cried. "I got the door open! We have to get back now!"

Clio grabbed Britt's hand and hauled her to her feet. Britt shook her head in what looked like shock and relief.

"Are you okay?" Britt asked.

"I'm fine!" Clio tugged at her. "The door!"

"It's really open?" Lilah asked.

"Yes! Or...well, it was. I can open it again. I used my heart charm." Clio uncurled her hand, which had clutched the charm in a white-knuckled grip.

Britt watched her with an expression Clio couldn't read. It made Clio uncomfortable, but she was too anxious to get back to the door--before it could disappear or be altered or otherwise block the exit.

"Come on!"

Britt exchanged a glance with Lilah, but didn't resist when Clio pulled her onward.

"You got the door open?"

"Yes!" Clio frowned. "How many times do I have to say it?!"

"But you didn't go through it."

"Duh."

Clio picked up the pace, hoping to spur on Britt and Lilah. They were both acting like they didn't get that *this was it*.

Maybe they were just shell-shocked. Clio had to admit

that the idea of freedom was a heady thrill, especially now that Britt was with her.

"Clio." Britt's voice had lost some its usual confidence. She pulled back at Clio's arm, forcing Clio to stop.

Clio whipped around in irritation. "What?" she demanded.

Britt pulled her necklace over her head. She held it out at Clio, letting the small die swing back and forth.

"Here."

Clio's eyebrows drew together. "What?"

"Take it," Britt insisted.

Clio's eyes flew wide. "But that's your--"

"I want you to have it. I'm...sorry. About earlier. You were upset, and I didn't really help things. And...what you said--" Britt shrugged and pushed the necklace at Clio's open hand. "I *do* want out. I want us to get out together. And I like you, all right? So..." This last declaration was accompanied by an uncomfortable shift and eye roll, but Clio was dumbfounded.

Clio stared at the necklace.

"I can't take--"

With a clipped mutter, Britt forced the necklace over Clio's head. The weight of the die settled below the hollow of Clio's throat.

Clio touched it tentatively. Lilah looked on with a veiled expression, but Britt seemed satisfied.

"Let's go."

Britt took off down the hallway. After a couple of seconds, Clio followed with Lilah behind her. Clio watched Britt's long legs propel her around a corner.

Britt's yell gutted Clio as she turned the corner herself.

The thud of pounding boots filled the air as a sea of black-clad, faceless prowlers surged into the corridor. Britt was already in their midst, surrounded on all sides--only flashes of her white tank top peeked out through the hands and bodies that hopelessly outnumbered her.

Clio was only allowed a split second before Lilah yanked her back around the corner. Clio opened her mouth to scream

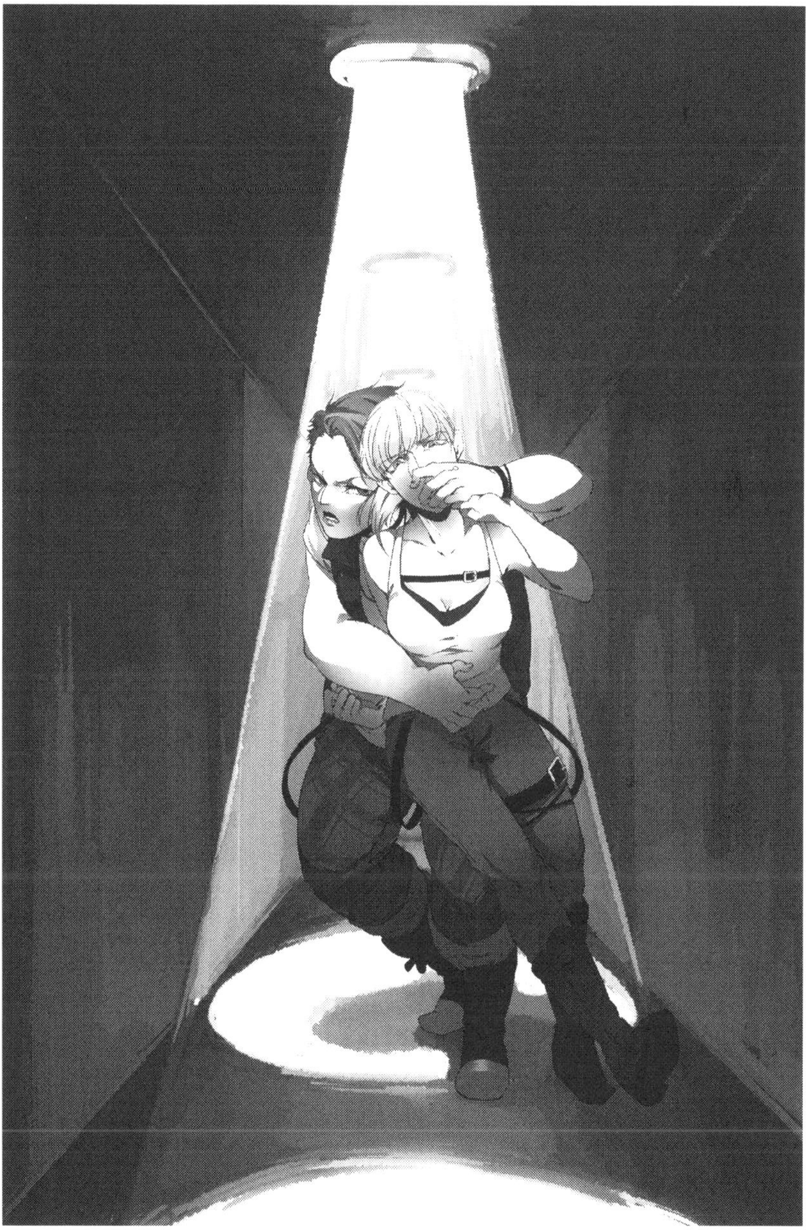

Britt's name, but Lilah's hand clamped over her lips with surprising strength.

Clio struggled as Lilah dragged her back down the hall. Her tenacious grip tightened as the lights in the wing went dark.

A door opened. Clio was jerked back; she felt the displacement of air as the door whispered shut in front of her face.

"Shut up," Lilah hissed before she pulled her hand from Clio's mouth. She kept her other hand gripped tight around Clio's wrist. "You can't help her right now."

"We *have* to help her!" Clio hissed back.

"You really want to risk it?"

"*Yes!*"

Things had happened too quickly for full terror to kick in, and Clio's pulse was racing madly. This couldn't be happening again. Not when they were so close to getting out.

Clio pulled furiously at Lilah's grip. "Let go of me!"

Wherever they were, heavy footfalls and shouts bled through the door. Lilah didn't let go. She was silent a moment, but then Clio felt Lilah's bangs brush against her face.

"I know how to help her," Lilah murmured.

"Then tell me how!"

"I'll do it on my own. It's easier that way." Lilah paused. "But first...I want your charm."

Clio's mouth dropped open. "What?"

"You heard me. I want the charm that opens the door."

"But...we can all--"

"There's not a lot of time," Lilah said coolly. "Make your choice."

Clio opened her mouth, but only a shaky breath filled the darkness between them. Her fingers crept up to the new necklace she wore.

Why had Britt given it to her? It made no sense. Now... now Britt would be truly lost in this awful place, if she didn't have her own talisman to get her through.

Why, Britt?

To prove herself? To prove her *friendship?* Because Britt

had thought they were about to escape?

Could Clio really give up her own talisman to *Lilah?* She'd never fully trusted the woman.

The darkness was a blessing. Clio didn't know what her face looked like, but she *definitely* didn't want Lilah to see it. The charm cut into Clio's palm as her fist tightened.

"You...you promise you can help her?" Clio whispered.

"Yes."

A sense of inevitability washed over Clio. Somehow, it didn't make her despair.

A stubborn little flame inside her flared--or maybe it was just bitter determination not to give in. There had to be another way out. Nothing was perfect...not even the Gauntlet.

And if she got Britt back, they could find another way out later. Just like this door had shown up. Getting out alone, without Britt, would be just the same as losing. The exit wouldn't be a win. And Clio wanted to *win.*

Clio's fingers slowly uncurled. In the dark, she found Lilah's hand.

It was less difficult than she expected to hand the charm over. This was all just a game, after all. A hollow laugh escaped her.

"What's so funny, Clio?" There was curiosity in Lilah's voice, layered over something else. Mocking amusement, maybe, that she couldn't conceal.

Clio really hoped she had done the right thing. But she still hadn't figured out the rules, if there were any.

"Easy come, easy go," she said by way of an answer.

"You're finally getting it." Lilah laughed softly. "In fact, you hit the nail on the head."

Something clicked behind Clio, and a wash of warmer air enveloped her. Lilah's hand planted against Clio's chest and shoved hard.

Clio tumbled backward and fell into darkness.

♦ ♣ ♠ ♥

The sweet scent was overpowering. Lovely, but almost too fragrant. It made Clio's nose itch.

Clio unwillingly exerted the effort to rub the back of her hand across her nose. Something brushed against her fingers, and the cloying scent intensified.

Her eyes blinked open into a soft green world. Long vines were entwined above her head, sprinkled with petite white-and-yellow flowers. One such strand dangled just above her face, responsible for the tickle that had woken her.

Dappled sunlight made Clio squint, though it was a hazy light she quickly adjusted to. Mindful of the headache that throbbed as soon as she sat up, Clio scanned her environment. An amazing realization finally penetrated.

She was outside. Not in some crumbling little courtyard, but *truly* outside.

Grass grew thickly beneath her. The sky stretched broad and blue above, and for some reason, she was napping under a verdant tangle of honeysuckle. A cobblestone road wound its way between two rows of buildings that had at some point fallen, into mild, picturesque decay. Masses of ivy clung to the walls. The gentle deterioration and silence spoke to the buildings' deserted state. Only the hum of insects disturbed the quiet.

Clio put a hand to her forehead. The skin was warm, but not hot. The ache throbbed and spread at the base of her skull.

Lilah had pushed her. She had fallen down a shaft, through a spray of some sort of gas that had hissed out, moist and cool. She couldn't remember anything after that.

But here she was. She twisted around, wincing at the bright flare of pain. There, behind a dangling mass of vines, was a small door.

Locked, of course.

Her fingers caressed the rusty ironwork. Had she tumbled out of that? She gave a short laugh. The Gauntlet's back door was much less imposing than the front.

Her smile faded into a rueful twist. She wasn't getting back in this way. Her lips pressed into a thin line. What was

Lilah's game, really? She could only hope Lilah would keep her word about Britt, because there wasn't anything Clio could do to help her right now.

Clio touched Britt's necklace again. Britt had given it to her just before the attack...almost as if she'd known what was coming. Maybe she had. Clio's chest tightened.

"I'll come back for you, Britt," Clio promised softly. "No matter what." She didn't know how, but nothing seemed impossible now.

She was out.

Clio climbed to her feet. She staggered around like a frail old lady.

She was *out*. She spread her arms wide and breathed in the scent of the honeysuckle. The light breeze teased her hair.

Clio spun slowly until her gaze hit a crumbling mosaic on the wall, high above the small door. A girl in a foolscap slept under the flowering branch of a tree. She was watched by a figure who sat in a straight-backed chair. Male or female, Clio couldn't tell. The sitting figure wore long robes and a featureless gold mask. A path stretched away from the sleeping girl.

The hum of the insects grew louder, driven to a momentary frenzy. Clio turned and looked at the disused road. Far in the distance, past the line of old buildings, Clio could see the hazy shadow of high walls.

Realization dragged down the brief, momentary hope that had lifted Clio's heart. This wasn't the city she knew. She *wasn't* out.

Her breath caught at the impossible scale of what she was seeing. It was too incredible...another city. A city *within* her city.

A city inside the Gauntlet.

Could it exist in the midst of millions of people going about their lives? The real world, the real city, was still outside of this place, walled out by the labyrinth she'd just been shoved out of.

Wasn't it?

Clio took a shuddering breath, a wave of dizziness bringing her hands to the warm skin of her face again. "I'm not out of it yet," she whispered.

When the faintness passed, she stared at the mosaic a little longer. They were still watching her, and she was still their fool. The message was clear.

In a flare of defiance, Clio swallowed and shrugged.

It didn't matter. They would do whatever they wanted, whether she agreed to it or not. But *she* was going to do whatever she wanted, too.

Maybe they wouldn't like *that* in the end. She had more than one purpose now.

All she could do at that point was advance on their game board. Clio spared one last look at the little door for Britt, then turned her back to the wall and began to walk.

♦ ♣ ♠ ♥

Chapter 5

♦ ♣ ♠ ♥

Clio heard it before she saw it--the sound of water. The muted whisper gave her the strength to shuffle her tired legs. The dryness in her mouth seemed to increase tenfold at just the promise of a drink.

"I *know*," she groaned.

She was thirsty...and hungry. It had been two days since she'd eaten anything like a full meal, and half a day since she'd gulped water from the spigot on a crumbling, empty building in one of the silent neighborhoods she had passed through. It was still mind-boggling that she'd seen no one, heard no signs of life.

All this for some screwed-up playground. It had truly begun to sink in how rich or powerful the people running the Gauntlet must be.

She knew that if she didn't find something to eat and drink soon she would be in real trouble, as her current shakiness and irritability attested. Thinking about whether or not she could beat the game was far down on her list of priorities.

The sound grew louder as the narrow lane funneled into a small, open square. A bubbling fountain stood in the center, streaming water from the pursed lips of a stone fish that arched over the structure. She stumbled toward the fountain eagerly and cupped her hands underneath the fish.

The water was cool and clear when it touched her tongue. She had expected some sort of chemical tang, but the taste was pure pleasure. Nothing had ever tasted so good; she drank with messy gulps until her stomach began to cramp.

The water also eased the pinched, empty feeling in her stomach for the moment. Clio sighed and lay down on the broad rim of the fountain, replete with satisfaction.

The late morning heat of the sun made her feel lazy. It was hotter than it should have been, considering the sun wasn't at its zenith yet. But it still felt good to lie there and listen to the relaxing cascade of the water.

Just for a bit.

Her eyes focused on a sweep of clouds as they drifted slowly across the sky. She lost track of time.

The sound of distant music gradually crept into her awareness. Clio suddenly realized that the song she was hearing had been going on for some time. She also noticed that the sun was now high overhead. When had it crept so far?

She still didn't feel an urgent need to worry, so she focused on the music, trying to make out the tune and the instruments. A reed instrument, she thought, or pipes of some kind. It sounded old-fashioned and woodsy, somehow. The muted sounds grew clearer.

A languid heaviness seemed to weigh her limbs as she slowly sat up. The music was definitely getting louder. She felt a growing urge to locate the source, and she stood up, weaving unsteadily on her feet before finding her balance.

A shout of nearby laughter made her whirl around. She caught a bright flash of color at the mouth of one of the narrow lanes that radiated from the square. But when she turned to look, nothing was there.

A tinkle of bells rang behind her, and she turned again. There--a shocking face was framed by the paneless square of one of the windows. The grinning mask seemed to stare right at her, and her heart squeezed hard.

The crowned figure wore a brightly colored costume of red, gold and blue. The jangle of bells sounded again with a tilt of the head, as if acknowledging her fascinated gaze.

She walked toward the building, not taking her eyes off

the figure until she passed through the doorway. But when she entered, there was no one inside. She took a few steps through the dusty air and peered through the window, as the figure had done.

She gasped. Not one, but two identically costumed figures stood on the fountain's edge in exaggerated poses that mimicked the statue of the fish.

Clio laughed, a thought growing inside her. There were filigree ornaments adorning the tops of their crowns. One figure had a heart, and the other a spade.

"Jack?" she asked aloud. She paused a moment, then added, "Jack?"

She giggled. A distant part of her brain was dimly astonished at her reaction, but the sound made the two figures spring to life again. They leapt down from the ledge, bells ringing, and danced comically in front of the window. Their antics made her dizzy, and she put up her hands.

"Stop!"

They didn't speak, but instead darted inside to appear in the dusty doorway. Their warm hands seized hers and they drew her outside into some frantic version of ring-around-the-rosy. Clio couldn't help it--she started laughing helplessly until she was breathless, especially when she realized the unseen musicians had switched their tune to match.

The high-pitched notes grew faster and wilder. Clio began to feel a little nauseated, but the Jacks--if that's who they were--kept spinning.

"No...stop...I can't..."

They stopped dead. Her hands were still gripped tightly, and she swayed between them. Then their fingers began to slip away. Alarmed, she reached for them, but involuntarily weaved away from them with drunken steps.

"Round and round and round she goes..." said the Black Jack.

"And where she stops, nobody knows," said the Red Jack.

But were they *her* Jacks? She couldn't be sure. The voices were somehow off, but...everything about them seemed so familiar. Their masks grinned at her in flashing snatches as the world still whirled around her. She fell to her knees.

The two figures darted away, bells tinkling, down different lanes. They threw flirtatious gestures behind them that beckoned her to follow.

"Wait..." She wanted to chase them, but which one?

She felt ungainly as she rose to her feet, but the music changed again, and she found herself lured to the sound of the lively tune. It seemed to flow inside her and loosen her limbs. Her hips swung as she walked, and, without realizing it, she began to hum along to the easy rhythm.

The lane turned and twisted, but spilled out several blocks later into a small park. The music swelled to a festive decibel that echoed around the little wilderness, sheltered within a ring of abandoned buildings.

The park was overgrown with a riotous tumble of vines and flowers and uncut grass. A few tall trees sat sentinel around the perimeter, surrounding a stone table laid with delicious foods.

Clio ran to the table without thinking. She grabbed a cold, purple plum and bit into it. Its unreal sweetness burst across her tongue, and she slurped greedily, unmindful of the sticky juices that dripped down her chin. She ate it to the core, licking her fingers before reaching for a shiny red apple.

Before she could take it, someone grabbed her wrist. She was pulled into a spinning waltz by the spade-crowned Jack. The grinning mask peered down at her with a blank jolliness that could have been sinister, but just made her laugh.

She knew, deep down, that she shouldn't take all this in stride...but she couldn't make herself care. The air around her felt liquid; every motion and thought was organic and irresistible. It didn't matter if these were fever dreams or drugged hallucinations. This was the most fun she'd had in ages, and she felt amazing.

Everything was amazing.

The tune quickened, and so did her feet as her partner guided her expertly through the steps. From the corners of her eyes, she saw other figures darting in to prance around the park. She craned her head to get a better look.

Her head whipped back as she was passed to a new partner. Clio pouted, but didn't struggle, as the new masked figure shifted and multiplied in her vision. How many people were here now? She found herself changing partners again and again as part of the long chain of the dance.

Everyone was in costume, their masked faces beaming with red-painted smiles. Waxed, rosy cheeks, and sharp chins and noses poked at her from all directions.

The laughing crowd pressed bits of fresh fruit past her lips--peaches dipped in honey; pomegranate seeds; figs split open to display soft, pink flesh. She accepted them like a fledgling bird in mindless enjoyment.

Somehow, it was night already. Old-fashioned streetlights cast illuminated circles around the park, and the sky was filled with stars. Clio was sure she saw a naked man dash across the grass and disappear into the branches of one of the trees. She heard feminine laughter up in the branches overhead, but no one else seemed to notice or care.

Her current dancing partner seemed to grow. His wax face melted and reformed again and again, shuffling through a number of faces.

Clio stared with rapt attention until it morphed into the bulbous-eyed mask of a prowler. She gasped and staggered back; the other dancers weaved around her, seemingly unmindful of her horror. The prowler-masked figure stepped toward her.

She turned and tried to run, but was snatched and passed from hand to hand. She was twirled between countless bodies until she landed, breathless, at the head of the stone table.

Two tall figures sat there, silent behind their featureless gold masks.

She could see that one was male and the other female--they wore nothing but sheer white togas draped over their straight forms. They were young...or at least not old. They looked like beautiful statues, sitting so still.

Clio suddenly noticed that the woman held a golden cup in her smooth, graceful hands. She raised it in silent offering, the golden rim inches from Clio's lips.

The moment seemed heavier than any other. Everyone around Clio grew silent.

What is this? Clio thought through the fog in her mind. *Was any of this even real?*

She reached up with the back of her hand and pressed it against her cheek. The skin was hot, feverish. The dancers spun in her peripheral vision, tumbling her thoughts.

The cup lifted higher. The liquid inside was as golden as the chalice, thick and viscous. Clio caught the scent of honey and the sharp edge of spice. Her hand drifted down to accept it when a flash of dark arms caught her eye.

She jerked her head up. A tall woman in a simple gown disappeared into a knot of revelers. She wore no mask, only a circlet of leaves around her close-cropped hair. Her face was turned away.

"Britt?" Clio breathed, and turned to follow.

It *was* Britt. It had to be. Unless Clio was hallucinating now, seeing what she wanted to see... An ember of resentment began to burn inside her.

An arm slid around her waist.

"Drink," a male voice murmured in her ear. His hand covered hers and together they reached for the cup.

The voice made her shiver. It sounded like the liquid in the golden cup--smooth and thick with secrets. She didn't resist as he helped her bring the cool metal to her lips. She drank tentatively at first, then took a deep draft as the heady taste surprised and delighted her.

"That's it." The voice rang with approval and Clio glowed. She didn't protest as he began to sway her to the new music that rolled out across the throng. It included a slow, percussive beat that charged her body with an electric hum.

One by one, the streetlights went out, and there was only the music and the dark and the rustle of moving bodies.

Something thumped at her feet. She didn't realize it was

the man's mask until his warm mouth closed over hers.

A rush of adrenaline made her tremble, shock or pleasure or something else. She'd never been kissed so slowly and deliberately, as if her every reaction was being explored. It felt good...but something made her pull away.

She stumbled in the dark, pushing past entwined bodies, until she was pulled into another embrace. She was kissed again, then spun into another pair of arms and another set of lips. She was kissed and passed again and again, like a dancer in a line. Male, female... *Both,* she thought, but her blood was racing. She couldn't think.

She was surrounded now. Fleeting touches made her gasp and turn, but they were growing bolder. Unmistakably carnal sounds began to rumble around her. The shadows seemed to shift and change.

She shrank away from the touches. *This isn't real,* she reminded herself. She looked up at the moon, searching for one clear thought. The round face of it reminded her of Lilah.

"She took my heart," Clio whispered.

"You can have mine."

Clio spun around. Red Jack stood there, a hand clasped in melodramatic fashion across his chest.

"No, take mine," Black Jack offered with a courtly flourish.

"No, mine," said another voice from the darkness.

"Mine, mine, mine, mine..."

The voices assaulted her from all sides. Clio clasped her hands over her ears to shut them out.

The vibration from the drumming bled through her feet and up her spine. It grew heavier, wilder. She backed away from the reaching hands, her own hands slipping from her ears and letting in insistent voices.

"Not real," she muttered fervently.

Laughter peeled from the throng and their shadows began to close in. She stared blindly, repeating her mantra like a spell.

She was suddenly yanked away from the encroaching circle and pulled into a dark lane. Darkness flooded her vision as a large hand engulfed hers.

A new voice--familiar somehow--resonated in the black. "Do you want to stay?" he rumbled.

She shook her head numbly. He must have felt it, because he wrapped his hand more tightly around hers.

"Then run."

He pulled her swiftly down the black street with sure-footed confidence. Her hair streamed behind her and she stumbled to keep up. She found herself laughing, out of breath, from the sheer thrill of it. The sensation of the cool night air on her skin made her feel more alive than ever.

He finally pulled her into some dark doorway. She bent over to ease the painful stitch in her side, still laughing.

Her chin was grabbed and raised, but she didn't know why. It was too dark to see anything. She *wanted* to see him, whoever he was. She raised her hand to touch him, but he gripped her wrist and held it down. The action was firm, but strangely gentle.

"Are you going to kiss me?" she breathed. Her chin lifted in almost unconscious anticipation.

The fingers around her wrist flexed. Then she heard an exasperated snort; her arm was abruptly released.

"Time for you to sleep it off," he murmured.

"But I'm not sleepy," she protested.

"It's all right," the voice soothed. "Sleep."

Clio closed her eyes.

♦♣♠♥

"Mmm..."

Clio rolled over. She pulled the thin sheet up over her shoulder until it was tucked snugly under her chin. She was unwilling to open her eyes just yet, despite the light that penetrated her lids and told her it was daytime. The bed was too comfortable...

Her eyes popped open.

She was in a *bed*.

Clio abruptly sat up. She didn't recognize this small room, nor the mysterious bed that had materialized under her. The place was clean; sunlight streamed through an open window that let in a light breeze. A pitcher of water and a glass sat on a small table next to the bed.

She clenched her fingers into the sheets. Flashes of the night before danced through her head.

She tried to piece together a coherent sequence of events from the surreal fragments, but only succeeded in frustrating herself. She could only remember bits and pieces--and none of it made sense.

"Those bastards drugged me again."

God, she couldn't be sure if *any* of what she remembered was real. She couldn't even be sure how much time had passed; for all she knew she'd been sleeping here for days. If she wasn't more careful, she'd start believing her whole time in the Gauntlet was a hallucination--that she really *had* lost it and was actually far away, wearing a straitjacket in some rubber room.

She wasn't very hungry, though. Maybe some of the food had been real. She looked at the pitcher of water, then to her boots sitting by the wall.

Someone had brought her here. She had no idea why.

"Whatever," Clio muttered. "I'm not sticking around to find out." She scowled and got up to put on her boots.

The drugs weren't completely out of her system yet--lazy contrails of light floated in her peripheral vision, and she still had a strange sense of disconnect with her body. The water was tempting. Her mouth felt like cotton, but she wasn't voluntarily dosing herself up for their amusement again. She pulled her boots on and headed out.

She didn't recognize the area. She squinted at the sun and grimly headed east, as she'd been doing all along.

The weird vision effects made her paranoid. She spent too much time jerking her head from side to side, trying to catch imaginary things that seemed to lurk in the corner of her vision. It wasn't until a few hours later that she felt mostly normal again, though a throbbing headache and low-grade nausea hit her hard.

Clio was more than ready to hole up in one of the cool buildings and rest. She was so distracted by that desire, though, that she didn't hear footsteps as she turned a corner.

She looked up and stopped dead.

Three intimidating men halted in front of her. They looked as surprised as she felt. Two of them flanked the one in the middle--a tall, young man with tan skin and piercing eyes.

Clio realized, with a sinking feeling, that it was too late to run. When she took an instinctive step backward, they all tensed. Clio swallowed. She felt frozen and tongue-tied, and her stomach crawled with nervous anticipation.

Maybe they'll be friendly...?

The tall man in front didn't seem pleased by her presence. He was *very* good-looking, his brown eyes framed by long, thick eyelashes any girl would kill for. He looked her up and down and seemed to find her lacking. His broad shoulders squared.

"What are you doing?" he snapped. "You shouldn't be here."

So much for friendly. In her confused, nauseated state, his rude tone irked her. She threw out her chin as her fear melted into anger.

"I'm just passing through," she snapped back, frustration getting the better of her. She was so tired of being tossed around by this stupid place. "What are *you* doing?"

His eyes narrowed. "You should mind your own business," he said flatly. He jerked his thumb over his shoulder. "This way is off-limits. Turn here or go back the way you came."

He spoke with the self-assurance of someone who was usually obeyed. Clio glared.

"Why should I? Who do you think you are?"

He stepped closer. "Someone who knows a lot more than you."

"Wow, thanks for that detailed explanation."

Ellery Prime & T2A

He ignored her and crossed his arms over his chest, managing to look bored and irritated at the same time. He loomed over her, still blocking her way.

Clio was torn. If he was telling the truth, then she probably *didn't* want to go that way. On the other hand, she couldn't just go back--she wanted to put space between her and the creepy room she'd woken up in.

Her frustration exploded in her chest. "I have to keep going!" she insisted. "Why can't I go that way?!"

"Just consider this area private territory and stay out. That's all you need to know."

"How can it be private territory? Do you *own* it? Isn't this still the Gauntlet?"

"Stop being unreasonable," he returned in a clipped tone.

"I am *not* unreasonable!" Clio threw up her hands. "You're just a player here, right? Well, so am I, and I *have* to go this way!"

He expelled a sharp breath. "You don't know anything," he murmured as he threw a subtle signal to the men behind him. His two goons moved closer. "We can do this the easy way or the hard way."

Clio's pulse began to race. She took a step back.

The man suddenly cocked his head and went very still. After a moment, Clio heard it, too--the sound of boots marching on asphalt.

She gasped when he grabbed her arm. He pulled her swiftly away from the open promenade and into the concealing shelter of a side street.

"Let go!" she hissed. "What are you--"

Clio ended up against the brick wall with a hand clamped over her mouth. The sound of marching got louder, so she didn't struggle. Only then did she realize that the other two guys hadn't followed them.

She heard voices, sharp and cold. The marching stopped and indistinct words were exchanged. The hand over her mouth pressed harder; she glared up at the man, but he just narrowed his dark eyes in warning.

After a few moments, the marching resumed. Not long after that, the two missing men finally joined them in the alley. They nodded at their leader--if that was what he was.

He let out a breath. He released her and stepped back.

"Who were they?" Clio asked.

"Grays," he said offhandedly. He jerked his chin at her, indicating that she should follow him down the narrow street.

She burned with irritation. After a moment's hesitation, she ran after him.

"But who--"

"They're headquartered in the town center," he said, cutting her off. "There's an ugly, square building you can't miss. Stay away from it if you know what's good for you."

A sharp whistle drew his attention to the far end of the alley, where the two men stood guard. He stopped in his tracks.

"Last chance," he warned. "Leave now, or they'll get their hands on you."

"But--"

"Do you *want* your mind tampered with?"

Clio's eyes widened. "Is that what they do?"

"Go or don't," he replied. "It's up to you." He sounded as if he was done with the conversation.

Clio took a faltering step away, and then another, but she stopped and clenched her fists again. "Where am I supposed to go?" she demanded.

"That's your problem."

"Yeah, well, thanks for nothing!" Clio spun on her heel, tacking on an "Ass!" under her breath.

Apparently, he heard it--he even gave a short laugh. Clio looked over her shoulder.

"Just stay on the perimeter, as close to the outer walls as you can. Keep your eyes open." He dropped a significant glance to her arm; Clio tensed, her hand wrapping around the wrist where her charm bracelet dangled.

"They say fortune favors the fool," he murmured.

He motioned to his companions. He jogged after them, out of the alley, and the three turned out of sight. Clio stared angrily.

"I made it this far, jerk!" she called lamely. She knew he was well out of hearing range.

Sure, she'd had help, but *still*. The average person would have curled up in a little ball after seeing half of what she had. She'd been doing pretty damn well, right?

The sound of approaching, synchronized footsteps convinced her that *now* was not the time to ignore advice out of spite.

She ran the other way.

♦♣♠♥

Clio cupped her hands above her eyes to lessen the glare from the sun. A small group of people passed in front of the building she hid in.

Their nondescript clothes were an ugly gray and looked vaguely like some sort of uniform--button-down shirts and pants tucked into black boots. They walked in a tight formation, looking straight ahead.

Grays? she wondered. She got a good look at their faces as they passed, then immediately she wished she hadn't.

They could only be described as creepy. Their expressions were eerily blank, and they seemed more like windup dolls than living people. It made her think of the droolers, only with more coordination, and she wondered if there was any connection.

But these people seemed more...more *something*. Higher functioning, maybe, which almost made it worse. She *expected* mindless people to shuffle around aimlessly--not march around like living robots. It made her wonder about whoever was programming them.

She shuddered. That guy had mentioned tampering. This place could be so sick.

She got a bad shock when the group stopped abruptly. They peeled off from each other to head for the vacant buildings on either side of the road. It looked like a systematic search. For her?

Did that guy sell me out?!

One of the blank-faced men was headed right for her.

Clio's heart rose up in her throat. She ran through the building and out the back.

She didn't stop until she'd put several blocks behind her. When she inched along a wall and peeked, panting, around a corner, her stomach sank.

The streets were barricaded with fences and human guards--if she could call those creepy robots "human." Even the building entrances along the line of the blockade were secured or guarded.

She knew she needed to backtrack through the streets and come up with a different plan. When it got dark, she could try to slip through. She would just have to hole up somewhere and wait...

But when she backed around a corner to hide from a patrolling group, she didn't pay attention to what was behind her. She turned, then froze.

Another group of men--wearing darker uniforms and acting much more coherent--chatted in a loose circle on the street. One of them turned and looked right at her.

Stupid, Clio!

He gave a shout. She took off running.

They must have *really* been searching for her--every street she ducked into was swarming with gray soldiers, like ants that had crawled out of the cracks in the cement. When someone grabbed her, she kicked and screamed, but several more swarmed in until she was drowning in gray.

"Don't... NO!"

She was hefted up by two men in the darker uniforms and dragged through the streets. They ignored her curses and any attempts to talk--they just frog-marched her under the fancy arch that fronted the town square.

On the far side was an imposing, ugly building. She was sure it was the one she'd been warned against.

"Dammit!" she cried in frustration.

Her appearance didn't seem to cause much of a stir. A few cold stares were directed her way, but she was quickly dragged through a door and deeper into the complex. She grabbed at doorjambs and walls and anything they passed in the dark hallways; her fingers bruised as the men yanked her free.

She gasped when they paused in front of a holding cell. A dozen droolers were crowded inside it, crouched or shuffling aimlessly. A man in a white lab coat scribbled at a clipboard.

One of her guards released her. She cried out and tried to leap away, but the second guard shoved her against the wall, pinning her in place. She watched helplessly as the first guard disappeared down the hallway.

The guard who still pinned her looked to the man in the lab coat. "When did these come in?" he asked.

"Early this morning. They did a roundup last night." The man in the lab coat seemed irritated.

"We haven't finished processing the last batch."

"There's been an increase in quota." The man jabbed at his clipboard and scowled.

"It's because they've been interfering again," the guard muttered.

"Overstepping their boundaries. They should stay in their precious sanctuary, if they know what's good for them."

"I heard they took a scouting detail last week."

The man in the coat spat. "They won't be able to reverse the process this time."

"They say he's good," the guard said doubtfully.

The man in the coat turned an angry red. "We've been told not to discuss it. If you're so intrigued, why don't you join them?" He walked away stiffly, without another word.

The guard cast a dark look after him, then turned his glare on Clio. Clio recoiled against the wall.

He pushed her roughly down the hall and through a white room that made her blood run cold. It held a chair with numerous straps, and machines whose purposes she didn't dare guess. She was almost happy to be thrust into a separate cell-

-complete with bars, a small sink, and an open metal toilet.

Another luxury accommodation, courtesy of the Gauntlet.

The guard disappeared into the attached room. After several minutes of silence, she was sure he was gone.

She looked around for anything like a surveillance camera. She didn't find one, but she knew it could just be hidden. She scoured the cell for any sign of a concealed exit, but it seemed her luck had taken a permanent vacation.

It had been dehumanizing to be so utterly ignored, to be treated as if she were mindless already. She shuddered at the memory of that chair covered in straps. She didn't want to end up there.

Clio curled up in the corner of the cell and watched the door. After an endless wait and no better plan in her head, she drifted off into uncomfortable sleep.

♦♣♠♥

She woke to someone in surgical scrubs hovering over her.

She yelped and shot up from the floor. The figure wore a mask, but she was pretty sure he was male. He closed in on her and gripped her arm.

"Wait," she begged as he steered her from the cell. "Don't do this. Please!"

He ignored her. But his grip was less bruising than that of the guard, and he was alone. Her desperation jumped on that.

"I-if you let me go, I'll give you one of these." She held up her bracelet. "You pick which one."

The hooded figure just prodded Clio out into the hallway. Her right leg was numb and turning prickly from the awkward position she'd slept in; she limped in front of her escort because she didn't have much choice.

When they turned down the corridor that led to the processing room, panic hit Clio. She dug in her heels.

"Please--I'm not one of them! I'm not a drooler. You can't!"

A snort came from within the depths of the hood. It was the first sign that a real person was under there, and that he might actually have a personality.

"I'll give you *two* of the charms," she bargained.

The figure lifted a gloved finger to his lips. "I'll do it for free," he whispered.

Clio gaped.

Hope flared in her, but she tamped it down with healthy mistrust. "Wh-what do you mean?" she asked warily.

"I *mean* that I'm busting you out." A thread of humor ran through the voice. "I've always wanted to say that." He tilted his hooded head. "What did the stamp say to the envelope?"

"What?" Clio asked, more surprised than meaning to respond.

"Stick with me, kid, and you'll go places."

Clio stared. This guy had either escaped his own "processing" session and was wandering the building with his screws loose, or he was just messing with her and leading her to her own personal nightmare.

"Where are you taking me?" she hissed.

"Shh. No time for a chat." He gently took her arm and pulled her down a hallway that--thankfully--led away from the medical wing.

Clio shut up for a moment as a pair of gray-clad soldiers passed them in the hallway. They didn't even look at her. When the soldiers disappeared around a corner, she leaned in to whisper, "Why are you helping me?"

The man in the scrubs shrugged. "We're always watching them. If we don't keep them in line, they start making trouble for us. And something funny's been going on lately. When I saw them bring you in, I figured you had something to do with that; I couldn't just leave you here." His voice turned grim. "You've seen some of what they can do."

Clio's mind raced through the conversation between her guard and the man in the lab coat. "Are you...are you from that place they were talking about?" she breathed. "That sanctuary?"

The man stopped, ignoring her for a moment as he pressed a random spot on the wall. A panel slid open to reveal a keypad. He tapped in a number and a door opened.

A utility tunnel lay beyond it. He laughed as he climbed down and continued into the featureless corridor.

"Well, I never *called* it a sanctuary," he said with a modest cast to his voice. "But I guess it's nice that people think of it that way."

Clio's suspicion still weighed like lead in her gut. "You knew about this tunnel," she accused.

"Oh, I've been here a long time. I've picked up some useful tricks here and there."

"How long?"

"Four years."

"Four *years*?" Clio felt sick.

"Don't worry about it. I made that decision a long time ago."

"You mean...you *chose* to stay here?"

He nodded, and Clio found herself wishing she could see his face. There was no reason he needed to stay hidden now, was there? Unless...her imagination began to get the better of her. Perhaps he'd been captured before, and they'd done some sort of twisted experiments on him. Maybe he wore that mask for a reason other than disguise.

"Cat got your tongue?" he suddenly asked.

Clio started. "Ah, sorry. I just..."

"Can't imagine why someone would stay?" He sounded empathetic, but she still felt awkward.

"Well," she murmured. "I've heard some reasons why already. But, to be honest...yeah."

"You probably noticed that there are two kinds of people who end up here." He sounded a little weary. "Those who... rise to the occasion, and those who don't. Or can't."

Visions of vacant eyes filled her thoughts. Clio shuddered.

"Yeah," she said after a moment. "I noticed."

"I wanted to do something about the ones who can't."

"Wow, that's...pretty incredible." And it was a far cry from Lilah's reasoning.

Clio snuck a glance at him, struck by a sudden thought.

She tried not to raise her hopes too high. "Do you think...?"

She stopped talking as they reached the end of the corridor. He touched the wall again; another panel appeared. "Sorry," he interrupted gently. "We'll be out of here in just a sec."

When the door slid open, he turned to her. He gestured for her to go first, so she did. Slowly.

"Do I think what?" he asked from behind her.

Clio took a breath. "I have a friend," she tried. "She's still back in the Gauntlet...the main building part, I mean. And the prowlers--I think they've got her. I escaped, and I couldn't get back in again, but I promised myself that I would help her. I'm just not sure *how*."

To her chagrin, Clio's voice quivered a little. She stared at the floor as she mounted the steps that led out.

"Gotcha. I'll help you figure it out."

He sounded so sure, so *kind,* that Clio had to bite back tears. A weak smile clawed at her lips as she emerged into the fresh air.

A man dressed in gray stood near the exit. She was startled into a scream when he peeled away from the wall. He had a short, dark mohawk and towered over her. The drab uniform did nothing to hide his impressive physique. He looked like he could break her in two.

She backed away and ran right into the arms of her rescuer. "Don't worry," he reassured her. "He's with me."

"What?!" All her fears and mistrust flared to life again. She jerked out of his hold.

"I got him out of the facility a long time ago. He's really loyal, though he doesn't talk much. Some things are harder than others to reverse." He slid an arm around Clio's waist and stepped forward. "Sunshine, meet..." he stopped expectantly and waited.

Sunshine? Was he kidding?

"Um...Clio."

Not a muscle in Sunshine's face twitched. But her rescuer rolled her name over his tongue, as if testing it.

"Clio," he hummed. "I've been rude. Excuse me." He tugged off the surgical cap and pulled the mask from his face.

He was *gorgeous.* His dark, beautifully curved eyes stood out against his pale face. His hair was dyed a soft chestnut--at least, she thought it was dyed, since he seemed to be Asian. But she saw no dark roots along his scalp and his hair looked soft to the touch.

Clio was instantly charmed by his infectious smile. And she'd thought he would look like Frankenstein's monster.

Oh, God, she thought. *He actually has* ***dimples.***

"I'm August," he drawled as he took her hand again. "I hope you'll like my little piece of the Gauntlet, Clio."

♦ ♣ ♠ ♥

Chapter 6

♦ ♣ ♠ ♥

"This is so amazing," Clio said for what felt like the hundredth time that day. She couldn't help herself. To say that Clio liked August's home was a vast understatement.

"It's like some...I don't know...medieval walled city in Italy."

"It is," August agreed with a hint of amusement. "You've been to Italy?"

Clio protested. "Oh, no--but it's how I always imagined it, from what I've seen and heard." She beamed at their surroundings.

The walled enclave really *did* seem like a hidden sanctuary. The miniature city within a city was a treasure hidden within the Gauntlet. She had to wonder how many layers there were in this place, and if she'd ever find the center.

August's warm chuckle made her blush; his fingers linked with hers to draw her farther along the cobbled street. She found herself hoping, in sudden fussiness, that her palm wasn't sweaty.

They started crossing a small footbridge over a running stream. Rows of stone houses were connected all around them, but each had its own pretty little doorstep and colorful door with an iron knocker. People obviously lived in them; some of the windows above the doors were open, with lines strung between the frames to hold fluttering sheets and assorted garments. She was curious about the people inside.

She wondered if their tales were similar to hers.

She could see a clock tower in the distance. She'd heard it tolling when she'd first woken up that morning--groggy in the little building just inside the city walls--and then every hour while August had led her deeper into the city. He'd been sure to stop along the way to show her particular points of interest.

It was the library that had really won her over. Now, when she thought about it, that was when her initial attraction to August had begun to rapidly grow into a crush, and when a tiny ember began to glow in the back of her mind that perhaps--under certain circumstances--the Gauntlet might not be so unbearable after all.

How could she resist floor-to-ceiling shelves stuffed with leather-bound books, curving staircases, and heavy old desks with deep leather sofas that just invited her to curl up in them? Especially when they came with a handsome young man lounging on top, wearing a smile that held a hint of something intriguing?

August had had a hard time luring her away from that particular delight. He'd only succeeded by promising her another visit soon, a surprise at the end of their journey, and an actual hot meal. Her stomach had rumbled in a very embarrassing way in response.

She finally caught a glimpse of the heart of the little city. "So that's where you live?" she asked.

"Yeah. I call it the town." He gestured to a structure in the near distance. "I'm in the building right in the middle; you can't see it from here, but it's next to a few other buildings across from a small commons. Typical set up--tacky sculpture in the fountain, statue of someone no one knows, park benches. No massive pigeon gangs, though, so it's safe to walk around without a hat."

Clio giggled. "That's good to know. I'm sure it's very nice." She took another sweeping glance at the quaint scenery and sighed. "I wish I could paint this."

"You paint?" August's eyebrows rose in curiosity.

"No," she admitted sheepishly. "I'm hopeless at drawing--even my stick figures are terrible. I just *wish* I could."

August chuckled.

"I can't carry a tune, either, just so you know."

That only made him laugh more. "You're cute," he drawled.

Clio made a face. "By cute, you mean I'm a dork."

"I would never say that!" August exclaimed in gallant denial. "You strike me as the *opposite* of a dork, actually."

August lifted the hand he still held and made an exaggerated bow. He placed a light kiss on her knuckles as she laughed, a little embarrassed.

"Are you ready to see the heart of our humble little home?"

"I can't wait."

He tugged her hand as she stepped off the little bridge, and again he turned his grasp into a loosely entwined grip as they walked along. Clio felt her cheeks warm, even though she wasn't sure he meant anything by it.

August glanced over his shoulder. "I wonder if I could convince Sunshine to hold an umbrella over our heads for shade." He looked up at the cloudless sky. "It's ridiculously hot out here."

Clio had come to find August's lurking hulk of a watchdog charming, in a bizarre way. It gave August an exciting air that she wasn't immune to.

"Shh," she whispered. "I don't think he'd enjoy that."

August pursed his lips in thought. "I guess I could just ask him to walk right behind us. His looming shadow should be enough."

"You're awful," Clio said lightly, stifling another giggle. "But he'd probably do it. He obviously worships the ground you walk on." She hesitated. "Can you... Can you tell me more about what they did to him, and how you...helped him?"

August was silent a moment, and Clio began to worry that she'd offended him by asking something too personal. But when she began to apologize, August flashed her a reassuring smile.

"I'll tell you all about it soon," he promised, looking apologetic himself. "It's just that now isn't the right--"

Clio's head bobbed up and down. "Sure--I get it." She cast a quick look back at Sunshine. "It was rude of me to ask, anyway. But I..."

"You want to understand. Who wouldn't? I'm planning to show you everything I've learned." He gave her hand a quick squeeze. "It's not that I don't trust you, okay?"

It was uncomfortable having her thoughts so easily read, but his assurances *did* make her feel better. She responded with an uncertain smile.

"It's okay. I mean, I'd understand if you *didn't* trust me--but I'm glad you do." She squinted at the clock, trying to calculate the distance at a brisk walk. "We're close, right? I'm starving."

August smiled again, and the tension melted out of the moment. Clio reminded herself to tread carefully with her questions.

Fifteen minutes later, they reached a small court. The surroundings and buildings were somewhat stately, despite their small scale and picturesque facade.

August was greeted by almost everyone they encountered. Clio couldn't help but notice their enthusiasm and, well, deference. She caught August glancing at her when one particularly fawning young man went on and on about some improvement August had recently made.

She bit her lip to keep from laughing; August kept sending surreptitious looks of exasperation her way. Despite that, he was unfailingly friendly to everyone.

"It's like you're the king," she commented when they had a moment alone again.

August smiled wryly. "You're *really* gonna make fun of me once I change my clothes."

"Why?"

"Let's just say that some of my less loyal subjects," he raised his eyebrow dramatically, "accuse me of being a little... flashy with my wardrobe."

"Clothing fit for a king? Should I call you Your Majesty?" Clio teased.

"Visiting dignitaries are allowed a first-name basis," August drawled.

"I'm a dignitary?"

"Amazon queen, obviously."

Clio laughed out loud. "No, that would be my friend Britt." Her smile faded a little.

August seemed to notice. He placed a hand behind her back and nudged her toward a new corridor. "Let's get you settled, and then you can tell me more about Britt."

The night before, Clio had gratefully collapsed on the first available horizontal surface she'd been offered in the guardhouse by the wall. But this building--where August lived--seemed *much* more accommodating. They passed common areas, like a kitchen and grand dining room, as well as a small number of private apartments. He didn't say, but Clio got the impression they were reserved for a core group of his trusted friends.

"And finally..." August drew out the moment with a fancy flourish of his wrist. She preceded him down the hall to a door with an old-fashioned brass knob. Sunshine silently followed several paces behind them, as he'd done all day.

"This is your room. I hope you like it. Mine isn't far." August's eyes danced in anticipation.

Clio looked at him in surprise. "I'm going to stay here?"

"Of course. What, did you think you'd be bunking in the guardhouse from last night?" August scoffed. "It's barely better than a broom closet."

"It's *way* better than a broom closet. I speak from experience." Her mouth curved in a wry grin. "It was like heaven after how I've been sleeping lately."

"We'll teach you to expect better around here." August flashed a smile that made her stomach flip-flop. "Go on. Take a look."

Clio's hand flew to her mouth when she opened the door. The room was as charming as the modestly named "town"--a huge window looked out over a manicured garden, right beside a plush, oversized bed that was so high it had a wooden stepping stool. A beautiful desk with a lovely inlay stood in one corner, along with a tall bookshelf filled with an array of books--which immediately filled her with greedy desire.

Now she knew why August had steadfastly refused to let her take any books from the library, no matter how she begged. For all that the Gauntlet could be terrifying, it could also be deathly boring; she was starved for any form of entertainment. She wanted to consume every last book on that shelf, no matter what kind of books they were.

Again, that faint ember flared a little brighter in the back of her thoughts--a seductive, uneasy pull. She still wanted to get out. She needed to find Britt. But...it was *so nice* to finally find something good and, on a more superficial level, beautiful. Her gaze flicked to August and then back to her room.

Overwhelmed, she joked, "What? No television?"

August laughed. "Sorry, but there's something you might like even better. Especially after I've dragged you around town all day."

"No--it was really nice! I loved seeing everything, and it's really beautiful. I think it's really amazing that you did all this--that you found it and made it better, and brought people here and helped them instead of...well, taking advantage of them or...or giving up. I really admire that."

August smiled at her, obviously pleased. Clio blushed.

She was gushing now. How many times had she used the word *really*?

"Thank you." His smile softened, as if he'd noticed her embarrassment. "I'm glad you like it here in our little town."

"You mean *heaven,*" Clio corrected.

August laughed again. "No angels here."

You could've fooled me.

The thought threatened to make Clio blush again, so she stepped forward and ran her hand along the bed's covering.

"I can see why people call this a sanctuary." The weight of everything that had happened seemed to settle on her shoulders; they slumped unconsciously. She curled her hand around one of the bedposts and leaned against it.

"You're safe here, Clio." The unexpected touch on her shoulder made Clio start, but when she looked at August, the concern in his eyes seemed...honest. She relaxed against the post, resting her temple against the smooth wood.

"Do we all get a bodyguard?" she teased, tilting her eyes toward Sunshine's shadow in the doorway.

"Not unless one adopts you, like Sunshine did me. But you won't need one here--unless someone tries to do you in for your private bathroom." A sly grin stole over his features, and he nodded toward the door she'd barely noticed before.

Clio's eyes grew wide, and she immediately ran to the door and threw it open. Moist, hot air washed over her, and she actually squealed when she saw an enormous tub, filled to the brim with hot water and bubbles.

"Oh...oh my God."

August shrugged. "I thought you'd like it."

"This is for *me*? Really?" A giddy laugh bubbled up her throat. "Tell me I'm not still hallucinating!"

"It's real--I promise."

The seriousness in August's voice brought a strange silence between them. It wasn't *exactly* uncomfortable, but Clio still felt her face heat.

She couldn't remember the last time she'd bathed. People could probably smell her coming from miles away. She brushed hair away from her face self-consciously.

"It's been so long, my grime has grime. I must look awful."

"You look very pretty, Clio." She glanced up to find August's face closer than before. Her stomach fluttered. "A little dirt can't hide that."

Suddenly at a loss for words, Clio gave a flustered, breathless laugh. August leaned closer, and he reached up to gently tuck a loose strand of hair behind her ear. Her heart began to pound frantically.

He was going to kiss her. She was sure of it.

"But Clio," August murmured, a mischievous grin curling

his lips. "Take that bath."

Clio gaped, then lightly smacked him on the arm, even as she gave a grudging laugh. "Fine. I get the message."

"You'll find some things you can wear in the other room. If you want, you can rest or nap awhile--we can wake you up in time for dinner."

"That sounds wonderful," Clio breathed.

"Great. See you in a few hours."

Clio soaked in the tub until the water went cold, then filled the tub up again with hot water and soaked some more. She finished it off with a shower, scrubbing her head until her scalp felt raw. It was, perhaps, the greatest day of her life.

The bath left her languid and sleepy, so she wrapped herself up in a fluffy towel and went in search of something to wear. A long, silky nightgown and matching robe lay on the bed. Clio touched them gingerly, wondering where in the world August had gotten his hands on them.

He'd mentioned finding several buildings that still had their furnishings, and scavenging other areas all over the outer city, but she doubted all his goodies had just been lying around. Maybe the Gauntlet had a shopping mall.

The gown felt heavenly sliding down her body. It wouldn't really do for dinner, though, and neither would her filthy clothes until they'd been cleaned.

She tried the armoire tucked into one corner of the room. Sure enough, it held quite a few items of clothing in Clio's general size. They were mostly dresses, which made her frown. Hard to run in those. And the prevalent style seemed to be dated--*very* dated. Come to think of it, the people she'd met that day had been dressed oddly, too. The clothes were more like costumes than everyday wear.

It brought to mind the theater where she'd scavenged for clothes. Suddenly, things began to make more sense. Maybe bizarre prop rooms were scattered all over the Gauntlet, just waiting for someone to find them.

Fine, she thought. *I doubt I'll be running from anyone at dinner.* She refused to let her guard down completely, but for the moment, at least, she seemed pretty safe in this place.

She fell asleep before she realized it, and woke up to a friendly woman knocking at her door. The woman said she was "there to help"--and convinced Clio to wear one of the fancier dresses in the closet.

"Everyone dresses for dinner here," she explained. "August likes it."

Clio frowned, but eventually resigned herself. "When in Rome..."

Clio still felt self-conscious when she left for the dining room. At least her hair looked nice--soft and shiny from the wash and a good brushing. Her bangs were getting much too long, though, and she nervously brushed them to the side before entering the room. She could hear the buzz of several voices, and, just as she feared, they all stopped when she stepped through the doorway.

Her embarrassment was short-lived; August appeared at her side almost immediately, covering any awkwardness with his banter. She greeted him with "Your Majesty," which earned her a beaming grin.

She relaxed a little, even though he introduced her around the room to a number of people whose names she couldn't remember two minutes later. Like the woman in her room had said, people wore elaborate outfits--some of the dresses skirted the edge of being full-fledged ball gowns, while the men in well-tailored suits distinguished themselves with splashes of color, brocade vests, and intricate neckwear.

For a moment, Clio had an unsettling flashback to the strange revel in the square. The similarities were almost too close for comfort, but she *knew* these people were real, and she supposed that every part of the Gauntlet had its share of weirdness.

August wore a sophisticated bit of flash that suited him. A gold pin with chains gleamed on his chest, accentuating the quasi-military cut of his jacket. He looked relaxed, completely in his element, and seemed to be enjoying the display of finery--including Clio's own, if the approving sweep of his eye was anything to go by.

Clio reminded herself of August's actions in the cell block. Grandstanding aside, he had to be really intelligent, considering what he'd managed to do for Sunshine. She was keenly aware of that when he suggested they walk in the garden before dinner.

"You clean up nicely, Clio."

"Thank you," she replied. "I feel almost human again." She did feel feminine and pretty, if a little silly. She tried *not* to think of what Britt would say about it.

"Good," he said with a hum. "I hope you enjoy it here."

His smile really was infectious. But after a moment, Clio's faltered.

"I feel guilty, being pampered like this."

August nodded. "Your friend. I haven't forgotten."

"Do you really think you can help her?"

"I'll do my best, and my best is pretty damn good, if I do say so myself." August draped a comforting arm around her.

She still felt like a heel for enjoying this haven and August's company, even if it was only temporary. Clio sighed and leaned into him. If he had a better chance of saving Britt than she did, then it was *good* to connect with him. She felt her guilt deepen a little.

"In the morning," August murmured, "tell me everything you know, and we'll figure something out. But for now, you need a good meal. You'll feel better."

"Okay." Clio gripped the edge of his sleeve with her fingers. "Thank you, August. For everything. I really can't tell you how much I appreciate it."

"It's definitely my pleasure."

The tease in his voice brought her gaze to his. And this time, he did kiss her.

She didn't have time to be nervous. His fingers came up to trail along her throat, while the soft, closed-mouthed kiss turned into two then three then more, heating up until her hands somehow ended up tangled in his hair. She was suddenly pushed up against the archway of some vine-laden, wooden trellis she'd barely noticed before.

The strong scent of crushed jasmine blossoms brought Clio back to reality. She pulled back, gasping, as her pulse raced madly. She could feel it fluttering in her throat; August traced the thrum of the beat with his fingertips.

"Clio..." His lips moved to replace his fingers. "Is this all right?"

Clio nodded, not trusting the sound of her voice. God, she barely knew him. This was probably a really bad idea--but she couldn't help it. She really liked him, and maybe she was a bit desperate for human comfort. She was definitely taking more chances these days.

Shivers stole down her spine as he pulled back to study her face. The look he gave her turned her blood to fire. The elegant planes of his high cheekbones contrasted with the rather filthy look in his eyes. The former delicacy of his attention all but disappeared, and his mouth was on hers again, hot and urgent and messy.

Clio moaned a soft sound against his lips, and she felt his hands tighten around her arms. "Clio...let's--"

"August."

Clio gasped and blushed down to her toes, instinctively pulling away. Someone stood in the open doorway to the dining room. The light behind him made it impossible to see his features in the dark.

Oh, God! She'd been embarrassed enough before knowing *she had an audience.*

August threw her a rueful smile and turned. "Chance," he called. "You're back."

"You wanted a report when I returned."

"Yeah, yeah." August waved his hand dismissively. "That can wait. Come say hi to our new guest."

Clio thought she saw the man hesitate in reluctance as he peeled from the doorway. Once he neared, she gasped in recognition.

"You!"

August raised an eyebrow. "You know each other?"

Clio stared at the man who towered over her. He wore the same irritating expression she remembered when he'd warned her against the Grays. The blank look in his eyes practically screamed *You don't belong here.*

"Not exactly," he said evenly. "We've met."

"Really?" August looked between them and cocked his head. "Do tell."

Clio waited, but the guy said nothing, so she tried to shrug it off. "I ran into him yesterday morning. He warned me against going forward, but, well...I still got caught."

August laughed. "Let me guess. Chance exhibited his usual levels of charm..." He bent conspiratorially toward Clio and added in a loud whisper, "...non-existent."

Clio giggled. "And instead of convincing you," August went on, "you proceeded to do the opposite of what he said."

"Not exactly. But it would've helped if he'd explained himself more, and not been..." Clio broke off before she called the guy an ass in front of August. "Um...so pushy."

August smirked at the guy, obviously enjoying the little drama playing out. "I told you--you scare people with that awful face you make."

"It was sound advice," Chance said coolly. "If she were rational, I wouldn't have to sugarcoat it for her to swallow it."

Clio glared. He was *definitely* an ass.

August put his steepled hands to his lips and snickered. "Easy, Chance. And Clio--he's not so bad once you get to know him." He gestured with his head. "Chance is my best friend and right-hand man around here. He's too damn serious, but he's a good guy. Chaaance," he wheedled. "Say hello to her. A *real* hello."

Chance's disapproving eyes fell on her again. "Hello," he said thinly. "You're lucky you made it here." He turned and headed for the dining room.

Clio grabbed a handful of her dress with her clenching fist.

"By the way," Chance called over his shoulder to August. "Sunshine's back."

"Perfect!" August put a hand on her lower back to guide

her inside. "I just need to have a quick word with him, and then we eat."

Clio hadn't noticed Sunshine's missing presence--but she was instantly relieved. She hadn't thought of him staring from the shadows while August's mouth was on her.

A shiver pebbled her arms. It was bad enough that Chance had seen them. She blushed again and reached up to smooth her hair.

When they walked through the door, she felt way too many eyes on her--and not all of them friendly. August took it all in stride.

"You look perfect," he murmured. Unfortunately, he immediately headed for another young man she recognized as one of Chance's partners from their first encounter. That left Clio standing with tall, dark, and irritating.

"Pour Clio a drink, won't you, Chance? You two can get to know each other." August winked and sauntered away. "Play nice. I'll be right back."

Wonderful.

Clio took one look at Chance's sour expression and turned away. There was a blonde girl across the room who kept sending her dirty looks, and Clio would have almost preferred talking with *her*. But she looked like she might bite, or scratch, or maybe pull hair.

"What would you like?"

"What?" Her gaze jerked back to Chance.

"To drink," he said with long-suffering politeness. "What would you like?"

"Oh..." Clio glanced at the other people milling around. "A glass of wine would be fine."

He procured a glass of white from a nearby table, and handed it to her with what she took to be a condescending smile. It rankled that she actually *did* prefer white, so she took it rather ungraciously.

"Thanks."

He raised one dark eyebrow. "You're of age, right?"

"I'm twenty-two!" Clio's indignation seemed to amuse

him because his mouth twitched.

She suddenly felt a tap on her shoulder and long fingernails dig into her arm. The dagger-eyed blonde stepped between them and flashed a fake smile.

"I'm Angela," came a voice like poisoned honey. "I don't think we've met."

Over the girl's shoulder, Chance raised an eyebrow. Almost in spite, she smiled sweetly at Angela.

"Hi, I'm Clio."

God, it was going to be a long night.

♦♣♠♥

Clio woke up with a throbbing headache and a queasy stomach.

"Ungh," she groaned into the pillows. At least they were soft and silky and cool to the touch--the bed was more comfortable than she remembered, even if she had no recollection of finding her way to it. She hadn't drunk *that* much, had she?

She knew she was a lightweight when it came to alcohol, and it *had* been awhile. And she remembered enough of the night before to know that any unusual consumption was completely justified. Between Angela and Chance...and God, there'd been dancing.

She moaned again, swearing to herself that she would *never* touch another glass of wine. If only her head would stop *pounding*.

"There's water on the bedside table."

Clio yelped and flew halfway across the bed in a flurry of sheets and pillows. It took a few seconds for her heart to drop from her throat and take up a frantic workout in her ribcage.

In that time, she noted several things: she was *not* in her bed, but apparently in August's. She wore nothing but an oversized, men's button-down shirt, as well as her bracelet and the necklace Britt had given her. August appeared to be completely naked, though she couldn't be sure because of the covers pulled up to the top of his hips. And she deduced that the town included a well-equipped gym, because August's trim body was *very* nicely sculpted.

"Sorry. Didn't mean to scare you." August smiled and swept back the covers. Clio went pink, but a pair of pajama pants hung low on the sharp curve of his hip bones. He came around the bed and handed her a glass of water and a few pills. "Aspirin."

"Thank you." She swallowed the pills and drank deeply, finishing the water in one draught. It made her feel marginally better.

She didn't want to ask the question that loomed large in her thoughts. She didn't even think she *could*. Not that she would be exactly upset if...if something had happened. But she would have liked to remember it.

She wanted to bury her face in the pillows again and scream. This was mortifying.

"I hope you enjoyed last night as much as I did."

Clio felt the flush bloom on her face and then spread farther. Oh, God, they *had*.

"Seeing you in action was an eye-opener. I didn't think you'd be so *aggressive*."

Clio stared at him in shock, sure that her face was absolutely scarlet by then. She could feel the heat coming off of it. "What do you mean?"

"So you don't remember?" August tilted his head and studied her.

"No." Clio shook her head in embarrassment. "I-I'm sorry!"

"Don't be," August said cheerfully. "Watching you put Angela in her place was the best entertainment I've had in a while. She deserved it for being ridiculously rude to you." His grin turned into a full-fledged laugh at Clio's dumbfounded expression. "Nothing happened between us, if that's what you're worried about. Well," he amended, "not much. You said you would sleep on the floor when we made it as far as my room."

Clio groaned.

"It was cute," August cooed. "I had to force some water and aspirin into you. Your hangover could be a lot worse."

"I'm *so* sorry." Clio dropped her face into her hands. "Really, this isn't like me at all."

"Eh, I've gotten shit-faced once or twice. Chance could tell you some good stories."

"Is Chance hungover, too?" Clio asked with perverse hope.

August snorted. "He's no fun at all these days. He's probably been up since 6 A.M. doing something productive and/or responsible."

Clio giggled.

"That's better." A finger slipped under her chin and tilted her heated face up. "You *do* get awful cuddly when you're drunk."

Cuddly. Clio breathed an internal sigh of relief. She could live with cuddly, but she was a little disappointed. She would've liked to remember *that,* too.

"So...Angela," Clio tried. "Is she your ex?"

"No." Definite amusement filled August's voice. "You don't need to worry about her. She won't bother you again." His hand traveled down to brush soothingly over her exposed collarbone, and then to toy with the metal die that rested near the hollow of her throat.

Clio felt a little weak-kneed, and not because of her hangover. She ducked her head.

"I hope I didn't say anything too nasty. I can't remember much past dessert."

"I think you're too sweet to say anything *really* bad."

The cheesy sentiment made Clio roll her eyes. "I do remember calling Chance an ass."

"Yeah, but that's true, and he knows it. No harm done there."

Clio laughed. It turned into a fit of giggles when her stomach rumbled loudly.

"Hungry?" August asked. "If you think you can handle it, there's breakfast out in the dining hall. Coffee, too."

"Oh, yes, *please*."

August gestured to one of her dresses, hanging off the door of an armoire. "I had that brought from your room," he explained. "Your other clothes are off being cleaned."

As usual, she felt a pang of discomfort at the massive dress. "I feel like an actor in a period drama," she murmured.

"'All the world's a stage,'" August drawled. "Embrace the drama."

"I'm not sure I like drama."

"You were pretty dramatic last night. You obviously just need the right motivation." His brilliantly white teeth flashed in a saucy smile.

Clio groaned. "I wish I could remember."

"Are you *really* sure about that?"

Clio thought about Angela's razor-sharp nails. "Um... maybe not."

"I could help jog your memory."

"How?" Clio asked suspiciously.

"By recreating some of the events of last night?" The look in his eyes was unmistakable, despite Clio's relative lack of experience. Her stomach fluttered.

"Which...ones?" Clio's voice petered out as August sat down next to her. His thigh brushed up against hers. "I thought you said we didn't..."

"Oh, we didn't do *that*, but like I said...you were very cuddly."

One hand slid up her bare thigh, while another slid beneath her collar and pushed it off her shoulder. Clio trembled when his thumb brushed the soft skin of her inner thigh. They obviously had *entirely* different ideas of the meaning of cuddly--not that she was complaining.

"Is it coming back to you?" August murmured, his breath leaving her skin moist and warm where he traced a path from her shoulder to her throat.

"No...no, it--mmph..."

He kissed her as he twisted around and pulled her on top of him; his back hit the mattress with a gentle thud. He

gripped her knees and daringly split them over his hips, his smiling lips nipping at hers.

Clio's mouth opened to his, and her hands unconsciously fell onto his bare chest. Oh...they must have kissed a *lot* the night before, because this felt incredible--not awkward like the garden, when she'd been too nervous to really let go. That had been exciting in its own way, but it was nothing like this. *Dear God in heaven,* August could *kiss.*

She could *definitely* get used to this.

♦ ♣ ♠ ♥

Chapter 7

♦ ♣ ♠ ♥

It was strange what a few weeks' difference made. Everyone Clio came across seemed to know her now, if only by sight. They paid her a subtle deference that she could only attribute to her closeness to August.

It made her feel a little weird, especially when someone would ask her to pass on a message for them, as if they were asking a great favor. At least there had been no more outright hostility. She hadn't seen Angela for days, and everyone else was distantly friendly.

Well, except for Chance. He was as blunt as ever, which was almost a relief, honestly. He reminded her a little of Britt.

Sunshine, of course, never spoke to her at all. She had no idea how he felt about her, despite how often she was in his company. He was like some bizarre appendage of August, which almost made it like she was dating him, too.

Maybe dating wasn't the right word, exactly. They couldn't go out to the movies or anything, but they were *together*. Everyone certainly saw them that way. Clio had all but given up her room to sleep with August in his. So far that was all they'd done; well, *mostly* all they'd done, but things were definitely leading up to more.

She smiled without realizing it, suppressing any other reaction to the warm tingle in her stomach that made her want to hug herself in self-conscious embarrassment.

"What's with the weird expression?"

Clio narrowed her eyes and tilted her head up. Chance loomed over the breakfast table, ignoring everyone else in the public dining hall. It was moments like this--when he stood before a backdrop of shuffling, laughing people--that really drove home just how damn stiffly he stood.

"You mean this?" She feigned a look of horror. "I was just remembering that you were about to show up."

"Cute." Chance poured himself a cup of coffee, and then walked off.

Clio jumped out of her chair. "Hey, wait!" she called after him. "I thought you're supposed to be my escort or whatever today."

"Then why are you standing there?" Chance kept walking, so Clio ran to catch up. She had to pump her legs quickly to match the stride of his long legs.

"I wish August wasn't busy," she muttered.

Chance cast a sidelong glance at her, but didn't react to that barb. "Why the sudden urgency to explore?" he murmured.

"Because," Clio replied, surprised to be asked, "I'm going crazy around here. I mean, it's nice, and I'm grateful to be here, but I want to *do* something."

He led her outside. They turned toward a wide alley between two buildings--Clio knew it was a shortcut to the outskirts of the main activity hub.

"Like what?" His sharp gaze turned fully on her. "Other than taking a scenic walk around town."

Clio scowled at him.

"Well, I want to *help*. August says people are looking for me right now, so I can't do much. But I want to. Either with getting Britt back or...or with...anything. Finding other people. Getting *out*. I'd *love* to find the ones who did this to all of us and..."

"And what?" Chance's amusement tickled his brow.

"I don't know," Clio said sulkily. "I'd like to use some of their methods on *them*."

Chance laughed without humor. "I can't see it."

"August said he'd show me his lab."

"Really?" It was a pleasure to see Chance taken aback for once.

August had told her that, besides Chance and himself, not many had had the privilege of seeing the lab--because as safe as they tried to make their little sanctuary, they couldn't be certain about who was trustworthy.

When she thought about that, she realized that he had very little reason to trust *her,* and the fact that he did was probably based on him liking her. It was flattering, but she recognized the risk he was taking.

"I asked him about how he...helped Sunshine," she murmured at last. "So he said that he would show me."

"I see." The forbidding expression was back on Chance's face, and a hard lump settled in the pit of Clio's stomach. Even if they weren't the best of friends, she'd thought they were getting along a little better. He obviously still didn't think much of her.

"I'm not-- I mean, I understand that it's not meant to be talked about," she offered. "And I *won't* talk about it. You can trust me. I just want to understand everything that I can about this place, and what the people behind it are capable of." Clio searched Chance's face, but his expression remained shuttered. "Sometimes I'm still really not sure if it's all *real* or all pretend."

"Does it have to be all or nothing? Maybe the point is that you'll never know."

Clio wasn't sure what to say to that, and Chance offered nothing else.

They passed through several streets that pretty much all looked the same. The fresh air and warm sunlight felt good, and the exercise made Clio feel better than she had in a long time. It would have been more fun with August, or alone, but she had to admit it felt nice that Chance wanted to protect her.

Chance had kinda gotten *stuck* with the duty, though.

"Sorry," she suddenly muttered.

Chance raised a quizzical brow. "For what?"

"That you got volunteered to babysit me."

"Who says I didn't volunteer myself?" She looked at him quickly, but his smirk made her roll her eyes.

"August said he'd have you do it," she retorted. "I tried to call it off because I knew you wouldn't be thrilled, but he insisted." Clio gave him her own version of a smirk. "He said you would complain about missing your patrol because you like nothing better than strutting around and intimidating people with your grumpy expression."

"The view is nice, at least," Chance said blandly. After a beat, and somewhat disappointed by his lack of reaction, Clio was about to agree--because they'd climbed up a gently arched bridge to see a pretty little view spread out below them. But then his mouth twitched up at one corner. "Even if you *are* wearing a stupid dress."

Clio gaped at him a second and then laughed. "*Thank you.* Ugh, I hate it. I like dresses just fine, but these are ridiculous. And these shoes. I would *kill* for my boots right now, but my clothes seem to have been misplaced."

"August enjoys the spectacle."

"Sure, it's fine for you guys. You get to wear *pants*."

"I'll keep an eye out for something from this century when I'm on a scavenging run, but you'll still have to convince August to compromise his extravagant fashion vision for our citizens."

Clio giggled, feeling a little guilty for it.

"So you've known him for a long time?" she asked.

"Since we got here. We ran into each other quickly and got along well. We had similar backgrounds outside; it made sense to work together. We figured we could beat the system in no time."

"But you didn't..." Clio said tentatively.

"Let's just say, we--August in particular--got distracted."

"By what they were doing to people?"

Chance turned away, looking out over the narrow pathways and intimate squares that spread out below them. "Yes. He was actually a neurobiology grad student--and top of his class. He might seem...like some superficial party boy at times, but he's extremely gifted."

"You said you had similar backgrounds."

"Yes. His focus at university was cognitive neurobiology, while mine was behavioral. We found one of the labs here and saw some of what the Gauntlet brass were doing. What they *had* been doing for decades. The older studies were fascinating, especially with the progression. August was...well... hooked."

Clio shivered in the heat. "So that's how he was able to help Sunshine?" she asked. "August was able to reverse everything?"

"Something like that." Chance pointed northeast. "Do you see that building with the tower at the corner?"

"Yeah, I do," Clio said, a bit surprised at the random subject change.

"They're scattered all over this walled-off section. Look." He pointed out a few more peaks to her, until Clio learned to spot the slender towers that rose far above the roofs of the other buildings. The outer wall, which she could see circling the entire sector, still dwarfed the towers.

"What about them?"

"They're completely sealed off. No one can get in. We've tried."

"Oh." Clio looked at him oddly. "Why do you want to get inside so bad?"

A snort accompanied Chance's tilted grin this time. "It drives August crazy to be told he can't do something. If he decides he wants something, he can't be talked out of it."

Clio gave a little laugh. "Somehow that doesn't surprise me."

"It shouldn't."

She glanced at Chance again, but he was still looking at the towers. "Do you think they're important?" she asked at last.

She wasn't prepared for the smile he turned on her. It was one of the few true ones she'd seen, and it took her aback. She realized how attractive he would be if only he showed that expression more often.

"I think they're intriguing," he murmured. "Don't you? A mystery to be solved. Isn't that what life is all about?"

Clio beamed, surprised by Chance of all people expressing such a sentiment. So even *his* hard heart could long for something.

"Yeah." She looked back at the towers. "You might be right."

♦♣♠♥

Raised voices were something Clio hadn't heard in a while.

Clio stopped in the hallway, her fancy shoes clicking against the hard floor. Everyone seemed to get along so well in the sanctuary that it was shocking to hear what sounded like a heated argument from somewhere. She couldn't make out the muffled words.

If the voices *hadn't* been coming from behind the door to Chance's rooms, she might have been able to resist the urge to listen. If Sunshine were there, it wouldn't have been possible--because she was pretty sure it was August in there, arguing with Chance.

But Sunshine had been gone for days, and August was being pretty closemouthed on the subject. Pushing aside her guilt, Clio quickly glanced up and down the hall before stepping up to the door and pushing her ear to the crack.

She only caught snatches, mostly when Chance's voice rose in greater ire.

"...unnecessary...distracting you from...beneath you..."

Her breath caught. Was Chance talking about her? He hadn't exactly made it a secret that he was disdainful of her, and, by extension, her relationship with August.

No, she was just being paranoid--surely he didn't hate her so much that he'd fight with August about it. It wasn't like she was interfering with what they had going. Except, Chance had been forced to watch over her, and August said he was working hard to find Britt... Maybe Chance really did resent that? He certainly sounded angry, even disgusted.

August's tone, on the other hand, was conciliatory and indulgent, which wasn't that surprising. He always said he considered Chance his best friend.

She wished August *would* get mad--then she could hear what he was saying. He calmly murmured something that made Chance even angrier. Chance snapped out August's name with sharp disapproval; she heard his next words quite clearly.

"Just send her away. Let her sink or swim on her own."

Clio went cold, her chest freezing over with what felt like a layer of ice.

Oh, God.

August's feet shuffled closer to the door. "You *know* I won't do that. I'm surprised you would even ask."

"August--"

"I won't send Clio away," August said mildly, though Clio could hear a thread of displeasure underneath. "Don't be stupid." His voice lightened again, and he added almost teasingly, "I need her."

Clio felt blood rush to her face.

Chance snorted. "Quit acting like a fool."

"You're so unromantic, Chance. It's no wonder you're single."

"Fine. Do what you want."

"I always do," August responded cheerfully.

"Just don't expect me to go to this farce of a party. I'll go out on patrol."

The sound of heavy footfalls made Clio panic, and she ran in the direction she was facing. Unfortunately, that was in the opposite direction of her room. She rounded the corner, took a few deep breaths, and then turned back around the corner, as if just passing that way for the first time.

August had his hand on Chance's arm, but he stopped talking as Clio approached them. She briefly met Chance's gaze, and then smiled at August.

"Hi."

August grinned at that bit of conversational brilliance. "Hey, Clio. We were just talking about you."

"Oh?" she asked a little breathlessly. "What about?"

Chance stared at her, stone-faced, but August ignored it. He released Chance's arm and took her hand instead.

"The party tonight, of course, and what everyone's gonna be wearing."

Clio cleared her throat. "I don't have any idea what to wear."

"We'll pick something together right now." He tucked her hand under his arm and led her away, calling over his shoulder to Chance. "And don't think you're getting out of it, either."

Clio waited until they rounded the corner. "Is everything okay?" she asked, keeping her voice low. "He seems mad."

August shrugged. "Don't worry about it--he's fine. Didn't get enough coffee this morning or something."

Clio smiled weakly, and August gave her an odd look. "Are *you* all right?"

"I'm fine," she hedged, trying to provide a plausible reason for her emotional state. "Just, you know, still worried about Britt. I feel like I'm not doing anything."

"You trust me, don't you?"

August looked rather hurt, which made her feel guilty for inadvertently criticizing his efforts. "I do!" she reassured him. "Really. It's just that...I feel like *I* should be doing more. I know *she* wouldn't sit around and let someone else do her work for her."

"You're really loyal, Clio, and that's impressive." He squeezed her hand. "But you have to worry about yourself, too. Just be patient a little longer."

Clio nodded and wiped at the few tears that had sprung up from talking about Britt again. He leaned close to her ear.

"Sweet Clio," he breathed. "It's gonna be okay."

The words cut through to her core. Clio suddenly choked out a sob, the flood of emotional relief drawing new tears from her eyes.

He pulled her into his room and kicked the door shut behind them. Then he pushed her onto the bed and held her, kissing her until she stopped thinking about the argument or Britt or anything else.

Gradually, the comfort became something else. Clio responded eagerly, for once not worried about how she looked or sounded.

She wanted him to touch her, to do everything, to not stop this time.

They made out on top of the bedspread, him pushing her skirt up her thighs as he leaned in between her legs, until she was dizzy from the lack of oxygen. His mouth moved to her throat, teased at her ear. She was breathing hard, confined by the bodice of the stupid dress. His hands were everywhere except where she really wanted them to be.

He didn't want to push her, she knew that--even though he was as turned on as she was. The evidence pressed insistently against her. She knew it was up to her to let him know that it was okay, which was endearing and little bit frustrating at the same time. It was too excruciatingly embarrassing to just ask, but *oh...*

"Do...do you want to...?" she breathed.

He pulled back, and he didn't look like much of a gentleman in that moment. His grin was filthy with the best kind of promise.

"Oh, Clio..." A delicious sort of shudder racked her at the lust he didn't bother to disguise. "I was hoping to wait--*trying* to wait until tonight, at least. I wanted it to be special." He inhaled sharply and pressed his face against her throat. "But I could eat you up right now."

His groan lit a fuse that raced all the way down to burn between her legs. Her breasts ached, and her toes curled into the sheets. She wanted...oh, she wanted his hands on her...his mouth. She wanted *everything*.

But you're in the Gauntlet, a small voice in her mind whispered. *You're in the middle of some twisted game. Is this really what you want? For your first time?*

Yes, Clio insisted to herself. *And I don't care anymore. It might be my first time, but, as screwed up as this place is, it could be my last time, too.*

She liked August so much, and he liked her. He *wanted* her, and he'd been holding back for her sake. The simple truth was she didn't *want* him to hold back anymore.

"I don't want to wait." Clio expelled a shaky breath. "I want...I want you."

She didn't have a chance to blush before August showed her just how much he'd been holding back. He managed to undo the intricate laces at her back with amazing dexterity, hiking her skirt up even higher with a roll of his hips.

August's hot, hungry mouth devoured hers, greedily sucking up her shallow breath. One of his knees pushed her legs higher, spreading her hips open.

His fingers dipped beneath the lacy edge of her underwear.

When a mortifying little moan slipped from her lips, August raised his eyes to grin wickedly. A hot blush traveled from her face and all the way down her chest. August watched it bloom, and then bent his head to follow it with his mouth.

"Your heart is beating so hard, Clio," August murmured. "I can hear it from here."

Of course it was. This was...this was overwhelming, unbearably exciting. It almost hurt, her heart, as it frantically beat in her chest. She couldn't answer him. She was all too aware of her own inexperience.

"Don't worry, sweetheart. It's so very flattering."

August chuckled, another dirty, little sound, and Clio marveled at how different he was from the gentlemanly persona he wore in public. She was fairly certain she liked it...*a lot.*

Then his thumb brushed very deliberately, and Clio's hips bucked. She felt his hot gaze on her as she tried to stay still and quiet, but he seemed to catalog her every move and sound until she was twisting on the sheets and her voice was reduced to threaded, pained pants.

It was terribly embarrassing the way he watched her so intently, but so very arousing, too. And, God, why did it feel so much better when someone else was doing it?

She flung her arm across her eyes and turned her head on the pillow.

"Don't hide," August chided.

Oh, God.

She reached up, tangling her fingers in his hair and pulled his mouth to hers.

"More."

♦ ♣ ♠ ♥

The full, red skirt of her gown swished around her legs as she spun and looked at herself in the mirror. For once, Clio threw herself into the spirit of it. She felt like she had in that first theater room--transformed.

She laughed and admired herself once more. The ball gown's bodice enhanced even her modest breasts, and the tight waist made her look curvier than normal. Even though she was playing dress up, she *looked* more grown-up--womanly.

She was still a little sore, but in a way that she liked; it reminded her of what they'd done. It had been messy and a little embarrassing, but mostly really good, if not exactly what she'd imagined.

What if everyone could tell what she and August had done? It seemed so obvious to her. Her eyes looked brighter, and she couldn't stop blushing and smiling stupidly every time she thought about it.

"I don't care if they know."

She laughed again and smoothed her hair, which was pulled back into a loose chignon, leaving only a few wisps free. Britt's necklace and the charm bracelet were odd accessories, but she would never consider removing them. They would have to do.

August had chosen the dress for her, and he'd helped

lace her it before kissing her thoroughly. He'd apologized for having arrangements to make and told her to come find him when she was ready. She only needed to put on the sequined mask. It fit over the upper half of her face, not doing much to really disguise her--but it did give her an exotic air.

She gave herself one last look. The high color in her cheeks suited her, and she looked happy--truly *happy*--which she hadn't felt since she'd been thrown into this madhouse. A small voice in the back of her mind whispered the once unthinkable thought that maybe, just maybe, it wouldn't be so bad if she stayed. For a while. If she *wanted* to.

But that was far too deep a thought to dwell on now. Clio took a long breath and released everything but her excitement to see August and enjoy the party. She was going to have some real fun tonight.

The party was in full swing when she arrived. All of the rooms that opened onto the garden were filled with revelers in fancy dress; there were far more people than Clio had seen all at once in any part of the Gauntlet. Music and conversation flowed energetically around her.

She moved from room to room, saying hello to the few people she knew well enough to discern behind the masks. She kept an eye out for August, but found Chance first. He wasn't in costume at all.

She nodded and tried to move away, but surprisingly he stopped her.

"Did you just get here?" he asked.

"Yes," she said shortly.

He had the nerve to seem a little surprised at her abruptness. Clio reminded herself that he had no way of knowing she'd overhead his argument with August.

She cleared her throat. "Enjoying yourself?" she managed.

She already knew the answer, but his pained expression made her lips twitch a bit, anyway.

"You could try, you know," she offered magnanimously. She was still in a spectacular mood, so she wouldn't let him ruin it. "Talk. Smile. It's not that hard."

"I'm talking to you, aren't I?" He *did* smile then--only slightly and for a split second, but she was struck again by how much that simple thing changed his whole appearance.

Clio frowned. She didn't get him at all.

"Well," she offered at last, "don't strain yourself."

"Are you all right?" He was staring at her way too intensely, and she shifted in discomfort.

"I'm fine," she replied. "Great, actually." She raised her eyebrow at him. "You're the one acting off."

"Oh?"

"Yeah. You're being all..." Clio floundered, "...nice."

The hint of a smirk was back, erasing the softer smile. That was more like it. Clio relaxed.

"How inconsiderate of me to confuse you," he muttered.

Clio bit her cheek to stifle the laugh that threatened to slip out. She was still pissed after what she'd heard him say about her.

He's not your friend, she reminded herself.

She lifted her chin and surveyed the room. "Have you seen August?"

The smirk vanished from his face. "No," he said thinly.

That was interesting. She wondered if they'd shared more words.

"Well," she offered. "I'm going to find him."

Chance was silent. Clio turned away without another word, stung again by his obvious disapproval.

"Clio, wait." His hand closed around her wrist.

She snapped her head up at him. "What?"

But he was looking over her shoulder. She craned her neck and saw August across the room, surrounded by a cluster of partygoers. His golden mask was shaped like spread wings. She tried to pull away, but Chance held on.

"Clio…"

She huffed. "What is it?" she snapped. She was at the end of her patience with him.

"Remember the bridge we went to?"

"Uh, yeah. That was, like, two days ago."

"It's on my regular patrol route."

"Okaaay..."

He seemed done with the conversation, because he let go of her arm and looked over her shoulder again. Before she could turn around, an arm slid around her waist, and August was at her side.

"Doesn't Clio look beautiful this evening?" His smile charmed her all over again.

"She does," Chance agreed readily.

Clio shot him a surprised glance.

August gave Chance a disparaging once-over. "*You're* not wearing what I picked out for you."

"I'd worry that it hurts my chances in the Best Dressed Contest tonight, but I know you always award that to yourself."

Clio stifled a snort, but August laughed freely. He ran a hand down the front of his white, gold-buttoned jacket with ridiculously ornate epaulettes.

"I'm glad to see you in a better mood," he drawled. "You've been boring as hell lately."

Chance let out a breath. "I've been told I should *try harder* to enjoy myself." His gaze slid to Clio a second, then, in a move reminiscent of August's theatrics, he bowed. "I think I'll go practice by the vodka."

August grinned and spun Clio around to face him. "I thought he'd never leave," he teased as he drew her onto the dance floor. She beamed and quickened her steps.

August swung her to the music until she was laughing breathlessly. She was beginning to see what he found so appealing about the spectacle of it all.

The food and drink and music seemed better than any before. Clio's customary shyness melted away. With August there to charm everyone, she couldn't help but feel charming herself.

"You sure know how to throw a party," she complimented, making a stab at a little curtsy. "This is fantastic."

"I like to think so." He spun her out into the garden, taking her from the heat of the crowded indoors. She leaned against the edge of a small fountain to cool down.

He gripped her chin. "*Now* we can have a little privacy," he said with a hum. "Did you miss me earlier?"

"Yeah," Clio replied honestly. "It was the longest hour of my life."

"I knew it would be. I should've warned you that I'm addictive."

Her giggle was cut off by a kiss, though it didn't last long as their masks kept colliding. They ended up laughing instead.

"Probably for the best," he commented. "Because I have some *news* for you, and I shouldn't let myself get distracted."

Clio straightened. "News? About Britt?" Clio hardly dared to get her hopes up, but August was smiling. "Did you find her?!"

"Let's play a game," August said with a teasing smile.

"What kind of game?"

"A classic--hide-and-seek. An old acquaintance of yours is hiding somewhere at the party, in plain sight if you know how to look. You get to find her." August snapped his fingers. "Oops! Shouldn't have let that little clue slip."

Clio's hands flew to her mouth. "Is she really here?" she breathed. "Can I look for her now?!"

August flashed his palms. "Wait, wait. If you find her before midnight, when we unmask, then I'll grant you one wish. If you don't, then you'll grant *me* one."

"August!" Clio threw her arms around August and hugged him fiercely. "Thank you *so much!*"

He let her go with an indulgent smile.

Clio ran back inside and pushed her way through the crowded rooms, keeping her head high to spot Britt more easily. She was taller than most of the people there--even the guys.

As Clio went through each room without success, the crush of bodies became frustrating rather than fun. Maybe Britt was circulating, too, and Clio just hadn't caught up yet?

She considered staying in one place for a while, but she was too impatient to just stand still and watch.

When she circled back to the garden, she poked her head out. August had disappeared.

So much for teasing out another clue.

Clio slid into a narrow hallway that connected to the next room and stood on tiptoe to crane her neck around. A hum of excitement grew around her, and she realized that midnight was about to chime. She pushed through a knot of people, not really caring if she lost the game--but she was tired of it and desperately wanted to see her friend.

As a clock chimed somewhere, she made it to another room: a small, intimate salon with low couches and dim lamps. It didn't seem familiar, and a strange chill ran over her when she stepped inside. Her eyes caught on something.

Her eyes widened.

She didn't see Britt, but she *did* see August wrapped up with some girl in a silver dress on one of the low sofas. The woman had a diamond tiara perched in the middle of blonde, piled curls.

Clio's head reeled, and the room spun with it. A sudden, sickening revulsion twisted her stomach.

No. *No.* This wasn't--*couldn't be*--happening.

They didn't notice her until she made some inarticulate sound, and August looked up, mask askew. He pulled it off and tossed it away. It landed in the lap of a girl sitting next to them on the sofa, but she didn't react.

The girl who'd had her tongue down August's throat looked up, though. Angela took off her mask with a vindictive little smile, her eyes shining with triumph.

August flashed his perfect teeth. "Clio...right on time. Oh, wait a second--it's 12:01. You lose."

"Where is she?" Clio asked dully, suppressing the flood of hurt and loathing she was afraid to even acknowledge. "Where's Britt?"

"Oh, she's not here. *You* assumed that."

"But you said--"

"I said you could find an old acquaintance here this evening," August interrupted. "It wasn't a lie."

Clio's fingers curled. "Why?" she breathed, unable to keep herself from voicing the trite, pathetic question.

"Because it was fun." August chuckled. "And because you have something I want. Of course, you were a stupid little girl and gave away part of it. It's no good to me if it's not the complete set." He twisted one of Angela's gold ringlets around his finger. "I needed something to pass the time while I was working to find it. You *owed* me that much, really."

Clio swallowed down the pain. "My bracelet."

"Of course. Though, don't sell yourself short. I enjoyed every last inch of you, Clio."

His mocking smile made her skin crawl. She felt the onslaught of hot, furious tears ready to spill over, but she didn't want that. She didn't want to give him that, too. She had to focus.

"Then you found it," she said slowly. "The heart charm?"

August glanced to the silent, motionless girl on the sofa.

Clio's eyes widened. She knew the face under that mask. Ice raced through her veins.

"Lilah," she breathed.

"Time to unmask." August reached over and peeled away the woman's mask, revealing Lilah's round face. Clio moaned.

Lilah's once sharp eyes were unfocused, unseeing. Her jaw was slack. All of the brash, annoying personality was completely smoothed out of her face.

"Oh...oh, God," Clio said hoarsely. She backed up one step, two, until she bumped into a body that she knew was Sunshine's. It didn't matter. She couldn't take her eyes off of Lilah.

"What did you do to her?" Clio whispered.

"Don't worry." August smiled and rose to his feet as Sunshine pulled Clio's arms behind her back. "You'll find out."

♦ ♣ ♠ ♥

Chapter 8

♦ ♣ ♠ ♥

Laughter rose around Clio, mixing with the loud music as she struggled with Sunshine along the edges of the dance floor.

She tried to dig her dragging heels into the marble as more laughter and razor-edged conversation swelled around her. Sunshine eventually stopped fighting and simply tossed her over his shoulder. The humiliation flooded her eyes with angry tears, made worse by the glimpses of mockery on blurred faces as Sunshine strode past.

The jolting from his shoulder winded her, but she kicked and hit wildly until his fingers dug into her hip. "Be still," he snarled. "Or I'll dump you on your ass and drag you the rest of the way."

The shock of hearing Sunshine speak was more effective than the threat. Clio stopped fighting and raised her head to see someone drawing shut a door to the great hall. The music faded to nothing, leaving a dull sense of dread to settle in the pit of her stomach.

She was pissed off, too--*beyond* pissed. She was furious, and she entertained herself with the fantasy of punching August right in the mouth. She hoped she would shatter every one of his perfect teeth and destroy that deceitful smile like he had destroyed her.

A choked sound of hurt, helpless rage caught in her throat, and she shook her head defiantly, blinking away the hot tears that pooled in the confines of her mask. He *hadn't* destroyed her. She wouldn't give him *that* satisfaction.

"Put me down," she snapped. "I can walk."

Sunshine seemed to ignore her, but after he turned into the next hallway he dropped her to her feet, keeping only one hand clamped around her upper arm. The look he gave her stated plainly that she'd regret it if she gave him trouble.

Clio resisted, just barely, the urge to flip him off.

They soon came to a door and a stairwell that only went down. He pushed her through the doorway, and Clio had the sudden terrifying thought that she would find herself once more inside the Gauntlet she'd first encountered--dark halls and dirty rooms and something to fear around every corner.

But the walls stayed clean, and the lights were bright. They went down and down until Sunshine forced her into an antiseptic corridor. A fast beat took up residence in her chest as they passed door after door secured by key card.

Is this August's lab? she wondered.

Her fears were confirmed when Sunshine took out a card and swiped it in the reader next to a door labeled "Test Subject 1." He shoved her in and shut the door behind her.

She wouldn't panic. Clio took deep breaths and pulled off the mask that seemed stifling now. It fell to the floor unheeded.

She surveyed the room--quickly at first, and then more slowly. The machine in the corner looked purposely intimidating, with numerous electrodes and other disturbing, unidentifiable objects plugged into it. The narrow bed wasn't any better, with its sturdy leather restraints and metal fastenings. There was a large screen attached to the wall at the foot of the bed, and a door that led to a small bathroom. Her eyes narrowed, taking in the mirror surface of the light fixture in the ceiling.

Nothing else but the camera, she thought grimly.

She didn't let that stop her from exploring the room more thoroughly, but the search didn't yield anything useful. Clio gathered up the full skirt of the dress she now hated, especially when she thought of the way August had helped her into it after...

She couldn't finish the thought. Her stomach rolled with nausea, made worse by the sharp, antiseptic odor that surrounded her; she flounced onto the bed, scowling in a sea of billowing, red fabric. With her back against the wall, she glared at nothing in particular while her mind worked furiously, trying to figure out what the *hell* she was going to do this time.

Eventually, all the shocks of the evening caught up to her, and she dropped her head to her knees and cried. By the time her tears dried up, leaving her hollow and drained, she was practically dozing in the cradle of her arms.

"Aw...Clio. Do you miss me already?"

Her head jerked up, and she stared at the screen in alarm. August's smug face beamed at her in high definition.

"You sadistic creep," she said with all the contempt she could muster.

It only made August laugh. "Out come the claws! It's cute. Jealousy looks good on you."

Clio seethed, but she ignored his provoking remark to ask a more pertinent question. "What exactly do you plan to do with me?"

"Lots of things," August said cheerfully. "You wanted to learn all about my methods, didn't you?"

"Yeah, before I knew you were a psycho," Clio retorted, refusing to display her rising fear in front of him.

"Brave talk, Clio." August smirked. "But we both know just how weak you are. You've only made it this far because other people keep covering your ass."

His snide assertion silenced Clio. It was true. She'd done nothing but fall into one mess after another, and she was bailed out almost every single time. Her harsh self-assessment made her flush with shame and anger, and she glared at August with all the strength of her newborn hatred.

"But I *am* still here," Clio pointed out, lifting her chin. "I bet it bugs you, doesn't it? That I have *friends* who'll help me.

You only have little suck-up minions with their noses stuck up your ass."

"You say that like it's a bad thing. If I wanted, *you* would be a pretty little minion, too."

"Not without you completely messing with my mind, I wouldn't."

"I have no problem with that," he drawled with a nasty smile. "In fact, that's kind of the point. Why do you think I've given you the number one suite in the house?"

"Because you have to keep me happy or I'll tell everyone you have a tiny dick?"

His expression darkened, and Clio felt a thrill of triumph that she'd punctured his smug, taunting surface. Her exhilaration faded quickly when she saw the flash of pure cruelty on his face.

"I'm going to enjoy breaking down all your barriers, Clio. It'll be fun." August smiled again, showing the dimples that she'd once found charming. "I already punched my way through *one,* after all."

His suggestive grin made Clio feel ill.

"When I see you again," he continued, "I'll take your little trinkets just like I took *you*. Bet you'll be just as eager to give those up before I'm through with you." He nodded when Clio's hand clutched at her necklace, making the bracelet around her wrist jangle quietly.

She'd almost forgotten. Why hadn't he taken them already? Before she could ask, August's twisted smile widened.

"And then I'll remake you into whatever I feel like. It won't be much of a challenge--getting in your pants certainly wasn't--but I need *something* to pass the time. Maybe I'll even let you in my bed again. Angela wouldn't be too happy at first, but she'd come around soon enough."

"You're disgusting," Clio said through gritted teeth.

"We'll see how long you think so." His teasing grin faded and a colder, more calculating look appeared. "For now, let's start the process of...softening you up a little."

The screen went dark, but only for a moment--and then

a terrible cacophony of sound and light appeared on the display. Clio winced and turned away with her hands clamped over her ears.

How long it went on, Clio wasn't sure. Hours, maybe, and the room seemed to grow colder with passing time. The discord was impossible to ignore, even when she pulled the pillow over her head; the piercing noise passed through the thick material like it was nothing.

The visuals were even more disturbing. The undulating circles and waves in lurid colors made her eyes throb. When those segued into a rapid-fire blink of images that her eyes couldn't quite capture--but left her with vague, subliminal impressions of wrongness and sickness and despair--she felt queasy. She did her best to keep her eyes averted, but sometimes couldn't resist a quick look to see if anything had changed.

Her eyes eventually grew heavy, though it was impossible to sleep through the horrible noise. She would have fought against falling asleep, anyway, but this was unbearable. When it all stopped at once, and the room's sudden silence seemed to weigh down the very air, Clio sighed with relief.

However long the reprieve would last, it was a blessing beyond compare.

Wearily, she dragged herself to the bathroom to drink from the faucet and splash cold water on her face. She looked ashen in the harsh fluorescent light, her skin starkly pale against the deep red of her dress. Her hair had mostly come down from its pins and straggled around her face in an untidy cloud. Her eyes had dark shadows beneath them and were bloodshot and glassy. Even now, she looked like she was losing it.

She *was* losing it. Before long, she'd be screaming, if the current state of her nerves was any indication.

She pulled the remaining pins out of her hair listlessly. She stared down at the last one, pinched between her thumb and forefinger.

"I'll gouge out his eyeballs when he shows up," Clio muttered.

"Carve out his heart while you're at. After all, he's got one of yours now."

Clio spun around with a gasp. The man who stood there wore a fancy suit and a mask, but Clio recognized the voice immediately, as well as the wicked grin.

"Black Jack!"

Clio wasn't sure if she should be relieved or wary--but she returned his smirk with a rather vicious grin of her own. "I'm sure he doesn't have one. Maybe I'll carve out his ego instead."

"It *is* a bigger target," Black Jack agreed. "Pop it and he'll probably *ppbbbbplttt* like a balloon." His hand waved around wildly in illustration.

Clio laughed, and Black Jack laughed, too. On impulse, Clio stepped forward and hugged him tightly. He seemed startled, standing stiffly before he returned the hug with bemused indulgence.

"I can't believe I'm saying this, considering you got me into this mess to begin with...but it's good to see you."

"It wasn't *me*," he protested. "But I don't have time to defend myself. You've got to move. The video feed is on loop right now, and August is dealing with...a diversion."

Clio hesitated.

Shit always seemed to hit the fan when the Jacks showed up. Things *changed*. One thing she did know: *anything* was better than staying in that room for more of August's idea of fun and games. Maybe she would let Black Jack cover her ass again, but she'd do it with her eyes wide open.

"What about Sunshine?" Clio prodded, still on her guard.

"Don't worry about our friend Sunshine. He's got his hands full, too." Black Jack smirked. "I hate that guy. But we--"

Clio's gasp cut off Jack's words. "Are those my clothes?!" She rushed over to the bundle on the bed, which included her wonderful, beautiful boots. "Where did you get them?"

Black Jack eyed her strangely as she picked them up and hugged them to her chest. "Chance gave them to me."

Ellery Prime & T2A

"*Chance?* Is he here?" All her suspicions revived, and she gaped at Black Jack. "Why would he--?"

"Who do you think sent me?" Black Jack said impatiently. "We've got to hurry, unless you want to wait around until August shows up."

"No." Clio shuddered.

"Then get changed. *Fast.*"

Clio did, gratefully shrugging out of the dress--that felt like a mark of shame now--and into her old clothes, which made her feel immeasurably better. God, how could she have been such a fool? Now that August had exposed himself, it seemed impossible that she'd ever been so blind.

"Finally ready, Cl-Cl-Clio?" Black Jack's saucy grin was probably meant to provoke, calling her back to all those weeks ago, before she'd set foot in this place. "Need some time to do your hair and makeup?"

It worked. She'd come a long way from that hopelessly frightened person, even if some people still thought she was weak and clueless. She felt newly armed with her bubbling rage.

Clio scowled. "No, but I'm keeping these just in case I run into August." She snatched up a handful of hairpins, and Black Jack laughed and reached for her.

They slipped out of the room, her hand in his. It reminded her uncomfortably of her escape with August from the center of the Gray Men. She pulled her hand away quickly, ignoring Black Jack's questioning glance.

He didn't stop moving, and they swiftly passed through the sterile corridors until they reached an outer door. It was still dark out, but Clio thought she could detect a faint lightening in the sky to the east. *It must be close to dawn,* she thought. Which meant she'd been in the room for five or six hours.

Black Jack pulled her into a narrow alley and led her along with sure steps. He hushed her with a warning sign every time she tried to speak, so they went along silently for a good half-hour before he finally slowed the pace.

"Listen," he said softly. "Whatever you do, don't go toward the gate. They'll be looking for you that way. Find a place to hide and stay there. Chance will find you."

The sky had lightened considerably during their walk; Clio saw that they'd arrived at the same little bridge Chance had brought her to not that long ago. She frowned her skepticism.

"Why would Chance help me?"

"I told you--he's the one who sent me. He's been helping you all along." Black Jack cast a look at the sky, then a worried look back the way they'd come.

"What?" Clio's brows knitted. "But...*why?*"

"You can ask him. I have to go."

"No! Don't go. You've got to tell me what's going on and--"

"Sorry, Clio." Black Jack playfully chucked her chin. "I wish I could, but I've got places to go, people to see. Can't be rescuing beautiful damsels in distress twenty-four hours a day."

"I'm not a damsel in distress," Clio growled. "The deck's just stacked against me."

Black Jack grinned, but it faded fast. "I really have to get back. Just trust Chance. He said that you'd know what to do if I brought you here."

"You told me not to trust anyone once," she said miserably, turning away. "When I trust people, bad things happen."

"Come on, Clio." His mellow voice had an unusual edge. "Does everything always have to be so black and white with you? And what about Britt?"

The sharp question jerked her gaze to his. He nodded once and slipped away, despite her last, half-hearted protest.

Trust Chance.

Fat chance, she thought stubbornly. He didn't even *like* her.

Okay, maybe she wasn't being completely fair. He'd been cold, but not cruel. The major stick up his ass didn't necessarily make him untrustworthy. On the other hand, he was August's right-hand man, which put him squarely on Clio's kill list.

But...she'd thought August *did* like her. God, she couldn't even trust her own judgment. How was she supposed to figure anything out at this rate? The truth was, she'd finally absorbed the message Black Jack and Britt had tried to drill into her: *Don't trust anyone.* Her doubts weren't really even about Chance, though she still didn't get why he was helping her. She couldn't trust *anyone's* motives. Could she?

Yes.

Britt had *always* had her back. Clio's feelings toward Black Jack were mixed, but he'd definitely been more of a help than a hindrance, even if he was only playing a part--and she knew he was, on some level. His part seemed to work in her *favor,* so she didn't so much trust him as she trusted him to...move her forward and not backward. He'd spoken the truth to her so far, even when it was couched in riddles.

She wouldn't ever forget that this was a game again. If there was one thing she'd learned from her humiliating experience with August, it was that. And if she considered the Gauntlet a game with pieces and rules, Black Jack *could* be trusted to a certain extent. So maybe, in that light, Chance could, too.

Clio stood at the top of the little bridge and sighed. Exhaustion was taking over; trying to puzzle through everything was a strain. All she wanted now was some rest.

The shadowy mass of buildings gradually resolved into distinctive shapes as dawn broke. She saw the tops of the towers Chance had pointed out--that day of their walk--against the pink sky. Black Jack's words came back to her: Chance had told him that she'd "know what to do."

Chance had called those towers a mystery. No one had been able to get in.

"This area is part of his daily rounds," Clio whispered. A sudden certainty grew within her. "Did he know what would happen?" His weird emphasis on the towers made more sense if that were true, if he really intended to help her.

With the sun finally making an appearance in the warm

colors near the horizon, Clio made up her mind. If she walked quickly, she could probably reach the closest of the towers in twenty minutes. She gave her bracelet a speculative glance and twisted her wrist from side to side. The charms jingled like tiny chimes.

It was a risk, but it seemed liked her best option, even if she remained wary of Chance's involvement. At least, in some strange way, his abrasive bluntness felt comforting in retrospect--compared to the soft, meaningless nothings that August had spouted constantly.

And, Clio told herself with a touch of gallows humor, *if Chance turns out to be a creep, it's death by a thousand hairpins.*

The towers were farther away than she thought, and Clio had to resist the urge to curl up in some empty building and sleep away the fatigue of the long, horrible night. When she finally arrived at the nearest one, it rose up even taller than it had seemed from a distance. The structure had no visible entry points, just as Chance had described. Low stone walls projected from each side of the tower and connected to adjacent buildings, leaving only the front half of the tower easily accessible.

A facade of large, irregular stones presented an impenetrable barrier. The stones were old, covered in some manner of small, cylindrical fossils here and there. The concrete seams separated the stone and helped form a haphazard design. She walked a slow arc around the base of the tower, her fingers along the rough lines. She was looking for something--a mark, a sign, an imprint. It would be around eye level, if it existed. At least, that was her logical conclusion.

Her eyes were bleary from lack of sleep when she finally found what she was looking for--a depression hidden in the shadow of an overhanging curve of stone, near one of the connecting walls. The small indentation was shaped like a tiny spade.

She lifted her wrist to the spot and pressed the matching charm into the groove.

"Yes," she breathed in triumph when the impregnable

stone in front of her opened onto a softly lit alcove. It held nothing but a small stairwell that spiraled upward.

Clio stepped inside the door and it closed behind her.

♦♣♠♥

The tower housed her that day--and gave her some badly needed time to sleep. When she ventured out to the town again, she tucked herself into a well-hidden cranny in an alley to watch the streets. She had a feeling her escape would result in...movement.

She eventually spied Chance from her hiding place and saw that he hadn't come alone. Of course, if he was supposed be on patrol--most likely searching for her--then his men *would* be with him, but that wasn't much consolation. She slipped through the shadows to follow them, her suspicions running high.

Only when Chance ordered his group to split up did she dare to move closer. Unfortunately, the twisting streets had mixed her up, and she had to hurry to find her way back to the bridge before his goons spotted her.

A narrow lane Clio had been sure led to an avenue crossroads instead dumped her into a dead end. She cursed and tried to reevaluate what she was doing.

She wasn't sure she even *wanted* to get to Chance. She'd had more time to reflect up in the tower, and she knew she was taking a risk, but Black Jack's words had struck a chord. Neither Jack had ever given her the name of someone who could help her, after all. Her knowledge of the Gauntlet and the confusing power plays therein had huge gaps, but maybe Chance had reasons for helping her.

If she ended up accepting the help offered, she would take it with a massive grain of salt. It sounded like Chance had betrayed August, maybe. And Clio couldn't suppress the fierce desire to serve up August some of his own nasty medicine before she got the hell out of this place. She wanted to kick him right where it hurt with the boots Chance had returned to her.

No matter what, she couldn't stay in that alley. She twisted around to retrace her steps.

Her luck failed her when Chance's two men came around the corner without a sound. Their eyes widened.

Crap!

When she turned to run, they grabbed her and hustled her back toward the bridge. Her furious struggling connected her boots to their shins *multiple* times, but they only winced and remained silent. She started to use her nails.

"Let her go."

The commanding voice actually flooded her with relief. Clio twisted in the guards' grasps.

Chance.

The goons released her, and Clio quickly put distance between herself and them, not taking her eyes off Chance. He jerked his chin.

The two thugs split off again. Clio was left alone with Chance under the archway of the bridge.

They stared at each other a moment, Chance searching her face as if looking for something in particular. Clio's eyebrow rose.

"It took you long enough," she murmured cautiously. "I've been waiting around for hours--I wasn't sure you'd actually come. I wasn't even sure *why* you would."

Chance ignored that to continue pinning her with his intense stare. "Are you all right?"

"Oh, I'm having the time of my life." Her brittle laugh made him frown.

"I would have been here earlier." To Clio's surprise, he sounded mildly apologetic. "But things are...out of control at the moment."

"Because of me?" Clio asked quickly. "Is Aug--*he* coming after me?" Ugh. She didn't even want to say the creep's name.

"Yes," Chance said bluntly. "But he has other problems."

"Like what?"

"To get you out, we had to make sure August was distracted." Chance stepped closer, making Clio tense a little. "There was an attack on the facility where you were first taken."

"The Gray Men!" Clio gasped. "But *how*? You planned an attack there? Why would August care about that? I thought he hated them?"

"Yeah, no. That's his baby. One of his first...projects. He figured out how to convert some of the mind-wiped into the Gray Men."

Clio's jaw dropped. "But he was the one who rescued me from..." She trailed off, an angry blush suffusing her cheeks. "That *jerk!*"

"August likes playing games." Chance eyed her warily, possibly because her hands had curled into fists. "If it's any consolation, that particular lab is trashed now."

"You had something to do with that?" Clio asked incredulously.

"Yes." The corners of his mouth turned up. "With outside help."

Clio was stunned. "Who?" she demanded. "What did they do? What happened?!"

"They took out August's labs there. All the equipment, software, and chemicals. More importantly, the research and records." Chance shrugged. "It's only a temporary setback, and there are other facilities, as you saw, but August is furious."

"Isn't *that* too bad." Clio couldn't help the spiteful edge in her voice.

Chance frowned at her again. "Are you sure you're all right?"

Clio knitted her eyebrows. "I'm fine. Or I will be, once I can kick August in the balls once or twice. Thanks for my clothes, by the way. It was really nice of you to find them."

Chance actually looked flustered, and finally turned his gaze away. "Let's move farther out. We're too close to the center for comfort, and we need to talk."

Clio hesitated, then nodded. But she grabbed his sleeve before he started walking.

"Just so you know," she hissed, "if you try to pull some

big double cross on me at some point, I *will* break your nose, no matter what else happens. I promise."

Chance barked out a surprising laugh--a real one that showed his teeth and made the perpetual intensity in his eyes soften. Clio stared in fascination.

"Thanks for the warning." Chance gestured toward the street, and Clio stepped out to lead the way.

"Oh, just follow me. If we're gonna do this, you might as well come back with me to the tower, since you sent me there in the first place, right?"

She stomped off through the streets, trying not to worry about whether she was doing the right thing. Chance followed obediently--which was a nice change.

"I've never been inside," Chance hedged.

Clio thought she detected a hint of curiosity. "Maybe I should charge you admission. It's pretty incredible."

She could hear his amusement when he asked, "How should I pay?"

"Information," she snapped.

"What do you want to know?" he replied cautiously.

"Why are you helping me?" The answer to that question had never been made clear. "Black Jack said you've been helping me all along. What did he mean?"

The silence drew out longer than she expected. She cast a curious glance at him.

"He shouldn't have told you that," Chance murmured, sounding for all the world like a petulant child. It was so out of character that Clio almost laughed, except she really wanted to know what his deal was.

"Why not? Why can't you just tell me what's going on?"

Chance scowled and started walking faster. Clio had to trot to keep ahead; she wouldn't let him weasel out of an explanation.

"Well?"

"August...wasn't always like this. He's changed over time."

At Clio's skeptical look, Chance grimaced. "Oh, he's always been full of himself. But this place...exposed his character flaws. It allowed him to *indulge* them. There was always a temptation to go one step further, and this place practically encouraged him.

"He never questioned the mechanics of it. All the...*toys*, as he calls them, just waiting to be found. The research...the clues...all perfectly tailored to his interests. To his way of thinking, that was all his due. I've stayed with him because I guess I've been trying to keep him under some kind of control." Chance snorted. "Clean up his messes when I can't prevent them in the first place. He needs some sort of check, or even *I* don't know how far he could go."

Clio's jaw tightened. She understood the temptations of this place all too well by now.

"So what does that have to do with you helping me?" she pressed.

"I'm sure you've realized by now that the Gauntlet isn't some by-the-rules board game--where everything is neat and orderly and there's a definite conclusion. Not everyone in here is even a *player,* like you. They have roles to play, and they do it for whatever reasons. Who knows how much free will factors into that?" Chance sighed. "I don't know if this place was ever different, but it's been this way for a long time. And now there are...opposing interests."

Clio gaped. "So there really isn't anyone in control?" She gestured wildly. "Outside...back in the real world?!"

"That's not it." Chance shook his head brusquely. "There are 'controllers,' in a way, but think of it as...some people wound up this place and set it in motion, and then they walked away. Observing, but not interfering. Mostly, anyway--there are some things that they directly allow, and some things that are...enforced."

"Like what?" Clio demanded.

Chance's gaze dropped to her wrist. "It's true that you can't just *take* what someone's been given as their...token. Not without consequences."

Clio clasped her wrist, wrapping her fingers around the

small charms. "But August said he was going to take *mine*."

"No. He was going to *persuade* you to give them to him."

Clio shuddered. "Is that what he did to Lilah before he turned her into one of those *things?*" She went pale thinking about the vacant, slack look of Lilah's normally animated features.

"I'm sorry I wasn't there when August locked you up."

Clio was surprised at the sudden apology. She saw self-recrimination in his expression.

"I wasn't expecting it then. I thought maybe he'd..." Chance trailed off. When it seemed he wouldn't finish the thought, Clio grabbed his arm angrily and faced off with him.

"But you knew it was *coming?* You knew he was just playing a sick game with me?!" She trembled with the force of her fury, blinking back an onslaught of hot tears that made her eyes sting.

Chance hesitated long enough that Clio had her answer. She pulled back and stiffly turned away, wiping her cheeks with jerky motions. "Everybody knew, didn't they?"

She heard Chance take a step toward her, and she tensed; he stopped before touching her. "No. August doesn't confide in the *masses*." There was disgust in his tone, but Clio somehow knew it was aimed at himself. "I...I knew, but not like you're thinking. I knew he was planning something, but I thought there might actually be a chance that he was sincere... with you."

Clio laughed bitterly. "Right."

"August likes to play games," Chance said thinly, as if *he* had more right to be distressed. "But he actually seemed interested in you. That's why he didn't just take you when you first entered the Gauntlet. He wouldn't even give *me* a straight answer about what he intended to do, even though we argued about you a lot."

"I heard you," Clio whispered. "Right before the party. I thought you didn't approve of me--that you wanted him to get rid of me."

Chance looked surprised for a moment, and then a little

grim, but he nodded.

"And *you* liked him." Chance's face was carefully neutral as he made the statement, but Clio couldn't help but feel a flush of shame. "I knew you wouldn't believe me if I told you he was playing you. And I had to be careful."

Her cheeks heated with the truth of that as she looked away. "You're probably right."

"You've been a pawn since the beginning, Clio. More than you can even imagine."

Clio clenched her fists. "Tell me."

"Back in the beginning, when the prowlers took you, do you remember any of what happened?"

"Not much. I know they drugged me...and I remember voices." Clio's eyes widened. "Was that August?"

He gave a curt nod. "And me."

Shock drained the blood from her face, and she reeled back from him. He quickly threw up a hand.

"He wasn't intending to do much then--he just wanted to shake you up a little. Make you doubt your senses...your reality. And he planted a few triggers, but you were remarkably unsusceptible. I managed to undo most of his little tricks that stuck."

Her lips worked, but no sound came out. Eventually she managed, "Why?"

"Why did he do it? Because he could. Because there hasn't been a new player in a while, and because he knows there are outside forces who have set themselves up against him and the little corner of the Gauntlet he rules. August doesn't like it when people challenge his authority; he suspected you were sent to cause problems for him."

"*Me?* But I wasn't!" Clio protested. "And I thought you said that the people *outside* just observe!"

"I said *mostly*. And Clio..." Chance waited until he had her full attention. "How do you know that wasn't *exactly* what you were intended to do?"

Clio tried to digest that idea. She remembered the dossier she'd found before the theater--all the disturbing, intimate details of her life and personality. She'd definitely been handpicked for the Gauntlet, but...was it only to be a pawn in some internal struggle of forces? To be sacrificed to an egotistical king with a fetish for blondes?!

"But I'm...nobody!" she cried in frustration. "I'm not some brain scientist like you...or him. I'm not even good at surviving, like Britt. I couldn't help her! I could *never* help her!"

"Don't sell yourself short. Britt doesn't."

Clio went rigid. "Britt? What do you mean?" She grabbed his sleeve. "You've talked to her?!"

"Who do you think arranged for our little diversion?"

"Oh my God!" Clio gasped. "Where is she? Is she coming here?!"

"She's busy." He smiled at her excitement. "You'll see her again, I'm sure."

"*When?*"

"First things first." Chance lifted an eyebrow. "You still want to get out of here, don't you?"

"Of course I do," Clio said wearily.

"So that's what we'll do." Chance spoke like it was a foregone conclusion, which only served to irritate her.

"Sure," Clio snapped. "Because it's that simple."

"It will be once we get your heart back from August." Chance surprised her by chuckling. "You should have seen August rant when he found out you'd given it away. I've never seen him so furious."

"And how will we do that?"

"Leave it to me," was Chance's infuriating response.

"No! I don't want to leave it to *you* or anybody else!" She shoved his arm back at him. "Screw this! I'm *tired* of being led around by the nose. If that bastard has what I need to get out, then I'll go kick his ass and take it back myself!"

Chance paused. She wasn't sure if she saw admiration or amusement in his eyes. "I think you're forgetting a key point."

"Wh..." Clio didn't finish the question before she remembered. There was that little detail about not taking someone else's token...and the threat of enforcement if someone *did*.

Clio deflated. "Is...the heart considered *his* now, since Lilah gave it to him?"

Her shoulders slumped when Chance nodded.

"I can get it from him."

She threw up her hands at his calm assertion. "How?" she cried. "And...and...how can you even go back there? Does he know you've been helping me?"

Clio gasped. "He must know you warned me off. You were really warning me about *him* when you told me to stay away, weren't you? *Not* the Gray Men. You didn't want me going into August's territory. But those guys you were with. Do you think they told him?!"

Chance's features softened. "I told you--August's always liked playing games. He knows I don't approve of most of the things he does, and that...amuses him. The fact that I would warn you off just makes it more fun for him." He looked away. "He calls me his 'conscience.' Which, trust me, he's happy to ignore when it suits him."

Clio grimaced. "Does that mean he trusts you or not?"

"He trusts me. We *do* go way back, and his narcissism makes it hard for him to believe someone he...*favors* would betray him. And..." Chance hesitated, his mouth curving into a frown. "I've changed from when I first met him. I wasn't always so...scrupulous. I think he lets himself believe I'm just like him beneath the surface."

"So..." Clio said slowly, trying to make sense of everything. "You've been doing all this...helping me...because you feel kind of responsible for keeping him in line?"

Chance opened his mouth, looking slightly self-conscious, and hesitated a moment. "I--"

"*Chance.*" A low-pitched, urgent voice called from behind them.

Chance turned as one of his men ran toward them, a bit out of breath. "Sunshine rounded up a troop of the Grays after the attack," the man murmured. "They've split up and are making a sweep of the city. They'll hit this quarter in a few hours; August is hell-bent on searching every building."

"Head back," Chance told him tersely. "I'll join you soon."

Chance remained calm, though he took Clio's arm and propelled her much more quickly through the streets. "I'll see you to the tower before I go back."

"Do you have any idea what I'm supposed to do there?" Clio blurted. "I can't hide out forever."

"I'll come back as soon as I can. Do you have food and water there?"

"Yeah, it's actually pretty nice--"

"Good. Then I won't worry if I can't make it for a couple of days."

"But--"

"Clio," Chance said with a fierce urgency that took her aback. "Just stay there until I return. It won't be long. *Don't* leave--no matter what."

Clio scowled. She deliberated on the instructions, once again weighing the pros and cons of *listening to anyone ever again.*

I'm the only one who can access the tower, she reminded herself. The entry was dependent on her spade charm. It probably *was* the safest place to protect her from everyone...including Chance. If it came to that.

"Fine," she said through her teeth. "But if you're not back in two days, then all bets are off."

He shot her an exasperated look but didn't argue; the tower was already looming up just ahead. "Come on!" she cried, almost excited to share something that even *he* hadn't seen before.

She ran to the corner by the wall and pressed her charm into the small indention. She spun around to grin at Chance and was startled to see that he'd followed her so quickly. His curious gaze took in the stairwell that wound up within the tower, then settled back on her.

This close, he seemed even taller, looming over her as she stood in the doorway. Clio had a sudden, strange sense of déjà vu.

Feeling a little flustered, she gestured awkwardly. "Do

you want to come up?"

Chance's mouth twitched and he raised an eyebrow. "I don't know. Are your parents home?"

Clio gaped at him a moment, then laughed. "Your sense of humor picks the weirdest times to come out."

"So I've been told." Chance's smirk faded quickly; when he stepped back, Clio felt almost disappointed. "But I can't stay now."

Clio nodded. "Um...be careful, I guess."

"Don't worry about me." Chance's lips parted, as if he wanted to say something else. His eyes searched her face with that penetrating gaze she was becoming accustomed to, but in the end, he simply stepped back.

"Thank--" Clio tried to get out before the door closed. "--you," she finished as the door silently slid shut. It cut off her view of his intense, dark eyes.

That strange sense of déjà vu still lingered. Clio stood in the silence for a moment, facing the unbroken stone wall.

She finally began to climb the staircase, her fingers trailing the cool metal railing. Another memory rose up--the frantic, claustrophobic climb up the rungs in the dark when Black Jack had given her a helpful shove into the shaft.

"Games are often won by luck. When all else fails, trust in yours."

Suddenly, Clio felt her lips curl, not sure whether to be appalled or amused. Even that far back, the moves had been planned.

"Trust in *luck.*"

Right. Well, maybe she would, but maybe she'd also make some plans of her own.

It was her move now.

♦♣♠♥

Chapter 9

♦♣♠♥

Clio shook the cans of red and black spray paint, sending the balls inside rattling. The broad, unmarked wall presented an appealing canvas, and she pursed her lips and thought a moment before stepping forward and releasing the paint with broad sweeps of her arm. A satisfying hiss accompanied her efforts; she dropped one can and continued with the other. She finally stepped back and surveyed her handiwork with a smirk.

The signature logo she'd made for him dripped a little red paint to the right of August's name. *Every leader needs a symbol to represent him,* Clio had decided when she'd stumbled across the cache of paint cans. Fortunately for her and her limited artistic abilities, an asshole was exceedingly easy to render.

She'd spread it far and wide across his precious domain, thanks to the tunnels that spiraled off what she thought of as *her* tower. Chance was probably going to be pissed that she didn't stay put like he'd insisted, but she was tired of following other people's orders.

Besides, *technically,* she was still connected to the tower, since the hidden passages all led from it. Popping outside when she was absolutely sure it was safe was her risk to take if she wanted. She couldn't pass up the perfect opportunity to find out what was going on, and it had been an excellent way to spy on August. Indulging in a little guerilla warfare of her own was just an added bonus.

Scrawling *August stinks!* throughout his pristine little kingdom might not do much actual damage, but she was sure it drove him crazy nonetheless. At the very least, it showed other people that not everyone lived in fear of him. Okay, maybe she *was* afraid of him, but that didn't mean she wouldn't *fight* him. Maybe August wouldn't even figure out that it was her, and worry that he had more enemies to watch out for.

This was the first time she'd dared to venture so close to his inner compound, though. It was worth it--he'd see the message, and so would more of the people who surrounded him.

"Not so untouchable now, King Asshole," she muttered.

The sound of voices sent her hurrying back into the safety of the tunnel, but she watched from a tiny viewfinder that allowed her a fish-eyed view of the street. Two girls stopped and gasped; one of them giggled before the other girl shushed her and tried to rush her past the wet graffiti.

Before the girls could escape around the corner, three of August's goons showed up--wearing those quasi-military outfits that Clio now knew were *meant* to intimidate. The girls certainly looked afraid as they were questioned brusquely.

The goons eventually dismissed them. As the girls scurried away, Clio strained to hear the conversation of the three men.

She caught Sunshine's name.

"...take it to him, not August," the possible leader said firmly.

"He's just as bad," one of them grumbled.

"Trust me--you don't want to go *near* August right now if you can help it." The leader pointed to the graffiti. "He's losing his shit over *that*. With the skirmishes outside the gate, he's got a short fuse."

"You mean he's fucking nuts," the grumbler muttered. "He loses one girl and we all have to suffer."

That earned him a smack upside the head. "Shut your fucking mouth, moron. You don't want the wrong person to hear you talking like that." The leader jerked his chin at the man who hadn't spoken yet. "Get a cleaning detail on this. If Chance is back, we'll inform him."

"I thought we were supposed to keep him out of the loop for now."

"It's your job to think now?" The leader sneered. "But if you're so worried, *you* can tell Sunshine."

The grumbler's protest faded as the men rounded the corner; Clio's grin of satisfaction warred with her concern for Chance. None of her spying had yielded a glimpse or a word of him until now. She was worried about the implications of him being left out of the chain of command. Had August turned on him?

Her sense of fun faded. If Chance didn't turn up soon, what would she do?

The lead goon had mentioned that Chance might be around. Maybe she could find him before she returned to the tower.

"I'll just have a quick look," Clio murmured to herself. She wouldn't leave the tunnel unless it seemed safe enough.

She backtracked a little and took the branch that led toward August's main headquarters. A short stairway took her up to a narrow, street-level alcove that allowed her a decent view of the little square through some kind of decorative, tightly woven, metallic mesh screen. She wasn't sure what the exterior of her hiding place looked like, but she guessed she was between the walls of two rooms; she saw the outlines of milling people and heard the muffled, irregular sounds of life from both sides of her.

Her view of the square meant this building was the dining hall. If she waited long enough, Chance would have to pass this way, if he was in the area at all. She squatted down--quiet as a mouse--and squinted through the metal at the people passing back and forth.

They seemed more hurried than she remembered, their attitudes tense as they moved from place to place without a lot of idle banter. August probably *was* in a bad mood.

Clio chewed her lip, her worry for Chance intensifying along with her guilt. The guilt made her a little angry, too. She hadn't asked for any of this--if Chance was in danger, it wasn't because she'd done anything wrong. But the feeling kept her there long after her cramped legs had gone numb.

The sounds of muted chatter and clattering cutlery grew louder on either side of her as more people came in to eat at the height of the dinner hour. August, Chance, and even Sunshine were nowhere to be found. Gradually, most of the diners streamed away to other activities, and Clio grew hungry and sore.

She was ready to go back to the tower when August angrily strode into the courtyard. She gasped and ignored the pins and needles in her legs as she shifted to press her face against the metal screen.

Her heart thundered when Chance followed. He called out August's name sharply, and August wheeled around; August threw something that bounced off Chance's chest and clattered noisily on the paving stones of the square.

It was one of her paint cans.

August looked incensed, even from this distance--his perfectly put-together look was mildly disheveled. Even that was startling. She *had* gotten under his skin.

Clio grinned.

Chance ignored the can and watched August stalk away. Before August disappeared into the building, he spun around and raked a hand through the hair that fell forward over his eyes. It seemed to comb out the agitation he was radiating.

"Find the little bitch." August smiled coldly--Clio flinched at the venom in his words. "It looks like you need more *incentive,* Chance. After she gives me what is *mine,* then you can do whatever you want. You can have her, if you still want her."

Chance just stood there as August left. Clio stared at him, trying to make sense of what she'd heard. After a moment, Chance bent and picked up the paint can.

She felt a zing of adrenaline when he began to walk toward the dining hall. Clio was thrown by August's words, now unsure of herself *and* Chance. Was August just...just spewing hateful words, or was there truth to it?

Chance approached; she watched him with her heart in her throat. He stopped a few feet from the entrance at her left, gripping the paint can tightly in his hand while he scowled at it.

"Clio," he muttered in a low voice that she could hear from her position. "What the hell are you doing?"

He sounded pissed off, exasperated...and worried.

Clio took a deep breath. "*Chance,*" she hissed.

His head jerked up. He stiffened for a moment before he made a visible effort to relax and peer up at the sky, as if he were trying to determine the time of day.

"I'm over here," she whispered as loudly as she dared. "Behind the big bush by the wall. *Inside* the wall."

"*Inside the...*" His eyes flicked in her direction. He clenched his jaw and bent down to adjust the laces of his boot.

"Go back to the tower," he said in a low, angry voice. "This is pointlessly dangerous."

"Not when I'm being careful," she whipped back. "I'm not going to sit around forever."

"I told you to *wait* for just--"

"But I found these tunnels and--"

"Shh! I'll come tomorrow. Around this same time. Listen for once and *wait* there."

"Wait! *Chance*. I--"

Clio bit off her words when Chance stood abruptly and a few people she didn't recognize came out of the dining hall. She waited, but without even a look over his shoulder, he walked away with them and didn't come back.

Disgruntled and swearing as her legs dragged painfully under her, she climbed back down into the tunnel and headed for what she called "home" at the moment.

Chance's dismissal soured the entire day. She spent the rest of the evening stewing over his arrogance and the creepy offer August had made him. There was something about August's wording that shook Clio to her core.

"You can have her, if you still want her."

She...needed to think about that one. If Chance had ulterior motives...

Despite her concern, waiting for him in the safety of the tower seemed her best option for weaseling out the truth. Besides, it wouldn't exactly be a hardship to relax for once, especially after the less-than-stellar accommodations during most of her stay in the Gauntlet. The unexpected oasis she'd found at the top of the tower *was* pretty sweet.

So the next morning, she climbed to the top of the tower and just sprawled out under the sun. She lay in the heat until it filled her with a sluggish comfort. Her back, bottom, and the undersides of her legs felt almost weighed down by the pleasant warmth; unwilling to relinquish the lazy enjoyment of the morning, she rolled onto her back and let the sun warm her breasts and belly instead.

She had to admit, it gave her a thrill to be able to do so, knowing that she was the only one who had access to this place. If it was a reward for making it this far, Clio felt it was entirely deserved. The mature fruit trees surrounding the lush lawn that spread over the top of the tower provided her with fresh food, and the cushion-filled gazebo was a lovely place to sleep. If the outdoor shower enclosed along the curve of the wall had been a splash pool instead, her temporary paradise would've been perfect. As it was, she couldn't complain.

She wished she could mail August a postcard to rub it in his face. She fanned a hand across her eyes and grinned. Her smile slowly faded as she remembered her hurried parting from Chance.

Would he really come that day? What if something worse had happened between him and August? And...and did Chance actually have some sort of feelings for her like August had implied, or was that just August being obnoxious and awful?

Chance seemed to stick his neck out for her a lot, but considering how much she'd been manipulated already, she assumed that had more to do with her role in the Gauntlet's machinations. He didn't seem to like her much as a *person*. Then again, it wasn't like they'd ever hung out in a normal context, so it was hard to tell. She couldn't fathom why or how he liked her, if he actually did. She wasn't sure how that made her feel, honestly. Beyond wary and doubtful.

What if he came in here and tried to seduce her like August had?

Well, he could *try*. She wouldn't fall for something like that a second time.

"August has to be full of it," she thought aloud. Chance knew where she was--if he wanted to give her up to August, he would've done it already.

But what if August *wasn't* full of it? What if Chance *genuinely* felt something for her?

"*Augh!*" She pressed her face into her hands and vented her frustration by drumming her heels against the grass. Her stomach squirmed in something like anxiety.

Clio sat up and looked around. What if this was just another trap? Things with August had looked good, too. Even if it wasn't, this little resort was still keeping her from what she wanted.

Which is to get out, she told herself firmly.

The thought drove her to her feet. Chance wouldn't arrive for a while; instead of lying around like she was on vacation, she'd check out more of the tunnels. Maybe there was more than one way out of this nightmare.

She stood under the cool spray of the shower and then let the sun dry her skin. She got dressed and pulled her damp hair into a ponytail. Before she could finish putting on her boots, a small beeping noise almost made her lose her balance, and she hopped precariously until her foot slid all the way in.

She ran to the sound. A decorative plate on the wall had slid aside to reveal a small screen.

"Cool," she breathed.

The screen showed the base of the tower--where Chance stood. He stared at the wall before craning his neck upward, looking a little nonplussed. Some proximity alarm had apparently been set off by his presence.

Clio snorted a laugh. He was early, and he obviously hadn't given a thought to how he was supposed to get her attention. He was alone, as far as she could tell.

It took her a while to make it down to ground level; Chance looked immensely relieved when the tower opened up. He stepped in quickly, and they stared at each other in awkward silence.

By the look on his face, he wanted to lecture her. But whatever Chance was thinking, he seemed to shrug it off.

"You've been busy." His dry words sounded almost amused, if a bit exasperated.

Clio shrugged. "Would you just sit around if it were you?" she retorted. Without waiting for an answer, she started back up the stairs. "What are you doing here so early?"

He followed. "Change of plans. How did you know I was here?"

"Wouldn't *you* like to know," Clio hummed. She glanced over her shoulder, expecting to see his dark brows drawn together in a scowl--but Chance was smiling faintly instead.

"What?"

"Nothing. You seem more relaxed than usual."

"I do?" Clio shot him a slanted grin. "Well, I have been working on my tan."

She watched his gaze search her face and then drop to her bare arms and shoulders. His eyebrows rose, as if he wasn't sure if she was teasing him.

But when their gazes met again, he looked away like he'd been caught ogling her. Clio had to wonder about August's words again.

"Good to know you're not spending all your time defacing buildings," Chance said gruffly.

"Was he really mad?"

Chance gave a low chuckle. "You have no idea."

A savage grin curled her lips. "Good."

They made it to the top, and Clio was irritated that she was more out of breath than Chance. He stopped at the edge of the flat lawn of the tower and took it in silently. Clio watched his reaction with an odd sense of possessive pride.

"Are those guava trees?"

Clio laughed at his eagerness. "Yeah. There are all kinds here, but I guess I know which are your favorites now. Want some?"

She pulled a few guavas from the tree and washed them under the spray from the shower. He trailed after her to the gazebo, and she tossed him one of the fruits.

He bit into it and made a happy sound. "It's sweet," he mumbled around a mouthful of fruit. "It's been forever since I had fresh guava."

Clio laughed again, a little charmed by his boyish enthusiasm. She put the others next to him. "It *is* nice up here."

"I guess you weren't kidding about the sunbathing." August wiped a bit of juice off his chin with his thumb. "Now I'm *more* surprised you left here to go tagging."

Clio snorted. "Oh, that was therapeutic, too. But I started out just exploring the tunnels. It wasn't until I found the box of paint that I got the idea."

"It wasn't a bad idea, actually," Chance admitted. "It's made August lose his focus in some ways, and that's been... helpful. Of course, everyone else might not thank you. His famous charm is definitely cracking around the edges."

Clio winced. "I'm sorry about that. Is he...taking it out on other people?"

"Worry about yourself. He's even more determined to find you."

"Yeah, I heard." Clio kept her voice neutral, but Chance looked at her sharply. She wasn't positive, but it seemed like his face took on the faintest tinge of red.

He opened his mouth and took a breath, then closed his mouth again. She waited.

"I know you don't have a good reason to trust me," he said at last.

"You helped me get away from him," she offered.

He frowned, maybe wondering why she was providing him with points in his favor. "Yes, just like August helped you get away."

They exchanged wry grimaces.

"You know where I am, and you haven't told him."

"That's true." Another humorless smile crossed his face. "But I could have my own agenda."

He was telling her what they both knew and she'd considered already. She eyed him speculatively.

"So now you're telling me *not* to trust you?" she clarified.

"*No.* No, that's not it. I mean, I wouldn't blame you, I just..." He broke off and rubbed his hands nervously against his pant legs. "What you heard August say...I wouldn't do that. I won't try to trick you, or...sell you out...or..."

Clio leaned forward. "But this could all be a really convincing act for something *else* I don't know about. Make Clio think she's safe. Make her believe you're her friend. Tell her that you're working with Britt, someone you know she trusts."

Chance looked startled, and his lips parted, but he didn't speak. Clio continued.

"Make her feel grateful, keep her isolated until she gets

lonely enough to want a little comfort, a little human contact, and then...seduce her? After all, it worked before."

"*No.*"

Chance bit out the word so sharply that Clio jerked back. But she relaxed again and grinned at him in a challenge.

"No?"

"I'm not like August," he growled. "No matter what *he* thinks."

"Okay." Clio leaned back and snagged one of the fruits from the cushions. She took a bite, enjoying the sweet, mild flavor of the soft fruit.

Chance frowned. "Okay what?"

Clio shrugged. "Okay. You aren't like him. You won't sell me out and you don't want to seduce me."

She felt a little evil as she watched him avert his eyes and turn away.

"That's it? You...trust me?" Chance asked.

"That's what you want, isn't it?" Clio cocked her head. "It's all a gamble, anyway, since I can never be sure of anything in this damn place. Unless..."

"Unless what?" he asked warily.

Clio felt her heartbeat pick up speed. She'd only been testing him a little up until now. August's words still bothered her, but she *was* willing to trust Chance at this point--she had to play the cards she was dealt, and this seemed a safer hand than most. If she really wanted something like *proof* that she could trust him, maybe it was time to put all *her* cards on the table.

It was a huge risk that would pay off big...or end everything.

"Clio?" Chance looked nervous now. It was almost endearing, but Clio pushed *that* thought away.

She slowly slid the bracelet off her wrist. Chance's eyes widened. She reached for his hand that curled around his pant leg and spread the broad palm open.

"It's yours," Clio said carefully.

Chance gaped. A flush spread over his face and down his

throat, and for a moment he looked like he might choke on his own breath. Then he exploded.

"What are you *doing?!*" Chance snatched up her arm and shoved the bracelet back over her wrist. "This belongs to *you.*" He shot up and walked halfway across the lawn in agitation before spinning around to glare at her. "Don't pull a stunt like that again."

A sense of lightness bubbled up in Clio. A wide smile pulled at her face.

"I'm serious," he said sharply.

Clio fell back against the cushions and dissolved into full-fledged laughter. She wasn't sure what drove the instinct, but it felt *good.* The tension rushed out of her with every bubbling breath.

Chance stomped back over and stared down at her with that bewildered, angry look on his face...and maybe something else. Clio's laughter faded away.

She cleared the saliva from her throat. "I think it's obvious I can trust you now."

Chance's frown cleared, and a grudging smile of admiration took its place. "Yeah," he said quietly. "But *you'll* be the death of me."

"Don't even joke about that," Clio said, and she was half-serious. She reached for a guava and tossed it at him.

"Now sit down so we can figure out what we're going to do."

♦ ♣ ♠ ♥

The tunnels made their meetings a lot easier after that. They still didn't have a workable plan, and August had disappeared with Sunshine two days earlier. Chance didn't know where he'd gone, which worried both of them.

"Not that it matters," Clio muttered. "I still don't know how to get out of here."

"It's got to be somewhere in the tunnels," Chance said, maintaining an annoying sense of calm.

"I've gone over every inch a million times!"

"Be patient and try again."

Clio growled. "Easy for you to say."

"Maybe we just have to wait."

His practical answer didn't pacify her. She threw her hands into the air.

"You mean I can't find a way out because the mythical Overlords haven't waved their magic wand to make one appear?"

Chance snorted. "Something like that."

Clio kicked the wall of the tunnel and leaned back against the rough cement, crossing her arms over her chest. "This sucks," she grunted.

Chance looked out through the viewfinder as people walked on the street above them. He pursed his lips.

"Do you think I could get back to the first building?" Clio asked with little optimism. "Back where I came from? Maybe I could find the theater again and get to that exit on the map."

"Shh." Chance waved a hand at her. Clio scowled, but she moved up next to him.

"What?" she whispered.

He turned around abruptly. "I have to go."

"Already?" Clio cringed a little. *God, I sound whiny.*

"August is back."

That wiped away her self-pity in a heartbeat. "Did you see him? How did he look? Was Sunshine with him?!"

Chance jerked his head from side to side. "They said he just returned. And...that he seemed *happy.*"

Clio's stomach sank. Chance look worried, too.

"I've really got to go. I probably won't be able to get away until tomorrow."

"I'll meet you here," Clio began.

"No!" Chance said severely. "I mean it, Clio. Don't come here until you hear from me again. I'll try to get out to the tower tomorrow."

"You should take the spade charm," Clio offered. "That'll make it easier for you to get in, and I won't need it as long as

I stay in the tunnel."

"You want to just hand it to August now?" he asked witheringly.

"That would only happen if *you* gave it to him!" she snipped. "Fine. Since I thought I could trust you, I was just trying to help *you* for a change. But I won't bother anymore."

She turned to go, but Chance took a step toward her, reaching out a hand that stopped short of her shoulder.

"Clio...I just want you to be careful. I don't know what to expect if August's back and happy."

"I know." She had to tilt her chin up to meet his gaze, and her stomach faltered at the concern she saw in it. It softened her frustration.

"I'm going to talk to him. I might have a plan, but I need to see him first." His hand dropped, but Chance's eyes begged her to agree.

"All right," she said grudgingly. "But don't screw yourself."

"I won't."

They stood in uncomfortable, awkward silence until Chance moved away; that tight feeling in her chest eased with some space between them. He scaled the ladder to the street and exited through the small door that sealed behind him.

She was frustrated that this all seemed to be *another* dead end. Clio wanted to talk to Britt, but Chance swore she was outside of August's reach and creating a lot of headaches for him. If she could get back to Britt, she was willing to bet they could find a way back inside the building complex. They could both get out, and Chance could come with them...

She entertained herself with the pleasant thought as she gripped the rungs bolted to the wall that led up to the base of the tower. Then another thought struck her.

Her tower wasn't the only one.

She'd been distracted by *her* tower's attractions, by the tunnels, by the business of hiding and surviving and trying to work out what to do. It hadn't even crossed her mind to try and get inside *another* tower. None of the tunnels led to them, after all.

She wanted to smack herself on the head. Britt probably would've explored them all in the first freaking day.

She shed the self-loathing with a pragmatism Britt would have appreciated. It wasn't too late.

Clio considered some obvious facts. She would have to go above ground if she was going to try it. Chance definitely wouldn't approve.

Good thing he's busy with his own plan now.

She climbed to the top of her own tower to work out the best route to the closest one. She'd try all of them if she had to, but she wanted to hit the first one and be back before Chance returned. If she had good news, she would surprise him. If she didn't, he didn't even have to know about it.

Other than dark clouds that slowly rolled in and threatened rain, Clio's luck was good. She stood at the base of her tower's clone not half an hour later, her fingers gliding over the rough stone.

She whooped quietly when her fingers found a groove. The tiny spade fit like a charm, and Clio grinned to herself at the pun as her heart swelled in anticipation. The tower opened up to her; she stepped inside.

There wasn't a spiral staircase like the one in her tower, but an old-fashioned elevator that filled the wall of the tiny room. A control panel was mounted next to it, featuring a single button. It was the kind that lit up when pressed--but when Clio tried it, the button stayed dark.

She wasn't surprised. Surrounding the button, like points of a compass, were four indentations: a diamond, a club, a heart, and a spade.

She looked at her wrist and its four dangling charms. The joker in its foolscap caught her eye, and a moment of inspiration made her gasp.

Jokers are wild!

But when she tried to fit the joker charm into the heart indentation, her brief burst of hope died. It didn't fit.

Shit.

She definitely needed her heart charm back from August. It would let her into that elevator...and maybe let her *out.*

Maybe they could capture August and strap him to one of those chairs, so they could "soften him up" like he'd tried to do with her. She was almost frustrated enough to be capable of something like that.

Clio sighed. *But not quite,* she admitted. And it didn't matter--they couldn't even *get* to August, anyway. Chance said Sunshine was almost always with August, and when Sunshine was gone, a number of other guards took his place. August was never alone.

"Worry about that later," she told herself, reluctantly turning away from the elevator. The important thing was that she'd found her next move.

Her luck with dry skies held on the way back, so she retreated to her outdoor sanctuary atop her tower. If it wasn't going to rain, she wanted to wait there. She flopped onto the cushions of the gazebo gratefully.

She was a little winded, but not tired. She practically thrummed with excitement. *Finally,* things were moving again. She couldn't wait to tell Chance. She got up and paced nervously, trying to walk off her pent-up energy until he arrived.

When the proximity alarm beeped, she pounced on it. Chance was there. She pressed the screen icon that she'd discovered could open the tower remotely. Chance disappeared from view, and she prowled the lawn as she waited for him to climb the stairs.

The sharp peal of a siren made her jump.

It sounded like the test alarm for an advance warning system...or when a disaster was imminent. For a moment, Clio jerked her face to the sky, half-expecting a black funnel to swirl down from the dark clouds overhead.

The clouds rolled, but not one drop of rain fell. Instead, the siren stopped and August's voice took its place.

Clio went cold as she recognized the bright, smug tone she'd come to know so well. Even through the distortion of the broadcast, he sounded entirely pleased with himself.

Especially as he described his recent capture of Britt.

His voice cut off as his message to the "citizens" ended, but what he didn't say came through to Clio loud and clear.

If she didn't go back to him, Britt would suffer.

Britt would suffer.

Clio barely made it into the stairwell before colliding with Chance. He wrestled her out into the open, where the rain had finally begun to fall in an irregular patter of drops.

"Let go!" she gasped. She fought his hold as panic bubbled words up her throat. "He can have it! I don't care!"

"It's a lie," Chance hissed. "He's *lying.*" His arms tightened around her, but Clio still thrashed in his hold.

"He's been *hiding* things from you, Chance! Let go!"

A rough shake snapped her head back, and she stared at him wildly.

"It's a *lie.* He just wants to draw you out. *Listen* to me."

Clio took a shuddering breath, but the tension in her body didn't ease. "Britt..."

"He doesn't have her." Chance looked directly into her eyes, and Clio searched them intently, her fingers digging into his biceps as she struggled to work out the truth.

"How do you know?" she breathed. Her throat felt raw, and she barely noticed the rain splattering on her head and arms.

"I know," Chance soothed. "He doesn't have her."

"But--"

"You have to trust me on this one, Clio."

She wanted to. She wanted *nothing more* than to believe that Chance was right. He didn't elaborate, but his eyes softened in a way she'd never seen before. Desperate loneliness welled up inside her.

"He...really doesn't have her?" Clio whispered, her voice breaking.

She let herself sag a little when he nodded. When his arms came around her, she couldn't help the tears that came. She pressed her face against his chest, focusing on the tiny pats of rainwater that tickled her scalp until the relief sank in.

Britt...

She wiped her eyes and finally pulled away. The distress in Chance's face shocked her.

"You were going to run out without waiting for me," he accused. "You would've walked right into his trap."

"I didn't have any other choice!" Clio shouted.

"Yes, you did. You *do*! I thought you trusted me!"

Clio had never seen Chance so worked up. She pulled back from him and the hurt that radiated off him.

"I *do*, but this is different," Clio countered.

"It's *stupid,*" he snapped. "You think August would've let her go just because you showed up and offered to take her place?"

"I had to do *something*!"

"Yeah, turning yourself over to August--great plan."

His scathing disapproval hurt her, made her feel even guiltier because she could see how much she'd freaked him out. But her pride hurt, too. She hadn't planned to waltz into August's clutches, but clearly Chance was going to judge her on her first reaction.

She clenched her teeth. "I found the way out," she said flatly.

His eyes widened as the scowl dropped from his face. The rain had grown harder; rivulets dripped down Clio's face, and she had to blink water from her blurring gaze.

"It's in another tower," she clarified. She added, a little anxious, "But we need the heart August took from me."

She assumed Chance would yell at her for taking another stupid risk, but a resigned expression passed over his face. "Yeah," he murmured. "I figured it would come down to that."

"I...I was thinking...about how we could get it from him," Clio said tentatively. "I know he used to be your friend, and maybe he still is, but--"

"I'm going to steal the heart," Chance interrupted.

"Wh-what?" She could barely get the word out, she was

so floored by his sudden certainty.

"It's the easiest way." He looked up into the pattering rain, his eyebrows drawn together in thought.

Clio wiped water from her own face as she felt her clothes soak through. "Y-you can't *steal* it," she gasped as the rain pelted her with new fervor. "You told me yourself."

Chance shot her a sad grin. "I never said you *can't*."

"You said there are *consequences*!" Clio cried. "What are they?"

Chance sighed. "Rumor is you become an unwilling test subject to the powers that be."

"You'll become a *drooler?!*"

"Or worse."

"No!" Clio shook her head frantically. "Don't be stupid! We'll find another way!"

"It could just be a rumor," Chance murmured. "Maybe I'll get lucky."

"Chance, I mean it. *No*."

He had to be kidding. It was too crazy of an idea, and it didn't make any sense. He wouldn't do that for *her*. Not even if...

He leveled his dark eyes on her, his long eyelashes batting against the torrents of water from above. "Sometimes you have to sacrifice a piece to win the game."

"It's not worth it!"

"I saw this coming. And it *is* worth it if it'll get you out, Clio."

"Not to *me!*" Clio stepped forward and clutched his arms. "Why would you even *think* about doing something like that?!"

"Why would you think about rushing off to help Britt?" A tiny, self-deprecating smile curved Chance's mouth. "August wasn't wrong about everything."

Clio's stomach rolled. "Was it you?" she asked, her voice unsteady. "Was it you who kissed me at that weird feast with all the people in masks? Were *any* of them you?"

A look of regret passed over his face, and Clio wanted to

cry. He wouldn't see it in the rain.

"No," he breathed.

"But you got me away. That *was* you," Clio insisted.

"Yes." His eyes seemed to light up, and Clio watched in fascination as his features softened. "When you asked me to kiss you--even though you didn't know who I was--I was tempted. I wanted to...but not when you were half out of your senses."

She was hit with that sweeping sense of déjà vu that she'd felt with him before; it brought fragments of memories she couldn't quite clarify in her mind. But she remembered the feelings from *that* night. She had wanted him to kiss her, not because she was drugged and half out of her senses, but because he'd *wanted* to. She'd felt that. Because he'd wanted to and *hadn't.*

Clio laughed weakly as the sky opened up and seemed to dump all its contents on them at once. Chance looked at her like she was crazy, and that made her laugh harder. She reached up on her tiptoes and wound her arms around his neck.

She kissed him when his arms tightened around her, drawing her against his chest.

His mouth was warm and soft and eager, and despite the rain that made her break out in goose bumps--was it the *rain* doing that?--she didn't stop to breathe until she began to shiver. Chance pulled her into the shelter of the stairwell.

He started to speak, that obstinate cast spreading over his features, and Clio *knew* he would say this didn't change anything. He was still going to steal the heart.

She interrupted him with another kiss, unwilling to let him say it. Maybe she couldn't change his mind. Maybe he was going to be his typical hard-ass self and run straight into his doom.

But she'd be damned if she let him go alone.

She grinned against his lips. "Let's go find August," she breathed.

Ellery Prime & T2A

♦ ♣ ♠ ♥

Chapter 10

♦ ♣ ♠ ♥

Clio struggled to keep up with Chance's long stride. He seemed oblivious to the pace he was setting, clearly distracted by his thoughts as they made their way through the tunnels below August's stronghold.

"How are we getting to August's rooms without being seen?" she asked, the quick clomp of her boots echoing around them. "The tunnel only goes to the edge of the square."

"We won't need to," Chance said tersely. "The more people that see us, the better."

Clio shot him a look. "What are you talking about?" she asked. *Are you crazy?* she added silently.

"August has always been a little paranoid, but now he's got good reason to be. He's even better guarded than before, and I'm on his shit list at the moment. I can't get near him easily--not when he's alone."

"You should've mentioned that before we got here," Clio muttered. "So what are we going to do, then?"

"We're going to walk in through the main gate."

"*That's* your plan?"

Chance smirked. "Says the girl who was all set to run off and confront August when she thought Britt was in danger."

"I didn't intend to just waltz in," Clio snapped. "How is walking right into August's clutches supposed to help us?"

"We need to get him alone, right?"

Chance's calm demeanor combined with his inability to

get to the point made Clio grit her teeth. "*Yes.*"

"To do that, he needs to trust me." Clio stumbled as Chance stopped abruptly and turned to face her with an intent look. "So do you."

"Okaaay," Clio said. "How are you going to make him trust you?"

"By giving him what he wants." Chance looked almost apologetic when he shrugged at her impatient expression. "You."

"Ugh." Disgust crumpled Clio's face. "Don't put it that way. You make it sound like some sick prisoner-of-war fantasy you've cooked up."

"You know, sometimes you're pretty melodramatic." Chance gave a dry laugh. "But you have a point. Which means August will love it."

Clio snorted. "You're right about that."

She drew her eyebrows together as she tried to think of a better plan, but conceded that Chance probably knew the best way to manipulate August. Anyway, it was time to end this, and she couldn't wait to see the look on August's face when he realized just how screwed he really was.

"Fine," she said at last. "If you're sure it'll work." She shivered a little; her clothes and hair were still damp from the squall they'd been drenched in, and her ponytail clung unpleasantly to the back of her neck. The tunnel was cooler than outside--now that they'd stopped walking, she felt the chill.

"Are you cold?" Chance reached out and rubbed her arms from shoulder to elbow with his warm, broad hands. He didn't seem to be bothered by the dampness of his clothes, and his hair, being so short, was practically dry already. Only the slightly curling ends around the nape of his neck and his temples showed any evidence of the downpour.

Considering their current situation, it was a bit ridiculous to start wondering how curly Chance's hair would be if it were a little longer...but the thought struck her, anyway. He was standing so close now, his head almost brushing the low ceiling.

Clio blushed as she remembered how she'd kissed him so impulsively. She could feel the skin at the base of her throat flutter quickly over her pulse.

"I'm fine," she blurted, pulling away from the actually comforting warmth and hoping the dim light in the tunnels hid the flush in her face. "We need to talk about what happens once we get August alone."

"Like I said--I'll take the charm from him and give it to you." Chance's voice matched the imperious cast of his expression. His eyes narrowed as if he expected her protests and was warning her not to bother. "Then you get back to the tower."

A muscle jumped in Clio's jaw. This pissed her off so much. His attitude was the reason she hadn't listened to him when they'd first met--one of the reasons, anyway.

"Don't talk to me like that. Just because *you* say something doesn't mean we're doing it--especially when your idea is terrible, like this one is." Clio folded her arms across her chest. "We're not stealing it."

"It's the only way to--"

"It *isn't*," she said quickly, cutting him off. "Did you really think I was okay with you doing that? I have a better idea, but first I have a question."

Chance frowned. "What?"

"Why does he want my bracelet so badly? I never really took the time to think about it until recently, but..." Clio cocked her head and watched the look of surprise bloom on Chance's face. "I know why it's important to *me*--I want to get out. But does *he* want to get out? It seems like what he wants is right here, isn't it?"

A long moment passed before Chance answered. Clio's stomach squirmed pleasantly when an admiring grin lightened his features.

"You're right. He doesn't want to get out to *stay* out. But if he has your bracelet, with *all* the charms, then he should be able to come and go as he pleases."

Clio thought about that. August with exclusive access to

all the resources available in the "real world"--things that could give him even more power in the Gauntlet--was a scary thought. He could even bring in *people.*

Clio grimaced.

"Have you ever known anyone that made it out?"

The silence was even longer this time, but Chance finally nodded. "I've heard about people who did, but I've only met one of them."

"Did they come back?" Clio asked with wide eyes.

Chance nodded again.

"Who was it?" Somehow Clio knew what he was going to say before the name left his lips.

"Britt."

Clio's fingers lifted up to the small die nestled on its chain just below her collarbone.

Britt. It stunned her, but it also made a certain kind of sense. Britt's competence, her knowledge and bravery...it came from more than just her personality. She had *experience.*

But why did she come ***back?*** Clio wondered. And did that mean...Clio had *never* needed to save her?

Relief rushed through Clio, although it was twisted up in embarrassment. Maybe she'd overvalued what she could do for Britt. She seemed to...do that a lot, when it came to Britt. But if this meant Britt was okay, even now, even if Clio got out--that was what mattered.

And if Britt had left the Gauntlet before, she could leave again, right? And maybe she and Clio could meet on the other side?

The thought surged excitement through Clio, crushing any last regrets.

Clio looked up at Chance; one other thing still bothered her.

"Why didn't *you* get out?" she asked him. From what she'd seen of him, she couldn't picture him not trying, or giving up before he'd found a way.

Chance's short laugh, devoid of humor, startled her.

"I told you that when we--August and I--first found the

research about the experiments they were doing here, he was completely fascinated. I was, too, to be honest." Chance paced a few feet away and frowned, his eyes distant with memory.

"Well, we didn't find everything at once. Little discoveries here and there that all added up. It was...addictive. August was completely hooked, but as we uncovered more...unethical methods, I started to question what we were doing. I brought up looking for the way out again."

Chance scowled. "It made August angry. That was our first real fight. He said we were meant to be here--that we'd been chosen, and to leave was cowardly and stupid and a waste of our talents. We could take what we'd learned and push it even further, and *then* we could go back and show everyone what we'd done. I disagreed and tried to convince him that we should go back to where we belonged.

"And, well...it was like someone had been *waiting* for us to reach that point. Maybe we would've found the new wing, anyway, but the timing was too perfect."

"What was in the wing?" Clio asked with eager interest.

"A laboratory--better than state of the art, equipped with everything we needed to continue the research. Computers, drugs, records..." Chance met her gaze, a look of self-disgust contorting his face. "There was even a dormitory that dispensed food and water...for what you call the droolers. Test subjects. August was beside himself."

Clio sucked in a breath, one hand unconsciously pressing against her slack lips. "*That* convinced you to stay?"

"Not in my case, no. Oh, it confirmed to August that he was meant to be here, to take over the reins. He felt like he'd been given carte blanche to do as he pleased. I think he would've let me leave without him then, without fighting me on it--he was walking on air. But at that point, he couldn't just let me go."

"Why?" It was some trap of the Gauntlet, Clio was sure. That was exactly the way it worked--offering something that seemed too good to be true.

"We were only given a glimpse of the *wonders* that awaited us." The bitterness in Chance's voice was clearer now. "To access it, *both* of us had to use our version of your bracelet simultaneously. It was both of us or nothing."

A long silence ensued that Clio was a little afraid to break. But when Chance started walking again, she stepped quickly to keep up.

"So you did it, then. I mean...obviously," she said lamely.

"Yeah. August was wild; he wouldn't let up, and he did everything he could to convince me." His jaw tightened. "And I...let myself be convinced. I won't lie. A part of me wanted the knowledge, and to be on the cutting edge of something like that. We *could* change lives. Could've. Of course, there was a catch."

"Of course." Clio exchanged a look of pained amusement with Chance. They understood each other perfectly on that point.

"Our tokens...were taken in the process. We didn't get them back. We knew in advance that would happen, but August convinced me that when we were ready, we could find a way. He said that whoever had put us here wouldn't want us to rot away without sharing what we discovered."

"So...here you are."

"Yes."

"And August is ready now to...what? Publish a paper in some scholarly journal?" Clio scoffed.

"He's drained most of his resources here. Run into dead ends, and the Gauntlet hasn't coughed up anything interesting for a while. Not until you. He wants the freedom he has here, but he needs things from the outside, too--a pipeline he can control for information, drugs, equipment, people..."

Clio pursed her lips. "And he needs my bracelet for that," Clio said slowly, thinking over the implications. "So he can come and go."

Chance grunted. "Yes, but that's not going to happen. I'll take the heart. You'll leave, and both you and the bracelet will be out of his reach."

Chance's dogged persistence with that plan made Clio

scowl. "You think that'll make things *better?"* she clarified. "He'll get even angrier and crazier!"

"I can handle him," Chance said evenly.

"You'll be a drooler!" Clio cried, yanking his arm and digging in her heels so he was forced to stop and look at her.

"We don't know that for sure."

"Just listen, Chance. This place is crazy, and the rules are stupid, but from what I understand... Why...why can't I just take August with me?"

Chance stared at her blankly. His mouth opened, but nothing came out until he finally uttered a simple, "What?"

"I'm serious." Clio paced ahead, outlining her plan with broad gestures of her hands as she talked. "What if we, I don't know, tie him up or something. Instead of stealing the heart back, we take him to the tower where the elevator is. He gets to keep the heart, but we use our charms together, and we leave the Gauntlet together. Once we're outside, I'll destroy my bracelet. He only has one charm, so he won't be able to get back inside."

"And neither will you," Chance said quietly.

Clio jerked her head back. Chance was frowning thoughtfully at the ground.

"But...it could work," he murmured at last.

The fact that he'd given her plan even *that* much approval startled her. The shot of excitement made her clap her hands together eagerly as she stepped toward him.

"It could, *right*? I mean, he'd be let loose out *there*, but he can't be that dangerous without his thugs." Clio laughed gleefully. "He'd be so *pissed off*. He wouldn't have access to the kinds of things he does here. And maybe whoever is... *watching* this place, maybe they'd finally do something about him, too. I don't know, but it seems like the safest option. Don't you think?"

"I think..." Chance straightened, fixing her with one of his intimidating looks and sending her newfound confidence plummeting, "...that you're brilliant."

Clio's breath caught in her throat. She beamed. "Really?"

"Yeah."

Chance was wetter than he looked--his jacket was still soaked through--but Clio didn't mind at all when she plastered herself against him. This was apparently going to be a thing--Chance saying something that made her want to kiss him uncontrollably.

He seemed a little stunned when she pulled away, though his hands warmed her back through the thin fabric of her T-shirt. He seemed in no hurry to release her. "What was that for?"

Clio grinned. "You're a lot less obnoxious on further acquaintance."

One dark eyebrow rose. "Thanks?"

"Come on." Clio laughed and grabbed his hand. "The exit isn't far. We can figure out the details of what we'll say to him on the way, and you can start practicing your looming and stuff."

"I don't loom." Chance actually sounded insulted, which made Clio snicker. "I'm just tall."

They made it to the exit in about ten minutes, ironing out their plan as well as they could considering August's unpredictable nature. Even if things didn't go exactly as planned, Clio was still glad to be taking *action* for once; she felt both excitement and a real sense of hope that this time, things would go her way.

A quick survey of the area showed that it was clear. After they emerged from the tunnels, they looked at each other in nervous anticipation.

"Ready?" Chance asked.

Clio nodded.

Chance snorted, but Clio was amused to know, despite the nervous twisting in her stomach, that he *did* draw himself up and assume his most off-putting air. He gripped her arm to complete the look.

Clio let Chance tug her along somewhat, like she was at his mercy. It wasn't hard, considering how much faster he was and the strength of his grip--and that bothered her a little. But it seemed to work, since the two of them made it into the main square without being challenged.

A murmur of voices rose around them; Chance nodded at a trio of uniformed men as they passed. The flutter in Clio's stomach intensified as she heard them fall into step behind her and Chance. Someone darted into the building they were approaching.

She expected to see August waiting in the entry hall, but he wasn't there. They passed through the room, under countless curious stares, until another one of August's guards silently pointed them toward a salon.

August sat on an ornate wingback chair inside--one leg leisurely swinging over the edge of the intricately carved arm, his face dimpled by a smile. Sunshine stood next to him, glowering in counterpoint to his master's cheer. August's good humor seemed genuine as Chance dragged her into the room with their silent escort behind them.

Ugh. All of Clio's loathing for August hit her full force again. Her nose wrinkled as she looked at him, but he merely swept his gaze to Chance.

"You finally caught the little mouse," August drawled. "I was starting to think you weren't committed to the search."

"She found a bolt-hole," Chance said simply. "Ran out when she heard your announcement."

August laughed. "It worked!" He rose from the chair and fussed with his already immaculate clothing, flashing the new band he wore around his wrist--which dangled Clio's heart charm--before he pulled his cuff over it and gave his attention to Clio. She couldn't help but grit her teeth as his eyes roamed over her.

"She looks like a drowned rat." His eyes narrowed. "Why is she so cooperative? What did you do to her?"

"Nothing." Clio didn't take her eyes off of August, but in her peripheral vision, she saw Chance glance at her. "I just convinced her that I'm on her side."

It took a moment for the words to penetrate, but something cold settled in Clio when she turned to him in feigned shock. Well, mostly feigned. A nagging sense of paranoia helped fuel the act.

He's playing August, not me, Clio told herself. He'd rejected her bracelet. He *was* on her side. But the not unnatural fear of betrayal still made her hands tremble.

"You...you said this would save Britt!" Clio cried at Chance.

"It won't. Britt isn't here." Chance snorted, and his glare was disturbingly dark. "You were a fool to trust me."

Clio bit the inside of her cheek and tried not to panic. Then she realized she *should* look like she was panicking, and started tugging at Chance's grip and pounding his arm with her free fist. She hit him...maybe harder than she needed to.

"You bastard!" she shouted. "You lied to me!"

August found her reaction extremely entertaining, judging by his nasty, suggestive laugh. "Well done, Chance. Maybe there's hope for you still."

Clio's flaring fear twisted into anger, so she unleashed it on the man she *knew* was her enemy. She snapped her head to August.

"*Pig!*" she snarled. She lunged forward, ready to rip out handfuls of August's artfully styled hair and shove them down his throat.

Sunshine reached for her even as Chance jerked her back against his chest, holding her arms in an iron-like grip. He talked over her like she wasn't there. "She's mine, right? *No one*--" Chance turned his glare on Sunshine, "can touch her."

Clio's stomach churned. She looked up at Chance, but his eyes were locked on August.

August smirked. "Of course," he cooed, seemingly delighted by Chance's claim. "Once I've gotten what I want."

"You'll get it," Chance promised flatly. "She found a way out."

That wiped the smile off August's face. "What?" he snapped, unable to hide his avid expression. "*Where?*"

"Do you want to talk about that here?" Chance's head cocked only slightly, but August's gaze slid past him--to the silent guards and the people gathered in curious knots in the room behind them.

"No." August shook his head. "Not here." He snapped his fingers and strode out of the salon.

Chance followed, keeping a tight hold on Clio. Sunshine was right behind them. The guards brought up the rear, but they weren't allowed in August's room--they remained outside as Sunshine shut the door.

Clio tried to slow her racing heart.

August sat down for a moment, then almost immediately sprang up. He was practically shaking with eagerness. "Well?!"

"The west tower," Chance answered.

"The tower..." August's eyes narrowed, but then he gave a wide smile. "So she found a way in. You've been a busy girl, huh? No wonder we couldn't find you."

"I guess I found the corner of the kingdom not even the king can enter," Clio said through her teeth. She tried to flash a mocking smile.

August sneered. "You're boring me now. Give me the bracelet and you won't have to spend any more time down in my labs. Of course, if you *want* my attention, then I suppose we can do it the hard way." She tried to ignore the hard shine in his eyes.

"Can't do it," Clio retorted. "I don't have it anymore."

"You're lying."

"I'm not." Clio raised her bare arms up and away from her body. She added, as evenly as she could, "You're welcome to search me."

August stared for a moment; he snapped his gaze at Chance in dawning fury. "You didn't make sure she had it before you brought her here? Where did you hide it, you little--"

"She didn't hide it," Chance interrupted, cutting off August's burgeoning rant. "She gave it me." He slipped a hand into the pocket of his jacket and pulled out the bracelet.

August gaped almost comically, and then he began to laugh. Slowly, he clapped his hands. "I didn't think you had it in you."

"To be honest, I was just as surprised as you were." Chance didn't look at Clio, but she knew he was thinking about the moment she'd put all her trust in him. She nervously clenched her hands.

"I always knew how it would end," August said exultantly. "And I told you, even though you never believed me! But I was right. Now give it to me." August extended his hand, palm up, with exactly the audacious entitlement Clio expected.

Chance shook his head and tucked the bracelet in his pocket again. "After we're out," Chance countered. "We go together, *with* Clio. Then we part ways and I go with her."

A measure of relief rushed through Clio, especially as August's face tightened in a brief flash of anger. But it disappeared just as quickly.

"So *you're* the one being played, Chance." August shrugged. "Of course, if you really want to throw away everything we've built for *her*," his tone made his opinion of Clio's worth crystal clear, "then I won't try to talk you out of it, and I'll learn to live without your lovesick ass. I just have a few preparations to make first."

"No," Chance said sharply. "We go now."

Clio watched the tense standoff nervously, but August backed down first. He walked to the far wall and touched the side of a bookshelf; it slid aside.

"Fine," August said shortly. "Let's go."

Chance raised an eyebrow. "Through the labs?"

"No prying eyes." August smirked. "Coming?"

"After you." Chance pulled Clio closer.

August ducked through the revealed door, Sunshine following right behind. Chance pulled her through before she could hesitate.

The white, stark halls were exactly as Clio remembered. August stopped at one of the doors that lined the wall and glanced back.

"I need to get something from my office." He flashed his

teeth. "You don't mind, right?"

Clio threw Chance a wary look, but he only shrugged. "Stay out here," he told her before following August and Sunshine into the room. She clenched her teeth and stood just outside the door to watch.

August pulled a small case from a drawer. "Everything I'll need for now is in here. Well, *everything...*" He turned and leaned casually against the desk, "except for the bracelet." He grinned, and added lightly, "Sunshine, take it from Chance."

Sunshine was a blur of movement before Clio even processed the words.

She gasped when Chance staggered across the room from the force of the impact, his back cracking into a display case and sending things crashing to the floor. Sunshine was on him a second later, his hands squeezing Chance around the throat.

Clio screamed Chance's name and launched herself at Sunshine, instinctively dragging at his bulging arms. Chance's face was red, his eyes had gone glassy, and his hands grasped ineffectually at Sunshine's relentless grip.

August laughed behind them, and Clio almost choked on her terror. In another fit of desperation, she reached up--glad of her ragged, bitten fingernails for once--and raked her nails across Sunshine's face.

She had only a split second to see the white lines bloom to a bright red before Sunshine swept one arm back viciously and knocked her to the floor. She gasped, winded, and heard Chance rasp out a string of words she couldn't make out.

Sunshine slumped to his knees on the floor, his head lolling forward, and didn't move again. Clio stared in shock from him to Chance, who bent over his knees and sucked in gulps of air.

It was August who moved next--fury contorting any remaining charm in his face. He lifted a syringe over his head, poised to plunge.

"Chance!" she cried.

Chance looked up and caught August's wrist as it arced down. They grappled as the syringe hit the floor.

Clio scrambled backwards, trying to get to her feet, and her hand brushed something cold and hard--a statue that had fallen. Her fingers wrapped around the bronze figure.

She lunged toward August and swung as hard as she could.

The statue caught August on the temple; he crumpled just like Sunshine, only he fell all the way to the floor in a limp heap. Clio stared at Chance with wild eyes, her heart pounding fiercely in her chest.

"Wh-what did you do to Sunshine?" she blurted. The kneeling giant hadn't moved a hair.

"Trigger phrase. August's specialty." Chance smiled grimly. "He didn't know I had one, too."

Clio felt ill, but she was too keyed up to dwell on it. She watched as Chance knelt next to August and managed to hoist him over his shoulder.

"He's not dead, is he?"

"No. He'll live." Chance turned his dark eyes to her. "Thank you."

Clio stared back, feeling rather numb.

"He was going to sacrifice Sunshine to get the bracelet. Sunshine would've given it to him." Clio's revulsion broke through some of her quiet shock. "And he'd have it free and clear."

Chance grunted. "Come on. Let's get this over with. Bring the syringe."

Clio picked it up gingerly and followed Chance to another room. She opened the door for him and looked around at the medical supplies that lined the walls.

A dull thud made Clio jump. Chance had dumped August's limp body onto a gurney. She hurried to help Chance fasten the restraints, breathing easier once the wrist and ankles straps were attached. The three straps across the body were probably overkill, but she wasn't willing to take any chances--and neither was Chance, apparently.

August was already starting to stir; Clio took an involuntary step backward when his eyes opened. She could see the exact moment his confusion cleared. He jerked violently and spewed a litany of foul language, his gaze locked on her.

Clio recoiled.

"It's all right." Chance advanced on the gurney, holding a bit gag made of black leather and a long, slender bar. "You don't have to listen to this."

"Chance," August immediately began to plead. "Don't do this. It's always been us. *You* were the one who turned your back on that! We can finally do what we talked about--put our research out there, get the best of both worlds! *Chance...*"

Chance paused, but his expression was stony, even as August shot Clio a venomous look. "Don't let her come between us! You can't trust her. She just wants to use you!"

Chance gave a short laugh. He bent over August, who tossed his head wildly as Chance tried to force the gag into his mouth. Chance grunted impatiently and called Clio.

"You've got the syringe? If he doesn't calm down, just jab it in his thigh."

August shook his head frantically. "Chance...what are you doing? *Don't*. That's just a sedative. Until I could get you to listen to reason. Things will change--I swear. I won't hurt Clio. We can all work together--"

"It's too late," Chance said softly. "And we both know you'll say anything to get what you want. You'll *do* anything."

"Wai--mmph..."

Chance shoved the bit into August's mouth. August struggled until Clio moved forward at Chance's nod and held the syringe poised over August's leg. She swallowed hard, but shot him a look that promised she'd do it if she had to.

August's eyes rolled wildly, but he stopped resisting. Chance buckled the gag and tightened it until August could do no more than make garbled noises.

"Let's go. The sooner we get out of here, the better." Chance started rolling the gurney out into the hallway, and Clio followed, holding out the syringe.

"What about this?" she asked.

"We'll keep it." Chance took it from her and tucked it into

a pocket at the side of the gurney. "Just in case."

August struggled again, making guttural grunts around the gag, but Chance didn't even glance down at him. She jogged along as they wheeled the gurney through the hallways.

"Why are you so quiet?" Chance finally asked when all Clio did was glance at him.

She shook her head and shrugged. "I...I clocked August over the head." She started giggling, and it turned into full-fledged, breathless laughter. She had to lean against the gurney as she bent over from the force of it. "Did you see him just *drop?"*

A snarl from August made her laugh even harder. She looked down at his furious eyes, his disheveled hair, and the mortification on his face at his undignified state. He was *seething*.

"It was..." All of a sudden, her knees turned to jelly as whatever adrenaline had been fueling her disappeared. Clio sank down to a crouch against the wall, still laughing.

"Oh my God, it was so..." Clio gasped. "I thought... I thought Sunshine was going to kill you." The hysterical laughter went on long enough to make her stomach hurt. It was better than crying, though--better than the appalled nausea that made her want to throw up. Things hadn't gone as planned, exactly, but they were still alive.

Chance's eyebrows rose, and his mouth quirked. He walked around the gurney and held out a hand.

Clio grabbed it and let him pull her to her feet, a few stray giggles slipping out as she tried to compose herself. She leaned against him for a moment, appreciating that he understood her inappropriate release of emotion.

"And you say *my* sense of humor is odd," Chance said dryly.

"I'm sorry." Clio didn't mean it. "But that felt kind of good."

"I'm sure. But we need to get out of here."

Clio flashed Chance a smile. "Right." Despite everything,

her spirits were soaring now that they were finally on their way out.

They rolled August through the hallways to a different exit than the one Black Jack had taken her to. A small elevator--just big enough to fit the length of the gurney--took them to street level. They slipped out of the building and were able to navigate the alleys without seeing anyone else. The only tricky part was getting August into the tunnels that led to the tower.

By collapsing the leg-locking mechanism, they were able to slide him down into the tunnel. Clio's grip slipped at the end and August landed on the floor with a hard bump. He groaned.

"Oops." Clio kept a straight face as they raised the gurney onto its wheels again.

Chance snorted. "You're enjoying this, aren't you?"

"You have *no* idea." Clio felt like she had every right to enjoy a little revenge. She'd feel even better once August realized just what was going to happen to him. She wished she had a camera.

"You're kind of scary when you smile like that," Chance observed, one eyebrow cocked in mock wariness.

"Don't worry," Clio said cheekily, "I won't hurt *you*."

"That's good to know."

Clio was about to retort when a gagging sound stopped her. She looked down and saw August's face twisted in a look of disgust, obvious even with the slight distortion of his features caused by the gag. Apparently, August didn't appreciate their banter.

She made sure to aim for every rough patch and bump in the floor she could find, and they made good time through the tunnels. When they emerged to street level to make their way to the other tower, their pace slowed a bit; they still had to be wary about any people loyal to August. But no one appeared, and soon enough, the shadow of the tower fell across their path.

For the last time, Clio opened the door, and they pushed

August inside. He was all attention then, doing his best to take in everything from his limited viewpoint. His eyes roved greedily around the interior as if to consume all its secrets.

It wasn't like Clio wanted to keep him in suspense. She rolled him right up to the elevator and let him get an eyeful of the panel. His reaction was gratifying. His eyes widened, and he jerked at his restraints. Garbled words spilled out from behind the gag.

For once, Clio wanted to hear what he had to say. She reached for the buckles behind his head and peeled the gag away.

August's jaw worked as he stretched the muscles that had been locked in place, but he didn't speak yet. His fingers spread and stretched toward the display of symbols. His face was transformed by a simmering excitement that made no sense given that he was still strapped down and helpless.

Clio watched him with a revolted kind of fascination. He really *did* completely buy into his own hype.

"This is it, Chance," he said, his voice hoarse and throbbing with barely leashed exultation. "We can finally do everything we talked about." He ignored Clio completely, turning the full force of his charisma on Chance. "I know we've had our differences, but just *think*...just think what we can do now."

"Yes," Chance said softly. "I *have* thought about it." His fingers reached for the buckle of the strap at August's wrist, but he paused in the middle of loosening the leather strap. "It's you who forgot our plans, wasn't it?"

"No, I never did! I got sidetracked--I admit that. Maybe I did some things that I'm not proud of, but I was...I was angry that we were trapped." August spoke rapidly, his feverish gaze locked on Chance. "But that's over. We have everything we want now...everything we need. Chance, you can't abandon what we started now."

"What about Clio?"

August's eyes flicked to her for a moment, but returned to Chance. "She can come with us, okay? I'm sorry I stood in your way before. I was too focused on making sure we could get out of here--making everything we planned happen. I'm sorry." He rolled his head to meet Clio's riveted gaze. His expression appeared to exude such sincere remorse that Clio was almost impressed by his ability to lie so well.

"Clio, I know I didn't treat you well, but you know how this place can get you to. I had to find a way out. I *had* to."

She let out a breath. "Then you want to get out? Even with me?" Now that it had come to this point, she felt as if she was watching from a distance--above everything, yet also thrumming with a sense of secret knowledge, of superiority, of the deep-rooted amusement that came from knowing she held all the cards. Was this how August felt when he manipulated people?

"Yes." His earnest murmur, accompanied by a heartfelt grin that showed his dimples, was perfectly designed to emphasize his boyish charm. "We'll beat whoever's behind the Gauntlet at their own game. Finally. I know you want that."

"Yeah," Clio agreed. "I do." She nodded at Chance, and his fingers worked at the buckle of the restraint.

"Yes," August hissed, his fingers twitching in anticipation. "You won't regret this, I swear."

Chance lifted August's arm. The sleeve of his jacket slid down, exposing the chain bracelet that held the heart charm. August let him press the little charm into the matching groove. A slight magnetic pull engaged and it clicked in place.

Chance pulled Clio's bracelet from his own pocket while August watched, an avid gleam in his eyes. One by one, Chance removed the charms and pushed them into their slots.

Without any fanfare, the elevator door slid open.

It was empty and plain--an elevator that could exist in any building in the world, just like those Clio had first encountered in the Gauntlet. Her heart sped up and she looked at Chance.

This is it.

He nodded, a small smile playing about his lips.

A small click was the only warning before the magnetism that held the charms released. The heart fell and swung from the bracelet around August's wrist, while the other three charms clinked lightly on the floor. Chance bent over and picked them up, then passed them over to Clio along with the bracelet itself--from which the joker charm still dangled. "This is yours."

"What are you doing?" August cried.

"Don't worry," Clio said with a vicious grin. "You're still coming with us. It's just that it's going to be a one-way trip."

"He's going with *you*," Chance corrected her. He gave the gurney a push through the open elevator doors, ignoring August's fresh curses and frothing speech.

Clio froze. "Chance...no, you're coming, too."

"I can't just leave things like this. There's a power vacuum now, and August isn't the only one to worry about."

Clio's insides shriveled. "But *you* don't have to fix it all!" she said angrily. "Why can't anything *ever* be easy here?!"

"I've been a big part of the mess August made. I *have* to clean it up." Chance didn't flinch from her anger. "I never told *you* I was going with you," he pointed out.

"Yeah, but...but I thought..." Clio trailed off.

August started laughing, and they both looked at him with varying degrees of weary disgust.

"Looks like you're getting dumped again, Clio," August crowed.

Clio's eyes narrowed, but before she could retort, Chance pulled her forward into the open doorway of the elevator.

"I'm not dumping you," Chance said with an infuriating smirk, one that made her stomach flutter a little even as she frowned up at him. "Are you dumping *me*?"

"I should," Clio quipped. "Long-distance relationships suck."

Chance's expression softened, and this time, *he* kissed *her*. Even August's snide remarks couldn't ruin it.

Chance pulled back and smiled at her. "Try to resist the temptation to throttle him and focus on getting out."

Clio laughed. "No promises."

The smile faded from Chance's face, and he gently pushed

Clio backward. "Take this." He handed her a small envelope. "Open it when you're home."

She nodded, her fingers curling around the envelope. Her throat tightened, and Clio couldn't do anything but stare mutely as Chance took a step back and the doors began to close.

August thrashed and cursed behind her, but she barely noticed. She was finally leaving, after all this time, because of the help she'd received from Chance and Britt and Black Jack--even Lilah. She never would have expected her emotions to be so mixed when it came to this.

Right before the doors sealed, she reached out blindly toward the gap. "Chance!"

Her hand slapped impotently against the blank doors, and her head dropped. "Thank you..." she whispered.

The elevator took them down. The doors slid open and a long hallway stretched out before her.

Clio tucked the envelope away, took a deep breath, and wheeled August out of the elevator. Curiosity had shut him up for the moment. His head lifted as he peered forward.

Doorways lined the walls on both sides, and Clio could see that the doors to the rooms were half open. She didn't relish the idea of having to walk past each one. This place was clean and obviously well-maintained compared to the nightmare building she'd first been thrown into, but it was still creepy.

Her gaze focused on the far end of the corridor and the exit sign. The red letters were a bright beacon.

Clio began walking, her boots clicking on the clean tile. She glanced into the rooms as she passed them. All held neat beds--made with fresh linens--and small items of furniture that were dusted and bare, just waiting for an occupant. It was like a before and after picture, only she was seeing it in reverse order. The chaos and grime of her beginning had finally led to this.

August found his voice again.

"Clio, listen to me. I know you have every right to be angry, but I--"

"Shut up, August, or I'll drug you right now," Clio said mildly. "You said you wanted out, even if it was with me--so you're getting your wish."

His face screwed up in desperate anger, and his eyes rolled back a little as he tried to look at her. "But I-- *You* won't have any way to get back inside. Not unless we work together."

Clio laughed. "I have no intention of letting you get back inside. I'm going to take you through that exit door, and then I'm going to leave you there--wherever it is. Then I'll destroy the rest of my charms so you can never use them."

"You have no idea what you've been given! *This* is why you deserve to be treated like a pawn! What's so great about your life out there? You were so scared in here--you just scuttled around never thinking, never *seeing* the potential, just reacting to things like a dumb lab rat."

It stung. Clio couldn't help but lash back. "Isn't that exactly what you are, too?"

"I'm no one's lab rat," August sneered. "I made choices. I did things. *Brilliant* things. I didn't run and hide. And I'm not a hypocrite like you."

"I'm not a hypocrite," Clio said angrily.

"You cry about how badly you've been treated, but you've used plenty of people in here, or you'd never have gotten so far. You're just as willing to use people as I am--and then leave them behind."

"That's not true," Clio said with less confidence than she liked.

"It is. We both know it's true." August strained his neck to look at her. "But it's not too late."

Clio paused just before the exit and walked around the side of the gurney. "I never said I was giving up on the people in here."

"No? How are you going to help them? You need *me* to do that," August countered.

Clio watched a smug smile spread across August's face. "I'm so embarrassed that I ever found you attractive. Seriously." Clio bent down and grinned just inches from his nose.

"Keep the heart charm. Think of me every time you look at it. Remember it was *me* who kicked you out of your sandbox and *me* who kept you from going back."

"I'll make you regret this." August practically choked on the words as Clio leaned against the bar of the door and pushed. She began pulling him through. "No matter how long it--"

A shrieking siren pierced the air as the heavy door swung shut; the bright light beyond flickered and went out.

A familiar rush of adrenaline raced through her veins. Clio froze, one hand on the gurney, her face raised to test the air.

A sudden whoosh of something stirred the loose hair around her face. A hiss, loud in the dark, came from up high, along with a faint chemical odor. A moment later, her knees began to sink to the ground and her eyelids drooped.

A smile curved her lips before she hit the floor.

♦♣♠♥

The warmth was oppressive.

It woke her from her dream, but the light kept Clio from opening her eyes. It was too bright beyond her eyelids. Clio groaned and rolled away from it and into a blessed, cool dimness.

Wait.

After a moment, she forced her eyelids apart. She slowly turned her head, blinking rapidly in the light.

She was alone in a large room, lying next to a shaft of sunlight that streamed in through a stained glass window above a set of grand, red doors. The room was cavernous, but spotless. Surfaces were shiny and immaculate. Her heart leapt into her throat.

This was it. This was *The Building*--the first face of the Gauntlet, the building she'd entered on that fateful night she'd met the Jacks.

She was finally back at the start.

She pushed herself to her feet, then turned slowly in a

complete circle to take in everything. She half-expected to see the crazy old lady who'd given her the bracelet still huddled in a pile of trash in the corner.

But there was nothing. No lady, no rubbish, no rats--not even August.

She spared a brief thought for him, but he wasn't her concern past that exit door. This was *her* ending--back out the way she came. It made a Gauntlet sort of sense, she supposed.

All she had to do was walk out the door.

A strange reluctance made her limbs feel heavy as she crossed the last twenty feet. The clomp of her boots rang loudly in her ears.

She threw a look over her shoulder at the door at the far end of the entry hall.

"What would happen if I turned around and went back into that maze?" she asked quietly, although her voice still sounded loud in the empty room. No answer came, so Clio was left to wonder.

A dry laugh escaped her. "I'm not about to find out now."

She faced forward and pushed the huge doors open. Bright sunshine made her blink as she stepped outside. She sneezed three times as the sensation tickled her nose. A lovely breeze cooled her warm skin, and, even more wonderful, the sounds of people and not so distant traffic reached her ears.

She stumbled down the steps into the odd little neighborhood she remembered. Its squat buildings looked the same, but not ominous at all in the early morning light. She saw clotheslines adorned with white linens and bright clothing. She heard laughter, and two small boys ran across the courtyard, chasing a ball. A woman's voice called from somewhere.

Across the small square, she could see a vendor's stall at the end of an alley. Her nose told her it was selling pastries and breads. The sweet smell made her stomach growl. Clio realized that she was grinning widely.

"Everything's still here. Still the same."

She'd questioned her sanity more than once, but other than the fact that she was talking to herself on the steps of an abandoned--so to speak--building, this was reality. Normalcy. She appeared to have finally reentered the life she remembered.

The two little boys grabbed their ball and looked at her. Their heads bent together and they giggled. Clio didn't mind.

"Time to go," she murmured, and she walked down the steps.

At the bottom, her backpack sat innocently on the lowest stair. Clio sucked in a gasp of surprised pleasure. The unexpected sight of this mundane reminder of how she'd started out left her so disoriented that she had to sink down and sit on the steps.

Inside the backpack were all the little necessities of her life out here: keys, identification, money. Even the book she'd taken during a scavenging run with Britt was there.

All the realities of her old life slammed into her at once. Would her apartment still be there? Would her job? Would her family have come looking for her? What kind of mess would she be stepping back into?

She'd thought of those things before, of course, in the Gauntlet. But after the first couple of weeks, they'd become distant worries, almost unreal because her immediate problems were so much more compelling.

What was she going to do if everything was gone? How would she explain?

"Hey!"

Clio looked up to see a red ball rolling toward her. It bounced against her feet, and the two boys waved their arms wildly. "Throw it back!"

She stood up, slinging her backpack over one shoulder and hefting the lightweight ball in the other hand. She drew her arm back and threw. The ball arced high, and the boys laughed and ran, jostling each other as they vied to catch it.

A bemused smile crossed her face, and she began walking toward the alley and that delicious smell. *First things first.* She would have breakfast, and then she would see what happened after that.

She found herself noticing, as she made her way through

the city, the vividness of the day, the clarity of the speech around her. Even the facades of the buildings seemed to stand out in sharp relief. The cooing pigeons intruded stridently on her notice, as did all the pungent odors of the city.

But it was the people she noticed the most. The man she bought a pastry from--did he look at her just a little too long? The woman across the aisle on the bus--did she give Clio a knowing smile? Even those little boys in the courtyard made her think.

How did she know she wasn't still playing the game?

"Don't be paranoid," she said under her breath, though strangely, the uncertainty didn't alarm her. The too-fast race of her pulse put a bounce in her step, and she approached the brownstone walk-up that housed her fourth-floor apartment.

Her key fit.

The apartment was untouched. Her things were just as she had left them. The air was stale; she opened all the windows to let the morning breeze circulate through the small rooms. Clio pulled off her boots and backpack, sat on her couch, and put her feet on the small coffee table in front of it.

"I'm home," she said softly, testing the truth of it.

There was so much to think about--mundane things. Should she contact her job? Her family? But somehow, she wasn't worried. She had a feeling that it had all been taken care of.

A car honked on the street. Other sounds filtered through the open windows as Clio reached into her pocket and pulled out the envelope Chance had given her.

Her fingers smoothed over the unmarked surface. The envelope was light and thin. She pried up a corner of the V-shaped flap and tore it open. The only thing inside was a small card.

On its plain, white face, an address glittered in gold ink.

♦ ♣ ♠ ♥

Clio navigated the busy avenue with brisk steps. Her

freshly cut hair brushed against her jawline as the wind ruffled it. Over the last two weeks, the weather had finally begun to turn, and the clammy heat of summer had given way to crisper mornings.

The people on the street wore lightweight jackets or pullovers with hoods that could be easily removed when it warmed up later in the day. Clio was just happy it gave her an excuse to wear her boots.

Their magic seemed to work outside the Gauntlet just as well, making her feel ten feet taller and strong. A harlequin diamond-patterned scarf was knotted loosely at her throat, set off by her black sweater. She felt confident, enjoying the looks sent her way that told her she was striking as she walked with her head up and her eyes alert.

She felt ready.

Clio paused at the curb and raised her hand; a yellow cab pulled up beside her. The cab driver threw an assessing look at her over his shoulder when she gave him the address, but he turned back with a grunt of acknowledgment and drove.

They wound through an area of the city far from any stations of public transportation. This elite neighborhood seemed worlds away from the frenetic bustle of the parts of the city she knew.

They pulled up in front of a building that was tall and slender, a mere sliver compared to the high-rises of the city's common quarters. It was beautiful--glass and steel, almost too fragile to exist.

Her stomach churned as she stepped out of the cab. Every step toward the building's entrance made it twist a little more, and her hand trembled slightly as she pressed the intercom next to the door. She was highly conscious of the security cameras trained on her from both corners of the entryway.

A woman's voice acknowledged her presence--muted, but clear. "Yes?"

"I'm here..." Clio began, but she stumbled on her words. "I'm here to see..."

With a sudden flush of embarrassment, Clio realized that

as much as she'd rehearsed the things she wanted to say to whoever she found at this address, she had not planned how to introduce herself--or even how to get in the door.

"Yes?" the voice asked again in clear amusement.

That made Clio angry. "I'm here to see whoever's behind the Gauntlet," she said bluntly.

The silence went on for too long, and for a moment, Clio felt a sick sinking in the pit of her stomach. What if she'd come here for nothing? What if these people thought she was crazy or trying to scam them or God knows what? Maybe this was just a final way to trick her.

Clio frowned, but then she raised her arm to the camera and tugged at the sleeve of her sweater to expose her wrist. The joker charm--all alone--swung from the silver bracelet.

The intercom buzzed loudly, and Clio heard the locks on the door click.

"Enter. Take the elevator up."

"To what floor?" Clio asked, but no response came. She shrugged and went inside.

The elevator was at the side of a modern lobby decorated with abstract paintings and metal sculptures in twisted configurations. The interior of the elevator was paneled in mirrors. Only one of the buttons worked--the penthouse.

"Up." Her reflection grinned wryly back at her. It almost felt like a stranger's face, even though, except for her shorter hair, she looked the same as when all this had begun.

The elevator stopped smoothly and the doors slid apart with barely a whisper, opening directly onto what appeared to be a large, open living area. The furnishings looked expensive but lived in. Instead of the stark, postmodern lines she expected, the room exuded a subtle warmth and comfort that actually put her more at ease.

The doors on the far wall were retracted, opening almost the entire length of the room to a spacious terrace tiled in muted Mediterranean shades of blue and green. Clio stepped out of the elevator.

"Hello?"

She went farther in, but no one was in the room. Hallways branched off to either side of her, but she heard no sound from any of them. She went out onto the terrace and waited, admiring the breathtaking view of the sprawling city.

"So you've come to us at last."

Clio whirled around.

An attractive woman of indeterminate age watched her with a playful half-smile. She was dressed in a white, knee-length sheath dress and a pair of brown sandals. Her blonde hair was swept over one shoulder, and Clio was struck by a sense of familiarity.

"You were expecting me?" Clio asked, a hint of uncertainty creeping into her thoughts.

"Of course. Would you like to sit down?" The woman swept a well-manicured hand toward a set of cushioned lounge chairs. She took a seat in one and looked at Clio placidly. "We've expected you for the past two weeks."

Clio flushed. She wasn't sure if that statement was meant to be a rebuke, but she felt it, anyway--and felt the need to offer an explanation.

"I needed time to think," she said, her chin lifting slightly in unconscious defense of her choice.

"And did you?" the woman asked, curling her legs beneath her like she was preparing for a cozy, comfortable chat with a girlfriend.

"I..." Clio frowned, thrown off by the woman's casual demeanor. "Yes, I did."

The woman smiled that half-smile again, as if she were enjoying a private joke. "Please sit down, Clio. Would you like something to drink?"

"I don't want anything to drink," Clio snapped, almost immediately feeling guilty for her rudeness when she hadn't been treated badly. But the woman had called her Clio. She knew who Clio was, so that meant she *was* involved with the Gauntlet somehow.

Clio stood her ground and looked the woman in the eye. "I want to know who you are."

"Is that all?" Despite the irritating undercurrent of humor in the woman's voice, Clio was distracted by a sense of familiarity again. It was like trying to recall a word or a name on the tip of her tongue. Clio's thoughts were cut off when the woman offered, "You may call me Regina."

The woman--Regina--held out her hand, and Clio automatically stepped forward and took it. Then she frowned and let go.

"That's not what I meant," Clio said in sharp retort, "and you know it. I want to know what you have to do with the Gauntlet. Are you...are you the one running it? Are you the one responsible for putting me in there?"

"Responsible?" Regina tilted her head. "But you chose to enter it."

Clio balked. "I didn't *choose* it. I was chased into it!"

"You were chased, yes." Regina regarded her with a display of mild puzzlement. "But it was your choice to enter."

"You call that a *choice?*" Clio cried indignantly.

"Of course. You were given opportunities to turn back. I offered you one myself."

Clio scoffed and shook her head. "What are you talking about?"

"I offered to share my cab with you." Regina smiled, and Clio flashed back to that fateful day, before night had fallen and she'd wandered into unknown territory. Clio gasped, remembering the way she'd admired the woman's poise.

That was why Regina seemed so familiar--or part of the reason, anyway.

Clio's brow furrowed in frustration. "Are you trying to tell me that if I'd taken that ride, none of this would have happened?"

Regina merely smiled.

"But that makes no sense!"

"It doesn't?"

Clio got the feeling that the woman was studying her, as if trying to decide how much to actually reveal.

"I thought... Well, it seemed like you--or whoever it was--

wanted me in the Gauntlet," Clio said haltingly. "If that's true, why did you give me a chance to...avoid it?"

"Three chances," Regina corrected. "You were warned away by the man with the ice cream cart, and I believe you were offered a haven by two young men. As to *why,* well... the simple answer is that it makes the outcome so much more interesting."

Clio stared, hardly noticing as she sank into the chair nearest the woman. "So...so it was really just a game...some bizarre, twisted game?" Her face contorted. "*Why?* What's the point? Why did that man...the Jacks...any of them go along with it?!"

"The point..." Regina gave a curious tilt of her head. "You should ask them."

Clio opened her mouth. Nothing came out. There had to be a reason she was chosen by the higher-ups for the Gauntlet. They'd sent her in because of August, right? That had been her theory in the end. She'd been a pawn, but at least a pawn had *meaning.*

Was she wrong, or was she being misled *now*?

"Was *everybody* I met just playing the game?" she asked in a lost voice. "Just...playing a part?"

Regina released a soft chuckle. "Everyone plays a part every single day."

"Quit...quit *toying* with me," Clio cried, her face twisting in angry confusion. "Was *any* of it real?!"

"You ask that question like it has a meaning beyond what meaning we each give it." Regina bestowed a look on Clio that was almost sympathetic. "Can you tell me how it will affect you if I answer yes or no? Does it matter?"

"Yes!" Clio cried. "Of course it does!" Her hands spread in disbelief. "I... What I went through..."

She had invested *so* much--been taken away from her *life.* It hardly mattered if everyone seemed to think that her life was too mundane to be worth considering--it had been *hers.* Everything that had happened--especially with Britt, with August and Chance--had left a profound mark on her. If it was all just a lie, she didn't think she could cope with that. Every feeling revolted.

"What right do you have to treat anyone like this?" she asked in a tight, accusing whisper. "Why do you do it?"

"Because we can," Regina said simply. "Maybe we're simply bored." Her voice was almost kind. "Let me ask you this: will you believe my answers?"

"No," Clio said grudgingly, realizing it was the truth. "I could never take your word for it. But it's your fault I feel that way. Is that the point of the Gauntlet? To make someone doubt everything?"

Regina's lips pursed as if she didn't quite agree with that interpretation. "Everything that we experience is subjective. Perhaps one lesson is to learn that two people never completely share the same truth."

Clio shook her head in denial. "That's just a cop-out--a way to avoid responsibility for what you've done."

"I have no wish to deny what you call responsibility." The playful smile was back. "Those of us who...oversee the Gauntlet...have shouldered that responsibility for a very long time. We come and go, but the Gauntlet remains. It's much bigger than you can imagine."

That, at least, Clio could easily believe. "But what's it *for*? And why...why did you choose *me*?"

The woman threw back her head and laughed. "Always that question. It satisfies your vanity that you *were*, doesn't it? The 'whys' don't really matter, but let's just say that you were at a crossroads, and that those people are the ones who interest us most. You were perhaps...receptive."

Clio was startled when an older woman carrying a coffee service on a tray came out onto the terrace. Regina thanked her as she set it down on the table, then the old woman left as silently as she'd come.

"Receptive?" Clio asked as Regina poured two cups. "What do you mean, *receptive*?"

Regina seemed to disregard the question entirely. "Some people believe that a deity created the universe--wound it up like a clock and set it running, and then walked away to let it unwind on its own."

Clio frowned. "What does that have to do with anything? Are you saying that's what happened with the Gauntlet? Someone made it and wound it up, but then walked away? Then how did I end up there?"

Regina smiled. "Other people think that whatever mysteries the universe holds can only be examined by walking a path toward enlightenment, passing through a series of trials until they are initiated into awareness beyond that of the uninitiated."

"That sounds like a cult," Clio said warily.

"In a manner of speaking, I suppose you could look at it that way, though one without coercion, without form or formality." Regina set a cup and saucer in front of Clio. "Milk or sugar?"

Clio shook her head. "How can you say *without coercion?* I didn't actually choose to enter of my own free will, no matter what you say. It was just what seemed like the best choice in that moment."

"How is that different from *any* choice that you make?" Regina sipped her coffee, watching Clio over the rim of her cup. One eyebrow rose delicately.

"It...it *is* different," Clio said weakly.

"Because it made you feel like your heart was going to burst? Because it took you out of a comfortable, unexceptional existence and put something *vital* at stake?"

"Because it's *wrong,*" Clio flared. "It's wrong to play with people like they're toys, to force someone to make choices as part of a game they never agreed to."

"You think it's immoral."

"Yes!"

"So what is it that you came here seeking?"

"Answers! Honest answers. The things that happened to me, to the people I met--all of it can't be some elaborate play that they put on. The Jacks, okay. They were inside and out of the Gauntlet. *They* were playing a role--I knew that because they all but said it themselves, but it was still *more* than that, wasn't it? Even *they* were more than that. And the droolers... God, that wasn't faked. What's been done to them is beyond sick.

"And Britt! She got out and went back. It was to change things, wasn't it? What she found inside there? Chance said I was a pawn. Is that true? Was August really someone you sent in who got out of control? *Did* you want him out? Where is he now?"

Clio knew she was babbling, but she couldn't stop. The questions of the last several weeks--of the weeks before *that,* when she'd been surviving in the Gauntlet--rushed out of her all at once. She needed explanations. She needed *clarity.*

She needed...validation.

"What are you *really* doing with the Gauntlet? Who's in charge of it now? I don't believe for a second that someone started it up and walked away--someone's watching. You. There must be others, too. You interfere all the time, don't you, playing your God game? But maybe you've lost control, or maybe that's what you wanted all along. Do you even care about people who get hurt in there? Or... " Clio's hands curled tightly against her knees. "Or was everything really and truly just a lie? When is it going to stop? *Has* it stopped?"

"But you've already told me that you won't necessarily believe what I tell you," Regina replied. "So Clio...ask your questions, if you must, but I'll ask *you* again. Would my answers really change anything?" She leaned forward, and Clio was transfixed by the depth in the woman's clear, dark eyes. Her lips curved upward in the barest smile.

Clio closed her eyes. She thought about the question for a long time, focusing only on that and leaving her rage aside for the moment. And as she reflected on everything she'd gone through--everything she'd lost, and everything she'd *gained*--her anger finally began to dissipate. When she opened her eyes again, she felt her face relax.

"No, I guess they wouldn't. Anything you could say wouldn't change what I've already gone through." Her mouth curved in a mirror of Regina's expression. "I saw things and I felt things. *That* won't change."

Regina sat back as if satisfied, the momentary air of intimacy broken. "Will you go back to your job?" she asked swiftly. "You can, of course. All those sorts of things were smoothed over for you, as you've probably determined."

Clio stared, but after a moment, she smirked. The woman was playing another game with her. "No. I'm going back, which I'm sure you already figured out."

"Are you?" Regina looked and sounded genuinely surprised, though Clio didn't believe it for a moment. "But are you so sure the way will be open to you?"

Doubt was an unpleasant coil in Clio's belly for a second, but then she relaxed. "I think it will. After all, I made it out."

"Yes, but not with your *passport* intact." Regina's eyes dropped to the single charm on Clio's bracelet. "That earned you an audience here, but now it's nothing more than a memento."

Clio smiled. "I *thought* you'd say something like that. That's why I'm glad I was able to hang on to this." She reached up and pulled the scarf at her throat loose.

Britt's necklace dangled above her collarbone.

Clio held Regina's gaze for a long moment, and then Regina inclined her head. She rose from her seat; Clio followed suit.

"You're a good girl," Regina said, linking an arm through Clio's and drawing her inside. "So I'll give you this small caveat. The path, my dear Clio, is never the same twice."

♦ ♣ ♠ ♥

Clio thought about those last words as she ascended the steps to the Gauntlet. Regina had kissed her on the forehead before she'd left--formally, like a benediction, or perhaps an initiation.

Then Clio had found her way back to the stairs and the red doors.

She was sure there were other entrances, other methods of invitation. After all, the Gauntlet was bigger than the sections she'd been in. And she didn't know what was waiting for her any more than she had the first time she'd stood here, gazing up at the words engraved in the archway.

She didn't even know which of her motivations for returning were the most sincere. Did she want to help the people still inside--the people she counted as friends and those who couldn't help themselves? She did. But as her heartbeat raced faster and faster with each step she climbed, she also wondered if, truthfully, even *those* were merely excuses to keep playing.

The setting sun cast long shadows, and Clio's lips curved as she set her hand on the iron handle of the door and pushed.

Alea iacta est.

The die is cast.

end

Square One
A *Gauntlet* Bonus Story

Britt cursed and limped down the hallway, favoring her twisted ankle. It wasn't too bad; she would probably have full use of it back in a day. But it was annoying, and she was pissed off that she'd been careless enough to injure herself at all. That hadn't happened in a long while.

She needed to elevate her ankle and give it a good rest, so she was going to have to hole up for the time being. She had the option of crashing in one of the rooms she'd set up with a cache of supplies, but that wasn't what she wanted--not after the crappy mess of the last few days. Her back teeth ground together.

Being outmaneuvered never sat well with her, but she was especially miffed that it was that overdressed sociopath, August, who had managed to get the best of the situation. And now the latest game piece--some alpha male idiot--was in his clutches, despite all of Britt's efforts.

She was no stranger to inflated egos in the Gauntlet, but the way the new guy had disdained her advice had been especially obnoxious. He'd been determined to pull his tough guy bullshit from the start, and *then* he'd tried to cop a feel. She wasn't entirely sorry she'd lost him.

I should've turned him over to August right then and saved myself the trouble.

The smirk that slanted her mouth disappeared as quickly as it had come. Despite what a prick the guy had been, she wouldn't wish a trip to August's labs on anyone. But he'd rejected her attempts to protect him, and now she was limping, alone, through that dirty hallway.

She finally reached the dingy door, her frustration melting with the familiar sight. *Home sweet home.*

Her wry grin widened into smugness as she bent to work the lock, expertly manipulating two slim pieces of metal as lock picks. She still enjoyed exercising this particular skill, despite how long she'd been doing it. The tumblers clicked and Britt's tongue clicked approvingly.

A few days' downtime was just what she needed. She limped inside.

Her good humor disappeared when someone hurtled into her, making her stagger across the small room.

The body came with her, and Britt had the presence of mind to pivot, grasp her attacker, and throw the assailant with the existing momentum, along with an extra shove in the same direction. The initial spurt of adrenaline wasn't enough to override the pain as her bad ankle took the weight and crumpled beneath her.

Britt hissed in pain and fell to one knee, but her head jerked up. She narrowed her eyes at the girl sprawled on the floor in front of her; the stranger slowly pushed off the ground with a groan.

The girl glared at Britt beneath long, dirty, tangled brown hair. She looked short, but heavyset; her soft, Kewpie-doll face belied the strength she obviously had.

Britt wanted to wince as she catalogued the throbbing spots on her arm and shoulder, but continued to coolly assess the girl who had hit her like a ton of bricks. Strong, but untrained--the girl was sloppy as she gathered herself, leaving vulnerable spots open, and obviously had no second plan of assault. She wore tattered high-top sneakers, faded jeans, and a drab T-shirt as dirty as her hair. She looked like she hadn't bathed in weeks.

Fresh meat, then.

Britt suppressed a sigh, though not her irritation, and jerked her chin at the door. "Lock it," she barked before settling her back against the nearest wall and easing her leg out in front of her.

The girl's eyes widened, then squinted suspiciously. "Who the hell are *you*?"

Britt raised an eyebrow. "I'm the person you have to thank for the food you've been eating and the water you've been drinking." She gestured to the open cans and bottled water that sat in one corner. Britt had obviously interrupted the girl's meal.

Understanding flooded the girl's face, and she looked almost guilty for a second before her expression hardened. "I didn't know it was your place."

"Now you do." Britt pointed at the door again. "Lock it."

The girl's little Cupid's bow of a mouth pursed, but she did go lock the door. Her eyes flicked over to the empty cans of food.

"No big deal. I've got more," Britt said as she bent forward and carefully unlaced her boot. She eased it off, but couldn't help jostling her ankle. She grimaced and tossed the boot aside.

"What's your name?" The girl was crouched in the corner closest to the door, still peering out of her dirty tangle of hair. She stared at Britt warily, but with fascination, as if Britt were some exotic bug.

Britt repressed another sigh. She didn't leave the entry zone of the Gauntlet and its maze of dirty rooms and hallways unless she needed to; she'd been forced to this time by the last player's ineptitude, although there was no point dwelling on losses. She just hadn't expected another new addition to be waiting when she got back.

She didn't like what it meant that another player had been tossed in so soon. To her knowledge, it hadn't happened before; there'd always been time in between for adjustments and preparations tailored to the individual. This was bad timing.

Still, the girl seemed to have done fairly well on her own. Britt felt a grudging respect, even though it was mixed with a healthy skepticism.

She finally answered the girl's question. "Britt."

After the girl only continued to stare, Britt's eyebrows rose pointedly.

"Lilah," the girl offered at last.

"How did you get in here?"

Lilah's expression flickered, like she was trying to come up with a story that Britt would believe. "Um, it wasn't locked."

"Try again," Britt said flatly. Lilah had already started to bluster, but Britt's tone was enough to shut her up.

"Fine," she said after a moment. "Someone let me in."

"Someone."

"Yes." A defiant head toss flipped the dirty brown hair over Lilah's shoulders. "Didn't tell me it was yours."

Britt repressed a smirk. "Yeah, you said that. How long have you been here?"

The question made Lilah falter a bit. She bit her lower lip and shrugged. "A week, maybe. It's hard to keep track in here."

A week, Britt thought. *While I was wasting a month in the city, chasing after the idiot I lost*. She shook off the unpleasant feeling of not knowing what was behind the deviation. In any case, that other player was out of commission now, wiped out by August and his labs, leaving only one in play again--Lilah. Maybe it had been so obvious that the last guy was a lost cause that the timetable was stepped up. Britt frowned.

"So *who* let you in here?"

Stubbornness swept over Lilah's Kewpie-doll features again. "I promised not to tell. He said--"

"He?"

Lilah flushed, and Britt had more than a sneaking suspicion of who she was dealing with.

"*He* said what?"

"I told him I wanted to stay," Lilah grunted, her belligerence wearing on Britt's nerves. "And he said I could stay here as long as I want."

"What do you mean, you want to stay?"

"I *mean,*" Lilah said in a snotty tone, "that I don't want to leave here. The *Gauntlet,* or whatever you call it. He seemed to think I'd want to get out. I mean, yeah, those creepy people freak me out, but they don't really do much. And the guys with the masks scared the crap of me, but Jack's one of them, so--"

"Jack," Britt snapped.

"Oh..." Lilah clamped her jaw shut in a clear sign of guilt.

Britt snorted. "Which one?" she asked, although she was pretty sure she knew the answer.

"There's more than one?"

"Unfortunately."

Lilah turned pink, visible even underneath a week's worth of grime. "He seems okay."

"You have a thing for redheads, huh?" Britt smirked when Lilah's cheeks flamed even brighter.

I knew it.

Britt could imagine the annoying cackle of Jack's laugh as he'd dumped Lilah on her doorstep. She was going to kill the hyperactive fool the next time she saw him. Even if she *had* chosen to take an interest in some players, all she'd wanted to do that day was have a shower and a nap.

It wasn't unheard of for people to decide they liked it better on the inside, even if they never knew exactly what they were getting into. But they still needed to learn the ropes, and Britt needed to figure out what Lilah was really made of. If Lilah wasn't going to play the game herself, she'd end up being someone's pawn, one way or another.

Britt would just have to make certain Lilah was hers.

♦ ♣ ♠ ♥

She didn't pamper Lilah. If she wanted to stay, she'd have to learn to do it the hard way.

The next few weeks were almost typical, despite Lilah's vow that she didn't want to try to find a way out. Britt taught her how to scavenge, showed her a few safe spots and told her how to set up her own, cryptically explained the house rules, and--most importantly--got the girl to bathe. Not in her own private pool, though. Some things were sacred.

She secretly enjoyed watching Lilah both flounder and persevere. Outwardly, she was brusque and sparing in her praise and conversation. She couldn't let Lilah get too attached. She wouldn't be babysitting her forever.

But Lilah's overall competence certainly helped wash away the bad taste the moron before her had left.

"You think I'm going to change my mind, don't you?" Lilah, defensive again, crossed her arms and jerked her pointy little chin up at Britt. Britt stared down at her, slouched against the wall but still towering over the girl.

"I didn't say that," Britt muttered. *I may have thought it a few times, though.*

"You're thinking it."

Britt stopped at that.

Lilah's insight, although irritating, was potentially very useful. Britt was almost sorry Lilah didn't want to pit herself against the perils of the Gauntlet, but assimilation could prove better. Gaining another ally would improve her network. The way things were coming to a head, she'd need all the help she could get.

"You don't have any idea how dangerous things can get in here. You still think of it as just a game." Britt snorted softly. Usually, it was the other way around, and she had to talk people down from blind panic at the thought of being trapped. The instinctive urge for flight seemed to be entirely missing from Lilah, which made Britt wonder what the girl found so attractive about the place.

She didn't pry. Lilah's reasons were her own, and Lilah hadn't been nosy about *Britt's* reasons for being there, which suited Britt just fine. She only rarely accessed the files that existed for every player, preferring to go on her gut instinct rather than a compilation of information that might have no connection to actual truth. Trust was a rare commodity in the Gauntlet, so she wanted to try to foster some.

"*Life* is a game," Lilah replied.

Britt shrugged. "Just because you *want* to stay doesn't mean it'll be easy."

"I like it here," Lilah repeated stubbornly. Her long hair framed the huffy expression on her round face, which made her look even younger than she was.

Britt rolled her eyes. "Whatever. I already told you--you have something that's valuable in here, and that makes you a target."

"You said no one could take it from me," Lilah pointed out. She extended her small hand, revealing the ring sitting snugly on the plump middle finger of her right hand.

"That's true," Britt agreed. "But they could make you *want* to give it to them."

Instead of fear, a wide, self-satisfied grin spread over Lilah's face. Britt snorted again and began walking.

Lilah wasn't shy about her occasional liaisons with Red Jack.

"That's not what I meant. But I suppose we can add that to the list."

"You're just jealous," Lilah taunted.

"Not even close to my type," Britt said with bland disinterest.

"What *is* your type?"

Lilah's smirk turned toward her, and Britt raised an eyebrow. "Someone who knows how to mind their own business."

Lilah just snickered, but that stopped when Britt shoved her into an access panel and told her to crawl.

"I fucking *hate* these things."

Britt gave her a little kick. "I suggest you deal with your claustrophobia if you want to stay here."

Lilah tensed, but started crawling. Britt slid in to follow.

Lilah complained half of the way, making the effort to be a pain in the ass--her favorite pastime.

"Why can't we just *walk*?" she asked for the umpteenth time.

"Shut up or I'll send you down a direct shoot to the basement boys."

"Aren't they all asleep down there?" Lilah griped. "I don't see why we have to skulk around during the day, too."

"You know there's no direct access through the hallways," Britt said with fading patience. "Quit whining."

Lilah sulked until they climbed out of the shaft. Once out of the enclosed space, Lilah began to take big, dramatic gulps of air; Britt grabbed the back of her shirt and pulled her toward a door.

"Not in the mood, Lilah."

"Get off." Lilah swiped at her, and Britt let go.

"Okay, so we're going to go through this wing like I taught you. Separate and meet back here in about half an hour. You take that side."

"Fine," Lilah huffed as she began to stomp away.

"Also..." Britt waited for Lilah to look at her. "Keep an eye out for anything that might let you use that." She gestured toward Lilah's hand.

"But you said it'd help me find a way out. I don't *want*--"

Britt scowled. "That's *true*, but sometimes it'll just give you access to things. *Good* things. Things that will make your life a lot more comfortable."

"Really?" Lilah suddenly looked much more interested in the proceedings. "Okay, later."

Britt pinched her nose and inhaled a few times, indulging her own dramatic side for a moment. Everybody always argued. *Always.* Ungrateful little sh--

Lilah screamed.

Lilah had never screamed before. Not when around spiders, not when she'd seen one of the ancient and very full toilets in the building overflow, not when she'd accidentally locked herself in a room with a few of the hapless subjects who littered the Gauntlet like human flotsam.

Britt ran, her heart pounding harder than it had in ages. She hated this part. It was inevitable.

A door slammed inside one of the rooms, and a few seconds later, Lilah ran out into the hallway, slamming that door behind her, too. She sprinted away, her tattered high-tops slapping on the tile.

Before Britt could call out, the door opened, and her stomach dropped.

Shit.

Sunshine.

Confusion and anger made her blood surge. *What the hell is **he** doing here?*

It should have been against all the rules, even if August had shown himself to be more and more willing to bend them. Sending his favorite minion--not to mention most feared--was outrageous, even for August. He wasn't supposed to have *access* to the entry zone.

She couldn't help the faint trickle of apprehension that crept down her spine when Sunshine turned away from Lilah's footsteps and met her gaze.

His blank expression sharpened, and Britt watched his large hands curl.

She knew there was a price on her head. Maybe that would work out well for her for once--she could lure him away from Lilah. August showing his hand so soon did not bode well for the girl *at all.*

Britt wasn't going to let him win this round.

She took a step back and then another. Sunshine's massive shoulders tensed, but then his expression flickered, disdain smoothed into an impassive mask, and he turned and ran after Lilah with a swiftness that made Britt hiss.

She ran after him, down the long hallway. When she finally made it around the corner, she saw him posed in front of an open door, his large frame almost filling it. Beyond him, Lilah was cornered in a large, communal bathroom. Her middle finger lifted as she glared.

Britt had to admire Lilah's guts, even though she knew how badly this was going to end. But Lilah surprised her.

"You want this?" Lilah pulled the shiny ring off her extended finger. Sunshine's muscles flexed as he made a motion toward her.

Lilah grinned broadly, mocking him, as she let go of the trinket. It plopped in the toilet with a loud splash; she pressed the silver handle.

"Tough shit."

The loud rush of water mingled with Sunshine's howl, and he stepped menacingly into the room. Lilah's expression faltered, and Britt tried not to panic now that Lilah had eliminated any reason for Sunshine to go easy on her.

"You're going to be sorry." His words were chilling in the flat way he recited them, and Britt didn't doubt him at all. She could see that Lilah didn't, either.

Britt steeled her resolve. She wouldn't allow another loss, even if she had to settle for a draw.

"Hey, asshole," she called, reminding him of her presence. The goon's shoulders tensed, but he didn't turn around.

She still had value to August. He just needed to remember that. "Did your master let you off the leash to pick up his weekly supply of hair spray? I think I saw some in the supply closet on the second floor of the south wing."

His body coiled, and Britt was off and running before he could fully turn. His legs were long and fast, but so were hers. Besides, she knew this place far better than he did, and she was in full possession of her reasoning abilities.

She managed to wrench her ankle again before she finally lost him, but she'd led him well away from Lilah. Surely the girl had holed up somewhere until it was safer to find her way back.

Britt hauled her own tired ass back to the room she'd been sharing with Lilah. But this time, that wasn't going to be good enough. She deserved a real rest.

She entered the glorified supply closet and ignored the pathetic pile of blankets in the corner as she exposed the hidden panel that led to another shaft. Ten minutes later, she was falling onto a cushioning pile of exercise pads, managing not to screw her ankle up more.

The pool undulated invitingly, but she bypassed it to head

to the smooth wall. Her fingers tapped out a pattern, and a door slid open. She sighed with pleasure, stripping off her clothes as she headed to the shower across a thick, pale carpet that felt like heaven on her tired soles.

Later, wrapped in a purple terry cloth bathrobe and idly kicking her fluffy matching slippers behind her, Britt browsed the files open on a small screen. Her eyebrows rose higher and higher, especially when she read the message attached.

I think everything's about to hit the fan. Read this one.
ETA 14 weeks, 3 days, 7 hours.
Watch out for her.
-C

Britt read the files again, peered at the blonde woman in the photo, and shook her head. Things were going to get messy. She shoved the screen aside and dropped her face into the pillow. She was grinning. *About damn time.*

Sometime later, the screen beeped, waking her up from some fitful rest. Britt rolled over, rubbed her eyes, and opened the message. It had a picture attached.

Our friend J sent me this. Starting a trend?

Britt ran a hand over her close-cropped hair and laughed. It seemed that Lilah had received a reward, despite the loss of her ring--or maybe because of it.

The picture was a video feed still of Lilah with an electric shaver to her head, a pile of dirty brown hair on the floor and an assortment of hair dyes littering the counter. She wore new clothes and an expression of glee.

Britt would count this one as a win, after all.

end

Bonus comics

Bonus comics